"Peg Cochran has a truly entertaining writing style that is filled with humor, mystery, fun, and intrigue. You cannot ask for a lot more in a super cozy!"

—Open Book Society

"A fun whodunnit with quirky characters and a satisfying mystery. This new series is as sweet and sharp as the heroine's cranberry salsa."

—Sofie Kelly, *New York Times* bestselling author of the Magical Cats Mysteries

"Cozy fans and foodies rejoice—there's a place just for you and it's called Cranberry Cove."

—Ellery Adams, *New York Times* bestselling author of the Supper Club Mysteries

"I can't wait for Monica's next tasty adventure—and I'm not just saying that because I covet her cranberry relish recipe."

—Victoria Abbott, national bestselling author of the Book Collector Mysteries

Books by Peg Cochran

The Cranberry Cove Mysteries

Berried Secrets
Berry the Hatchet
Dead and Berried
Berried at Sea
Berried in the Past

The Lucille Mysteries

Confession Is Murder
Unholy Matrimony
Hit and Nun
A Room with a Pew
Cannoli to Die For

Farmer's Daughter Mysteries

No Farm, No Foul
Sowed to Death
Bought the Farm

More Books by Peg Cochran

The Gourmet De-Lite Mysteries

Allergic to Death
Steamed to Death
Iced to Death

Murder, She Reported Mysteries

Murder, She Reported
Murder, She Uncovered
Murder, She Encountered

Young Adult Books

Oh, Brother!
Truth or Dare

Writing as Meg London

Murder Unmentionable
Laced with Poison
A Fatal Slip

Berried Motives

A
CRANBERRY COVE
Mystery

Peg Cochran

BEYOND THE PAGE
PUBLISHING

Berried Motives
Peg Cochran
Beyond the Page Books
are published by
Beyond the Page Publishing
www.beyondthepagepub.com

ISBN: 978-1-950461-88-2

Chapter 1

The day started like any other.

Monica Albertson microwaved a bowl of instant oatmeal, sprinkled on some dried cranberries and ate it standing at the counter with a spoon in one hand and a mug of steaming coffee in the other.

She then kissed her husband Greg goodbye, scratched Mittens, her tuxedo cat, under the chin, and headed out the door of her cottage.

There was the whiff of autumn in the air on this early October morning. Dew sparkled on the grass and the air was chilly. The leaves on the trees were turning color and a few had already dried up and dropped to the ground. Monica pulled up her collar and stuck her hands in the pockets of her fleece.

She passed one of the cranberry bogs where Jeff, her half brother, and his crew were already at work. The bog had been flooded and the bright red cranberries bobbed on the surface of the water. She paused for a moment and watched as they hauled the boom across the bog, corralling the plump berries into an ever-tightening circle.

Jeff stopped to adjust the straps on his waders and must have noticed Monica, because he waved and shouted good morning. Monica waved back and continued walking toward the commercial kitchen, which they had recently added on to one of the farm buildings. Monica baked all sorts of cranberry goods to sell in the farm store, along with a cranberry salsa that was very popular with the local Cranberry Cove restaurants and was now being carried by an upscale chain grocery store. She had started out in the kitchen of her small cottage but had soon outgrown that space.

Monica had had her own small café in Chicago, where she'd served coffee, tea and her homemade baked goods, but when Jeff had needed help at Sassamanash Farm, she'd closed her business and headed to Michigan to lend a hand.

She dug her keys out of her pocket, selected one, inserted it into the lock and opened the door to the kitchen. The large room retained some of the early morning chill, but once she had the ovens going full blast, it would quickly heat up.

The space had been outfitted with industrial-sized appliances, a long counter for rolling and cutting dough and a table and chairs where Monica could take a break and eat her lunch.

She hung up her fleece on one of the hooks 0n the wall by the door and replaced it with an apron printed with bright red cranberries, although she knew she would still manage to get flour all over her clothes and sometimes even in her hair by the end of the day.

After measuring out flour, butter, sugar, buttermilk, vanilla extract, baking powder, salt and an egg, she blended the ingredients into dough studded with dark red cranberries.

She placed the mound of dough on a marble slab on the counter and eased her rolling pin across it, watching with satisfaction as the lump slowly became flatter and rounder with each pass. She blew a lock of hair out of her eyes, dusted off her hands and began to cut the circle into even triangles.

The door to the kitchen flew open as she was placing the scones on a baking sheet and Lauren, Jeff's fiancée, burst in.

Monica jumped. "You scared me."

"Sorry," Lauren said, brushing strands of her long blond hair back from her face. "I didn't mean to scare you, but I'm so excited." Her voice rose to a squeal.

Monica smiled with amusement. Lauren was bouncing on the balls of her feet and her cheeks were tinted pink with excitement.

"What has you so worked up?" Monica opened the oven door and slid in the sheet of scones.

"Sassamanash Farm is going to be on *What's Up West Michigan*. You know—it's that local evening show that comes on before the news. I contacted them about featuring the farm and I couldn't believe it when they replied." She paused to take a breath. "I know it's terribly short notice, but one of their guests canceled so they had an opening and anyway, they called to set it up."

"Isn't that the show hosted by that young blond woman—Betsy something-or-other?"

Lauren nodded. "Yes. Betsy DeJong. I pitched the story to one of their producers, and he loved the idea. Like I said, it's short notice. They're coming this afternoon to film the harvest."

"This afternoon?" Monica said in panic. "Does Jeff know?"

Lauren nodded again. "I just told him. He's quite excited." She frowned. "But nervous, too. He's afraid viewers will notice his arm."

Jeff had been injured in Afghanistan and had returned to Michigan with a partially paralyzed arm. It was one of the reasons Monica had left Chicago to come and help him.

"Will Jeff even have to be in the segment?"

Lauren nodded excitedly. "Yes. He'll be the one explaining to Betsy how the berries are cultivated and harvested." She frowned. "I'd better make sure he doesn't wear that ratty old Lions sweatshirt of his. Maybe I'd better run buy him a new one."

"Good idea," Monica said, brushing some flour from the front of her apron. "He'll want to look his best."

Monica couldn't imagine Jeff on television. Her half brother wasn't shy but he was quiet and avoided the spotlight.

"You'll be in the segment, too," Lauren said.

Monica gasped and whirled around. "What? Me?" She looked down at her worn jeans and her stretched-out sweater, which was pilled around the elbows. She'd never been on television and had never had any desire to be.

"They'll want you to give them a tour of the farm store and explain about all the cranberry goodies you make, especially your famous cranberry salsa. The whole segment should do wonders for business."

"Oh, dear. I'm hardly dressed for it."

Lauren looked Monica up and down, taking in the clothes she had thrown on that morning without much thought as to how she looked. "Don't worry. You'll do fine." But Monica could detect the note of doubt in her voice.

It wasn't encouraging.

Lauren had barely left in a flurry of excitement when the door opened again. Monica looked up as Kit Tanner walked in. She had hired him to help with the baking now that their orders had increased and it was becoming too much for her to handle by herself.

When she had first met Kit, he'd had his black hair shaved up the sides but left long enough on top to flop onto his forehead. Since then, he'd grown it out and now wore it slicked back in a ponytail. To go with his new hairdo, he'd also cultivated a beard—a scruff that he somehow managed to keep at precisely the length of three days' worth of growth.

"I'm going to be on television," Monica said glumly after they'd greeted each other.

Kit stood with both hands on his hips. "Honey, I always knew you were meant to be a star."

Monica laughed. Somehow Kit always managed to cheer her up.

"I don't know about being a star," Monica said, brushing some flour off the counter and into the palm of her hand. She explained about *What's Up West Michigan* coming to film the cranberry harvest that afternoon.

Kit clapped his hands together. "But darling, that's marvelous. What incredible publicity for Sassamanash Farm. Serious kudos to Lauren for arranging it, the clever girl. I guess all those marketing and PR courses she took in college paid off."

Kit looked Monica up and down again. "But darling, I do hope you're going to change into something a little more . . ." Kit waved a hand in the air.

"Don't worry," Monica said as she untied her apron. "I was just about to go back to the cottage and do just that."

• • •

By the time the film crew was due to arrive, Monica was dressed in a pair of clean and pressed jeans, a white shirt and the crewneck sweater her mother had sent her last Christmas and which had still been wrapped in tissue paper in the box it had come in.

She pulled on her fleece but didn't zip it—the sun was higher in the sky now and the air had warmed up considerably. She checked Mittens's food and water dishes then headed out the door.

There was no sign of the film crew yet. Monica felt relieved. She heard shouts coming from the nearest bog and began walking in that direction.

Jeff was standing hip-deep in the water surrounded by bobbing cranberries. The berries moved in bright red eddies as Jeff waded through them toward the edge of the bog. Dan Polsky, one of Jeff's crew members, was sitting on the bank. He had a plastic water bottle in his hand and was tipping it toward his mouth. Water dripped down his chin and he wiped it away with the back of his hand. Mauricio, who had been with Jeff since Jeff took over the farm, was squatting next to a tree stump and twisting the top off a thermos.

Lauren, standing at the edge of the bog, was deep in animated conversation with another young girl, whose long blond hair was blowing across her face. She brushed it away with an impatient motion and gestured toward the bog.

Monica wondered if she was with the film crew. The girl was wearing distressed jeans, a black moto jacket and had a phone with a hot pink cover clutched in her hand. There was a camera slung around her neck.

Lauren turned, saw Monica and motioned her over.

"Monica, this is Melinda Leigh," Lauren said somewhat breathlessly. "I've hired her to take some pictures of the farm for our Instagram account."

"Instagram?" Monica hadn't realized the farm even had an account. "Are we on Instagram? Is that really necessary?" Monica had barely caught up with Facebook, let alone other social media.

Lauren nodded. "Yes. It's important to have a presence on Instagram these days. Besides, the farm will make a spectacular subject." She gestured toward the bog, where the sun sparkled on the water and illuminated the various shades of the berries, which ranged from a deep cherry to a pale pink. "Mel is a brilliant photographer so I know she's going to get some great shots."

Melinda ducked her head as if she was embarrassed. She seemed shy, with slightly rounded shoulders and a habit of pulling her upper lip over slightly protruding front teeth. Monica thought there was an air of defeat about her.

There was still no sign of the crew from WZZZ.

"Do you know when they are coming to film?"

"Todd Lipton, he's the producer, called to say they were running a little late," Lauren said.

"Do I have time to go home and get a bite to eat?"

Monica was hungry, but at the same time felt slightly queasy at the thought of her upcoming television appearance.

Lauren waved a hand. "Sure, go get something to eat. I'll call you when they get here."

Monica was almost to her cottage when she heard a rumble in the distance. Moments later a red-and-white van with a large antenna on the roof and WZZZ on the side in white lettering came into view. It jounced down the road, which was barely more than a dirt path worn in the earth, and came to a stop in front of Monica's cottage.

A young woman stuck her head out the driver's-side window. She had a mop of unruly dark curls, thick straight brows and a ring through her nose.

"Are you Lauren?" she said. "I was told to ask for Lauren."

"I'm Monica Albertson," Monica said, approaching the van. "My brother owns the farm." She gestured toward her cottage. "Why don't you park in my driveway. You'll be out of the way of any farm vehicles that might need to come through."

Monica watched as the young woman expertly backed the van into the driveway and came to a stop. The driver's-side door opened and she jumped out.

"Jasmine Talcott," she said, holding out a hand. "I'll be filming the segment." She went around to the back of the van, slid open the door and pulled out a large camera, which she hefted onto her shoulder with apparent ease.

Monica was about to direct her to the bogs when she heard the purr of an engine and a bright yellow Mustang came into view. The driver pulled over and parked on the grass alongside the path. The door opened slowly and a slender leg in a red stiletto pump dangled out briefly before the other leg came into view and the occupant slid from the seat.

Monica recognized her immediately as Betsy DeJong, the anchor of the evening news as well as the host of *What's Up West Michigan*.

She was wearing the usual exaggerated amount of on camera makeup—blue eye shadow swept nearly to her brows, spidery false eyelashes, and bright red lipstick filling in her full lips.

Her highlighted blond hair was in a perfectly layered bob that brushed her cheeks when she moved her head. She was wearing a white dress with navy blocking on the sides that made her waist appear impossibly small and had a trench coat slung loosely around her shoulders.

She looked like a Barbie doll version of a newscaster.

The downturn of her mouth clearly indicated that she wasn't happy. She looked around her and sighed.

"Where are the bogs? I was told we were going to be filming cranberry bogs."

Monica smiled. "Welcome to Sassamanash Farm. The bogs are a bit of a ways down the path."

"I hope it's not far to walk," Betsy said in a querulous voice.

Monica smiled again and shook her head. "No, it's not far at all. This way." She motioned toward the path in front of her.

She was about to start walking toward the bog when she heard another car coming down the drive, its engine not as sleek-sounding as the Mustang's. A green and cream Subaru station wagon came into view and stopped in back of Betsy's car.

"That must be Todd," Betsy said, squinting into the distance.

Monica watched as a man in his early forties got out of the car. He paused to straighten his tie and then began walking toward them.

"That's Todd Lipton," Jasmine said. "He produces *What's Up West Michigan*."

Todd had light brown hair that probably turned blond in the summer sun and hooded hazel eyes. He wasn't tall but had the body of a swimmer, with broad shoulders tapering to a narrow waist. His pants were a bit too short to be fashionable and the collar of his dress shirt could have used a bit more starch.

He rubbed his hands together as he neared them. Monica could see that his thick glasses were smudged and that there was an eyelash caught in the corner of one of the lenses.

"Are we all ready to go?" he asked cheerfully. He had a rather nasal high-pitched voice. He smiled at Monica. "I'm Todd Lipton."

He shook Monica's hand.

"It's this way," Monica said, pointing down the path.

Betsy made a face. "Do we have to walk? Can't we drive the van to wherever it is we're going?"

"It's not far," Monica reassured her again.

No wonder she didn't want to walk, Monica thought as she watched Betsy pick her way down the dirt path, her ankles wobbling dangerously in her high heels. Monica couldn't remember the last time she'd worn heels herself and she certainly didn't miss it.

"Whose idea was this anyway?" Betsy grumbled as she stumbled over a rock. She turned and glared at Todd.

Todd's expression didn't change. "It's going to be a wonderful segment," he said in a soothing voice, pushing his glasses back up his nose with his index finger. "Your public is going to love it."

Betsy's face relaxed slightly.

Your public? Monica thought. Obviously Todd knew how to handle the anchorwoman, who was clearly something of a diva.

"Are we almost there?" Betsy whined again several moments later. "I'm cold and my feet are killing me."

"We're almost there," Monica reassured her.

The bog came into view as they rounded the bend. Jeff was waiting on the bank. Monica noticed he'd changed into the new sweatshirt Lauren had bought him and had combed his hair. Lauren was standing next to him, but when she saw the news crew in the distance, she raced over to them.

"I'm Lauren," she said somewhat breathlessly. She nodded at Todd, who smiled in return. "Jeff is waiting for you," she said and motioned toward the bog. "He's going to talk you through the process of cultivating cranberries. It's quite fascinating actually," she said brightly, obviously noting the look of doubt on Betsy's face.

Betsy stared at the bog, her forehead wrinkled. She pointed toward one of the workers who was busy guiding the boom.

"Is that Dan Polsky?"

"Yes. Do you know him?" Monica said.

"I used to." Betsy's face tightened.

Lauren hustled the group over to where Jeff was standing. Jeff smiled broadly and held out a hand as Betsy approached.

Suddenly Betsy's entire demeanor changed. She smiled, lowered her eyelashes and bit her lower lip as she took Jeff's outstretched hand, holding it a moment longer than necessary. Jeff didn't appear to mind.

Monica watched as an angry expression spread over Lauren's face. She turned red and it was obvious she was furious. She glared at Jeff briefly and then turned on her heel and stomped off.

Monica watched her go. She couldn't imagine what had gotten into Lauren—she was usually so levelheaded. Jeff was focused on Betsy and didn't seem to have noticed.

Jasmine, meanwhile, was fiddling with the lens on her camera before hoisting it to her shoulder. She looked through the viewfinder as she panned the bog and surrounding area.

She lowered her camera. "Whenever you're ready," she shouted to Betsy.

Betsy smoothed down her dress and touched a hand to her hair. Jeff looked nervous, Monica thought. He was nibbling on the side of his thumb—something he did when he was anxious.

Todd pinned a microphone to Betsy's dress and the camera began rolling.

Monica edged closer to the pair but was careful to stay out of the shot.

"We're here today at Sassamanash Farm in Cranberry Cove," Betsy began in her silken voice, "talking to Jeff Albertson, the owner. He's going to explain cranberry farming to us."

Jeff gave the camera a bashful smile.

While Jasmine was filming, Melinda was hovering nearby taking still pictures of the event and scuttling out of the way like a frightened crab whenever the camera swung in her direction. Monica supposed Lauren would be putting the pictures on the farm's new Instagram account.

"So, Jeff, why Sassamanash Farm? Does the name mean something?" Betsy tilted her head coyly.

Jeff took a deep breath—Monica could see his chest rise and fall—then said, "Sassamanash is the Algonquin word for *cranberry*." He gave a deprecating shrug. "It seemed appropriate."

"So cranberries grow in water?" Betsy said, gesturing toward the flooded bog. "Tell us about the process."

"Actually, contrary to what most people think, cranberries don't grow in water," Jeff said. "They actually grow on vines. We flood the bog when it's time to harvest them."

"Why do you do that?" Betsy tilted her head coquettishly and widened her blue eyes while looking directly at the camera.

"Once the bog is flooded, we go through it with a machine we affectionately call an egg beater." Jeff chuckled. "It dislodges the berries from the vine, and since there are air pockets inside the berries, they float to the surface."

"That's fascinating," Betsy cooed and made wide eyes at the camera again.

Jeff pointed to the bog, where two of his crew were now wielding the boom.

"The boom helps us corral the berries, which are then sucked out of the water into the pump truck."

"And they end up on our table at Thanksgiving," Betsy said brightly with a tinkling laugh.

Jeff laughed too and gave a mischievous smile. "Would you like to put on some waders and try your hand at it?"

Betsy giggled.

"I hope you're not afraid of spiders," Jeff said as he motioned for one of his men to bring over a pair of waders.

"Spiders?" Betsy's voice rose an octave.

"Wolf spiders," Jeff said succinctly. "They make their home in the vines and clean the vines of any insects. Once we flood the bog with water, the spiders float to the surface and run across the tops of the berries."

Betsy shivered dramatically. "No, thanks. I think I'll pass." She laughed and grinned at the camera as if sharing a secret with the audience.

"We're just about out of time for this segment." Todd looked at his watch. "We still need to film the farm store sequence and then we'll need time to edit before we go on the air tonight."

That was her part, Monica thought. She wondered how her hair looked. A breeze was blowing over the bog and she could feel strands brushing across her face. She probably looked a wreck.

Jasmine had lowered her camera from her shoulder and was looking at the screen.

"What did you get?" Betsy yelled to Jasmine, gingerly picking her way across the rough ground.

Jasmine held the camera so that Betsy could see it as well. As Betsy watched the screen her face began to cloud over. Her fists were clenched at her sides and her eyes narrowed.

"You must be the most incompetent cameraperson in the entire world," she hissed at Jasmine. "You always manage to make me look bad."

Her voice was getting louder. Monica was embarrassed for both Jasmine and Betsy. She'd never been the sort to make a scene herself and they made her uncomfortable.

"How many times do I have to tell you that my right side is my best side? Huh?" Betsy stood with her hands on her hips, her face inches from Jasmine's.

"I tried but you —" Jasmine began, but Betsy cut her off.

"I'm tired of your excuses. I'm going to talk to Gus when we get back. It's time they hired someone competent to film my segments."

Monica expected Jasmine to look crestfallen but she merely looked resigned, her shoulders slumped and the corners of her mouth turned down.

Monica knew that people in television could sometimes be difficult to deal with—the pressure was enormous and tempers were bound to get heated. But Betsy DeJong really took the cake. Jasmine seemed to take Betsy's ill treatment in her stride—Monica wasn't so sure she would have been able to do the same.

Chapter 2

"What now?" Betsy said, looking at Todd, her hands on her hips. She looked both bored and annoyed.

"We head down to the farm store for the next segment," Todd said brightly. "You were great, by the way. Just great."

Betsy grunted and continued to scowl.

Monica felt her stomach tighten. This was going to be her part. The only other time she'd ever been on camera was when a reporter had stopped her on the street in Chicago to get her opinion for a segment WSNS was doing on the current political candidates. It had all happened too quickly for her to develop a case of the nerves.

Jasmine was walking ahead of her, lumbering along with the heavy camera balanced on her shoulder. Monica caught up with her.

"Does Betsy always treat you like that? I don't know how you stand it. It's so unfair."

Jasmine shrugged. "There's a lot of competition for my job at all the stations. I was lucky to get this gig. Besides, Betsy's just upset about what happened."

"Oh?" Monica didn't think that was any excuse, but she didn't say anything.

Jasmine kicked a small rock on the path and sent it skittering off to the side.

"She was angling for this job in DC." She turned to Monica. "Did you know she's engaged to Bob Visser? He's running for Congress. She thought if she got the new position, they'd both be based in the capital. She had visions of a big house in Kalorama, the two of them hosting important parties, becoming part of the DC social scene — you know, the works."

"What happened?"

"She didn't get the job." A ghost of a smile played around Jasmine's lips. "Let's face it, it would be a huge leap from hosting *What's Up West Michigan* and anchoring the local news to having your own political talk show." She repositioned the camera on her shoulder. "Anyway, it's put her in an even more foul mood than usual."

• • •

Nora, who had run the farm store for Monica for several years, was behind the counter arranging a pyramid of cranberry jams and jellies when Monica and the crew arrived. Crates stamped with *Sassamanash Farm* were stacked against the wall and the display case was filled with cranberry scones, bread, muffins and Monica's signature cranberry walnut chocolate chunk cookies.

Nora was clearly excited by the presence of the film crew. Her cheeks were pink and her hands fluttered over the various jars she was arranging.

Monica noticed Jasmine looking longingly at the baked goods and smiled.

"Can I offer you something?" she said. "A muffin or a cookie?"

Jasmine grinned. "A muffin would be super. I was running late this morning and breakfast was nothing more than a cup of tepid coffee from the station break room."

Monica motioned to Nora, who pulled a piece of glassine from the box on the counter, reached into the case and selected a muffin. She handed it to Jasmine along with a paper napkin.

Jasmine took a bite of her muffin and closed her eyes. "Delicious," she mumbled, brushing some crumbs off her lips. She glanced at Betsy, who was waiting impatiently by the door. She finished the rest of the muffin quickly, tossed the wrapper and the napkin in the trash and picked up her camera from the table where she'd left it.

Once again, she held up the camera and panned the scene, moving this way and that, studying the various angles. Betsy was touching up her hair and lipstick and Todd was on his cell phone.

"Time to film," Jasmine said briskly.

"Where do you want me?" Betsy said to Todd, her expression bored.

Todd moved the cell phone from his ear and put his hand over the mouthpiece. "Let's start in front of those crates over there. Jasmine," he called to the camerawoman, "make sure you get the Sassamanash Farm stamped on the crates in the shot."

"Okeydokey," Jasmine said. She stood poised with her camera pointed at the spot.

Todd maneuvered Betsy into position and Monica noticed that she made it a point to aim her right side at the camera.

Lauren still hadn't returned by the time Jasmine was ready to film. Monica was worried—that wasn't like her. Had it only been Betsy flirting with Jeff that had set her off or was something else going on?

Todd clicked off his call. "Gotta run. Something's come up. I'll see you back at the station." He nodded at Betsy and Jasmine as he left.

The door had barely closed before it opened again.

"Surprise," came a hearty male voice.

"Bob! What are you doing here?" Betsy said.

He was tall—a couple of inches over six feet—and was wearing a well-tailored and expensive-looking suit, a white shirt and red tie. He appeared to be in his fifties and had the professional smile of a politician. Monica thought he looked familiar.

He breezed past Monica, leaving the scent of his woodsy aftershave in the air, went up to Betsy and kissed her on the cheek. Now that he was closer, Monica recognized him as Bob Visser, Betsy's fiancé and a candidate for senator.

"I hope I'm not disturbing anything?" He smiled broadly at everyone. "Just thought I'd pop around and see how my girl is doing." He put his arm around Betsy.

Betsy looked pained and patted her hair as if she suspected him of having disturbed it.

He turned to Monica and stuck out his hand, baring his perfect white teeth at her like a shark. "Bob Visser," he said.

Monica had never met Visser before but she recognized him from his commercials on television. He owned several luxury car dealerships—one just off the highway outside of Cranberry Cove, one in Grand Rapids and one in Kalamazoo—and starred in his own commercials for Visser Motors, which aired regularly on WZZZ and had made him a household face and name even before he began his run for the Senate.

Visser proceeded to go around shaking hands with everyone else in the room. Politicians never stopped campaigning, Monica supposed. Betsy looked irritated that Visser's attention had been diverted from her. *She'd better get used to it,* Monica thought. If he won the Senate race he was going to be a very busy man.

"How did you know I was here?" Betsy said after Visser made the rounds.

"I stopped by the station first and your sister Heidi told me," Bob said, straightening his tie again, although it was perfectly straight already. He winked at Betsy. "I'd best be off. I just wanted to stop by and say hello."

Had he really wanted to see Betsy, Monica wondered, or had this simply been an opportunity for a campaign stop?

Jasmine motioned to Monica and she felt her mouth go dry. She wished she had a glass of water. Jasmine smiled encouragingly at her and motioned to her again, a little more insistently this time.

Monica made her way over to where Betsy was standing. Jasmine clipped a microphone to the collar of her sweater and hooked the battery pack to the waistband of her jeans.

Monica felt as if her smile was glued on as the film began to roll and she was convinced that she didn't start breathing again until Jasmine put down the camera.

• • •

Monica felt a great sense of relief as she headed toward the farm kitchen. The crew from WZZZ had left, and she was glad that was over. It had been interesting watching the filming of the segment—although she could have done without having had to play a bit part—but she was ready to get back to work.

And she was starving. Fortunately she had some soup in the refrigerator that she could heat up.

She passed the bog where they'd filmed. The berries had all been collected and Dan was hip-deep in water reeling in the boom and guiding it toward the truck parked on the shore. Mel had her camera to her eye and was photographing the process. She saw Monica and waved.

Monica waved back and continued on.

There was a note on the counter from Kit when Monica reached the farm kitchen saying that he'd gone into town to deliver an order of cranberry salsa to the Pepper Pot Restaurant.

Monica crumpled up the piece of paper and tossed it in the trash, then went to the refrigerator to retrieve her container of erwtensoep—Dutch pea soup—a recipe that had been brought to West Michigan by the Hollanders, as they called themselves, who had originally settled the area.

She was about to put the soup into the microwave when she thought she heard the sound of running footsteps outside. That was odd. She listened again. Someone was definitely running down the path.

Before Monica could get to the window to see who it was, the door was flung open so abruptly that it bounced off the wall. Jeff stood panting on the doorstep, one hand clutching the doorjamb.

"What's wrong? Has something happened?" she said, looking at Jeff's stricken face.

"Body," Jeff gasped, trying to catch his breath. "There's a dead body. It's Betsy, that newswoman."

"What? Where?"

"Side of the road." Jeff still hadn't caught his breath. He was leaning over with his hands on his knees. He looked up at Monica. "Can you come?"

"Of course. Did you call the police?"

Jeff shook his head. "Not yet. I should have, but I was so startled I could barely think."

Monica grabbed her cell phone off the counter and dialed 9-1-1. Her call was answered immediately by a woman with a calm and soothing voice. Monica gave her the details and their address and clicked off the call.

She stuffed her phone in the pocket of her jeans and grabbed her fleece from the hook on the wall.

"Show me where the body is."

She trotted after Jeff as he made his way down the worn dirt path. Betsy's car was still sitting outside Monica's cottage, the screaming yellow paint job at odds with the muted greens, browns and reds of the nature that surrounded it.

"Up there," Jeff said, pointing ahead of them. His voice caught in his throat.

She lay sprawled on her back, her body nearly hidden in the tall weeds that grew alongside the dirt road. Her legs were bent and her knees flopped over toward one side. Although Monica couldn't see any signs of injury, blood matted the flattened grass by her head.

"It was her shoes that I noticed," Jeff said, pointing to Betsy's red pumps. "Otherwise I don't think I would have seen her."

Jeff's breathing still hadn't slowed substantially and he looked back and forth between Monica and Betsy's body as if his eyes were drawn to the gruesome scene in spite of himself.

"We'd better stand back," Monica said, crossing to the other side of the road. "The police won't want us disturbing the scene."

She looked around but didn't see any signs to indicate what might have happened.

Just then a patrol car came into view, its tires churning up a cloud of dust. It came to a sharp stop when it reached Monica and Jeff.

Both front doors flew open and two patrolmen got out, the belts around their waists heavy and sagging with equipment. The radio squawked from inside the car, sounding like the cries of an angry bird.

Their nightsticks flapped against their thighs as they walked over to Monica and Jeff.

The shorter one, who had a round face and freckles across his nose, said, "You reported a body?" He pushed his hat back on his head, revealing an angry red welt where the brim had been.

"Yes." Monica tried to keep her voice from trembling. She led them over to where Betsy lay.

As they approached, the taller of the two patrolmen put an arm out to stop Monica from going any closer.

"Detective Stevens is on her way," he said, his eyes scanning the area. "We're here to secure the scene until she arrives." He turned to his partner. "Got the tape, Gil?"

Monica stood off to the side with Jeff and watched while the men strung up black and yellow crime scene tape around the area where Betsy's body lay. The shorter one stopped, pulled a handkerchief from his pocket and wiped his face.

"That ought to do it," he said to his partner.

Stevens arrived just as the men were finishing up. She pulled off the road, killed the engine and got out of the car. She approached the scene slowly, looking all around as if mentally photographing it. She stood for several minutes looking down at the body, her arms folded across her chest.

She shook her head and walked over to where Monica was standing.

"You have the worst luck," she said as she approached, her face grim.

She looked thinner than the last time Monica had seen her, and several silver strands now wove their way through her blond hair, which she'd pushed behind her ears.

"I'll need to talk to you if you don't mind waiting." She looked from Monica to Jeff.

They both nodded.

Stevens was silent as she walked back to the body and stood examining it, her head tilting to one side and then the other. She pulled a camera from the pocket of her jacket and began snapping photographs as she walked around the body, taking in every angle.

She took the camera from her eye and crossed the road to Monica. "Do you know who she is?"

"Betsy DeJong. She's the evening news anchor and the host of *What's Up West Michigan.*"

Stevens stroked her chin. "I thought she looked familiar." She looked toward the body again. "What was she doing here?" She jerked her head in the direction of the bogs.

Monica explained about Sassamanash Farm being filmed for a segment on the television show Betsy hosted.

"Who else was here?" She squinted at the scene. "I imagine there were other people?"

Monica ran through the names of the crew that had come with Betsy, ticking them off on her fingers.

"Jasmine Talcott, the camerawoman. Todd Lipton—he's the producer of the show. Betsy's fiancé stopped by."

"Who's that?" Stevens raised her eyebrows.

"Bob Visser. He's running for Senate."

Stevens nodded. "He's the guy who owns Visser Motors. I've seen him on television." Stevens frowned. "What was he doing here?"

"He said he stopped by to say hello to Betsy." Monica took a breath. "And then there was Lauren, Jeff's fiancée, and Melinda Leigh, who is taking photographs of the farm for our Instagram account."

Stevens wrinkled her forehead. "Instagram?"

Monica shrugged. "I'd never heard of it either but apparently it's one of the newer forms of social media."

Stevens made a face. She was quiet for a moment. "Is that all? What about the people working on the farm?"

It hadn't occurred to Monica that this could have anything to do with Jeff's crew. What reason would they have had to kill Betsy, someone they didn't even know?

"There's me, Jeff of course, and his crew. You'll have to get their names from him." Monica motioned toward Jeff, who had gone to sit on a large rock alongside the road. "The only ones I know are Mauricio and Dan Polsky." Monica thought for a minute. "Then there's Nora in the farm store and Kit, who works with me. But he was off on a delivery in town."

Stevens was scribbling in her notebook. She stuffed it back in her pocket.

"I don't want to move the body until the medical examiner gets here. There's no obvious wound from this angle, but there is blood so obviously she didn't have a heart attack. I suppose we'll get some more answers when the ME has a chance to examine the body."

As if on cue, the sound of an engine reverberated in the distance and a car came bumping down the road, its frame groaning in protest as it hit a large pothole.

A man, who looked young despite his thick head of gray hair and gray beard, got out. He stood for a moment looking around then approached Monica and Stevens.

"Fortunately the previous ME, Dr. Van der Heide, retired a couple of months ago." Stevens shook her head. "Dr. Russo is much easier to work with." She smiled as Russo approached them.

"Good to see you again," he said when he reached them. "Although I wish it was under different circumstances." He looked around him. "This is beautiful. The trees are almost at their peak." He grinned. "I'm a transplanted city boy. I grew up in New York." He exhaled sharply. "Best get on with it, I suppose."

Monica turned away as Russo began to examine the body, talking to himself in a low murmur. It was quiet except for the raucous cry of a loon in the distance.

Finally, Russo turned and snapped off his rubber gloves as he walked back toward Monica and Stevens.

"Blunt force trauma to the head," he said succinctly. "I'll be able to tell you more when I get her on the table."

"The blow was from behind?" Stevens said. "Could she have fallen and hit her head?"

"No." Russo stroked his beard. "Someone did this." He turned back and looked toward the body. "Someone did this on purpose."

"So murder," Stevens said. "Easy enough for the killer to pick up a rock. They're all over the place. That would mean it probably wasn't premeditated. An argument that got out of hand, maybe." Stevens sighed.

She called to Jeff and motioned with her hand. "I'm going to need to speak with your crew," she said. "Everyone who was here while the filming was going on. Can you get them together for me?"

"Sure. We'll be in the processing shed. Monica can show you the way," Jeff called over his shoulder as he took off at a trot.

Stevens turned to Monica. "Is there anyone else here?"

"Melinda Leigh is around somewhere. She's still taking pictures. And Lauren, Jeff's fiancée."

"I'll need to speak to them as well then. But first I'll deal with Jeff's crew. I imagine they'll want to get back to work as soon as possible."

Stevens took a last look at the body, spoke briefly with the two patrolmen, then raised her eyebrows and said, "Shall we?" to Monica.

Monica led them back down the path, past her cottage, past the bogs, toward the building that housed the processing equipment.

"My husband has come back," Stevens said suddenly.

Monica was surprised. Stevens's husband had taken off shortly after their son was born.

"He wants shared custody of Ethan." She gave a bitter laugh. "I've finally gotten the hang of this single mother thing and he shows up."

"What are you going to do?"

"I don't know. Hire a lawyer, I suppose. There goes the money I was saving for a new roof."

By now they had reached the processing plant. The men were sitting around, slumped on overturned crates, their expressions wary. Mauricio was staring at his feet, his shoulders hunched as if for protection, and one of the other men was picking nervously at a scab on his hand. Monica supposed they were nervous. It wasn't every day that you were interviewed by the police.

Stevens's cell phone rang as they stepped into the room and she moved off to the side to answer it.

Jeff glanced at her out of the corner of his eye and then sidled up to Monica. There was a faint sheen of perspiration on his forehead.

"I can't find Dan Polsky anywhere," he whispered to her.

Chapter 3

Monica said goodbye as Stevens began questioning Jeff's crew and headed back to the farm kitchen to do more baking.

She opened the door to the kitchen and sagged against it in relief. It was an oasis amid the nightmare of Betsy DeJong's murder. Monica couldn't wait to sink her hands into some dough. Kneading and feeling it beneath her fingers, stretching it and hearing it snap and crackle was always soothing.

She was finding it hard to concentrate though and put twice the amount of flour necessary into the dough for a batch of cranberry bread and had to scrap the whole thing.

She kept thinking about Jeff. He had clearly been worried about Dan going missing just when Stevens wanted to question everyone. But why? Did he know something? Monica couldn't imagine how. Jeff had only met Betsy today.

Monica had made another batch of dough for cranberry bread — with the right quantity of ingredients this time — and was about to shape it into loaves when Kit returned from delivering the cranberry salsa.

He was agog when he walked in the door.

"Why is there crime scene tape up by your cottage?" he said breathlessly as he took off his jacket.

"Betsy DeJong, the host of *What's Up West Michigan*, was found murdered."

"Murdered!" Kit shrieked, and Monica could have sworn he was more excited than shocked. "What happened? Who killed her?"

"We don't know. She and her crew had all left when Jeff discovered her body alongside the road. The police have been here and they've questioned everyone, but of course they don't know what happened yet."

Kit gasped. "So the killer is still on the loose?"

"It looks like it. But they don't think it's random. Betsy was targeted on purpose."

"That makes me feel a little safer at least," Kit said. His glance darted toward the door. "Should we lock the door? Just in case?"

"If it makes you feel better."

Kit scurried over to the door and turned the lock. "I do feel better."

He smiled at Monica. "Better safe than sorry, my granny used to say."

Kit had never talked much about himself and Monica realized she had never asked.

"Where are you from?" she said, keeping her gaze on the dough on the marble slab in front of her.

"A small town in Florida near the Okefenokee Swamp."

"Why did you leave?"

Kit rolled his eyes. "Believe me, it was no place for a boy like me. Can you even imagine?" Kit posed with one hand on his hip.

Monica laughed. "I suppose."

Finally they settled down and went to work, side by side, mixing dough, rolling it out and baking it.

Monica glanced at the clock on the wall and realized it would soon be time for *What's Up West Michigan*. She wondered if they would even run the piece under the circumstances. But if they did, she didn't want to miss it. She wiped her hands on a towel, took off her apron and reached for her fleece.

Kit promised to close up when he was done with the last batch of scones and Monica headed out the door.

Monica was approaching her cottage when she heard a car engine in the distance. Was it Greg on his way home? she wondered.

Moments later the red-and-white WZZZ van bounced into view, slowing over the ruts and potholes in the road. It pulled up to the spot where the plastic police tape still cordoned off the crime scene. The door on the passenger side opened and Todd Lipton jumped out.

Monica watched as Todd walked toward her. There was a new cockiness to his step that she hadn't noticed before and he'd changed his shirt. The one he'd worn earlier in the day looked as if he'd slept in it, while this one looked as if it had just come out of the plastic wrap with its stiffly starched collar and cuffs. He was carrying a microphone and was panting slightly when he reached Monica.

The driver's-side door of the van opened and Jasmine jumped out. She immediately went around to the back of the van and reappeared with her camera on her shoulder.

Todd began speaking into the microphone.

"We're here at Sassamanash Farm in Cranberry Cove, where WZZZ anchorwoman and host of *What's Up West Michigan* Betsy DeJong was brutally murdered earlier this afternoon."

He looked at Monica. "Tell us. Are you the one who found the body?" He thrust the microphone at her.

Monica backed away slightly. "No, I'm not."

Todd looked slightly irritated. "Can you tell us who did find the body?"

Monica didn't want to say, but Todd had the microphone in her face again.

"My brother," she blurted out. "Jeff Albertson."

"But you were here when the police arrived, were you not?"

Once again the microphone was pointed at Monica. "Yes," she said somewhat reluctantly.

"You saw the body?" Todd smiled at the camera.

Monica shuddered. "Yes."

Todd walked over to the area cordoned off by the fluttering crime scene tape. Jasmine followed him and focused the camera on the spot where Betsy's body had been sprawled on the grass.

"This is where Betsy DeJong's body was found—in these weeds alongside this dirt road leading to Sassamanash Farm. According to the police, she was hit over the head, possibly with a rock."

Todd seemed to be taking a ghoulish delight in reporting on the scene where his unfortunate colleague had been murdered. Jasmine, on the other hand, looked rather pale, Monica thought, but her hand on the camera was steady.

Finally, Todd finished speaking and Jasmine lowered her camera.

Todd smiled as he walked toward Monica. "We'd like to speak to your brother," he said. "Where can we find him?"

"I don't know. He might still be at the bogs."

Todd began walking down the path toward the farm. He motioned for Jasmine to follow him.

Jasmine stopped briefly alongside Monica.

"Betsy's death has certainly given Todd's career a boost," she said. "Word around the station is that he'll be taking over her evening news spot as well as *What's Up West Michigan*."

That was interesting, Monica thought. An idea crossed her mind but she dismissed it. Surely Todd wouldn't actually murder Betsy in order to get ahead. She thought about it as she walked back toward her cottage.

• • •

Greg was pulling into the driveway just as Monica reached their back door.

"What's going on?" he said before he even took his jacket off. "There was crime scene tape surrounding an area just up the road from here."

Monica filled him in on Betsy's murder.

He put his hands on Monica's shoulders. "How awful. You should have called me. I would have come right home." He put a finger under Monica's chin and tilted her face up. "Are you okay?"

Monica took a deep breath. "Yes. I'm okay. I'll be fine."

Greg glanced at the clock. "What time is the show on?"

"In forty-five minutes," Monica said. "I'll start dinner and then we can sit down and watch it."

Monica went out to the kitchen while Greg turned on the television in the living room. She was washing lettuce for a salad when there was a knock on the door.

"We thought we'd come watch the show with you," Jeff said when Monica opened the door. He had his arm around Lauren but Monica thought her expression was strained.

"Come in," Monica said.

They all bustled into the living room. Monica and Greg got comfortable on the sofa and Lauren sat in an armchair with Jeff on the floor at her feet, his head resting against her legs.

Monica tried to gauge the mood between Jeff and Lauren but it was hard to tell. She did think she detected some tension in the air though.

The show was about to start. Greg pressed a button on the remote and the television crackled on. Monica held her breath as he flipped to the correct channel. Part of her wasn't looking forward to seeing herself on television and part of her was dying of curiosity.

Before the tape was run, Todd Lipton came on the air to announce that they were mourning the passing of Betsy DeJong, who had died that afternoon in an unfortunate accident. He went on to narrate a short biography of Betsy—her childhood, college days, early career. The segment was complete with old photographs the station had been able to gather together in astonishingly short order.

In suitably somber tones, Todd announced that they were about to air Betsy's final segment for *What's Up West Michigan* and then the tape began to roll.

Monica thought Jeff did a splendid job—his nervousness seemed to have evaporated like dew on a hot morning, and the injury to his arm wasn't even remotely apparent.

"Bravo," Greg said as they cut to an exterior shot of the farm store.

This was her moment, Monica thought. She could only hope that she'd done half as well as Jeff.

The segment seemed to last forever and then suddenly it was over.

Greg turned to Monica. "Well done, honey," he said and kissed her on the check.

"Everyone was great," Monica said as she let her breath out in relief. "Jeff, you were wonderful."

"You looked like a natural." Greg smiled.

"Would everyone like a glass of wine?" Monica said.

Greg raised his eyebrows. "We should have champagne, but sadly I didn't buy any, so wine it is."

Monica got up and headed toward the kitchen.

"I'll come help carry the glasses." Jeff jumped to his feet and followed her.

Monica took a bottle of white wine from the refrigerator and opened it while Jeff got glasses from the cupboard. Monica was quiet. She had the sense that he wanted to tell her something.

"Did you ever find Dan this afternoon?" she finally said as she poured the wine.

Jeff took a deep breath. "Yes. But not until the detective had already gone." He frowned. "He said he went to get something to eat, but that's not like him. Normally he would let me know. Dan's the kind of guy you can count on, you know?"

"So it was just bad timing?" Monica said as she picked up two of the wineglasses. "Nothing suspicious?"

Jeff hung his head. "I wish I could say there wasn't anything suspicious about it."

"Do you think he was trying to duck having to talk to Stevens?"

Monica found that hard to believe. She didn't know Dan, but Jeff always spoke so highly of him.

"Besides, what involvement could he have had in Betsy's death?"

Jeff's head shot up. "I don't know, but I heard Dan and Betsy arguing before the filming of the segment at the farm store. They were standing by the processing shed. And it wasn't just a spat—it sounded serious."

• • •

Later, as they were doing the dinner dishes, Monica told Gregg about her conversation with Jeff.

"I suppose you would first have to find out what connection there is between Dan and Betsy," Gregg said as he dried a wineglass. He gave an impish grin. "Because I know you're not going to be able to resist investigating this."

Monica laughed. "You know me too well." She plunged her hands into the soapy water in the sink again. "I'll need to find out if Dan grew up in Cranberry Cove. They said on the program that Betsy did." She scraped at a bit of potato that had stuck to the baking dish. She'd made roast chicken, butternut squash and scalloped potatoes for dinner.

"Maybe they knew each other at school," Greg said as he opened a cupboard and put the glass away.

Monica paused with the sponge in her hand. "I'll have to find out if they're close in age. They look to be. Because if they both grew up in Cranberry Cove, it's probable they did know each other in school."

"But just because Jeff heard them arguing doesn't necessarily mean that Dan had anything to do with Betsy's death," Greg said as he picked up another glass from the draining board and began to dry it.

"That's true." Monica lifted a plate out of the sink and sudsy water ran down her arm. "But you have to admit he did have opportunity."

"Now I guess you'll just have to identify a motive."

• • •

Monica was putting on the coffee the next morning and Greg was still upstairs in the shower when there was a knock on the door. She wasn't completely surprised to find that it was Detective Stevens.

"I've just started the coffee," Monica said as she led Stevens into the kitchen.

Stevens glanced at the carton of eggs sitting out on the counter and the frying pan waiting on the stove.

"I won't keep you long. I'm hoping you can help me reconstruct everyone's movements yesterday."

"Sure," Monica said, grabbing two mugs from the cupboard. "How do you take it?"

"Black would be fine." Stevens sank into one of the kitchen chairs with an audible sigh.

Monica filled the mugs and carried them over to the table.

"Can you remember who left when?" Stevens said as she blew on the hot coffee.

Monica closed her eyes as she tried to picture yesterday afternoon.

"Todd Lipton left first," she said finally. "He's the producer. He got a phone call, and when he hung up he said he had something to do at the station." She frowned. "Of course, he could have come back."

Stevens's mouth quirked into a small smile. "We'll be sure to ask him."

Point taken, Monica thought. It was clear that Stevens was letting her know that Monica should leave the investigating to her.

"Then what happened?" Stevens took a sip of her coffee.

Monica stirred hers absentmindedly, swirling the glug of milk she'd added into the dark brown liquid.

"Jasmine left as soon as the filming was complete. She'd come in the station's news van. Betsy left a few minutes after she did. She had her own car."

"What about the young girl. Melinda . . ." Stevens began paging through her notes.

"Melinda Leigh," Monica said. "She didn't leave until later. She was still wandering around taking pictures. She blotted up a bit of coffee that had dribbled down the side of her mug with her napkin. "But I doubt Melinda and Betsy even knew each other."

"So she said when I talked to her."

"You sound as if you don't believe her," Monica said.

Stevens shrugged. "People lie. Especially to me. And they have all sorts of reasons, most having nothing to do with their guilt or innocence or even the case in general."

"You mentioned that the victim's fiancé was there." Stevens held her pencil poised over her pad.

"Yes, Bob Visser, but he came and went before the filming was finished."

Monica nodded.

"What was he doing there?"

"He claimed he wanted to stop by and see *his girl*, as he put it." Monica scowled. "Frankly, it seemed more like a campaign stop to me."

Stevens laughed. "That's a politician for you. Always campaigning." She pursed her lips. "I suppose he could have come back as well to lie in wait for Betsy."

"How did he know that there wouldn't be anyone else around? That the film crew had already left?" Monica said.

Stevens pursed her lips. "Maybe he didn't. But he did find her alone. And perhaps they had an argument. He got frustrated. No one was around so he picked up a rock and hit her. Maybe he didn't even mean to kill her but his anger got the best of him."

Stevens sighed and stuffed her notebook into the pocket of her jacket.

"Sorry to have disturbed your breakfast," she said as Monica led her to the front door and said goodbye.

Greg was coming down the stairs as Monica closed the door. His hair was still damp from the shower and slightly tousled, and Monica found it terribly endearing. Not for the first time, she thanked her lucky stars that she and Greg had found each other.

"Who was that?" Greg said after giving her a kiss.

"Detective Stevens."

"I guess I shouldn't be surprised. She was bound to be back. Did she fill you in on the case?" Greg asked teasingly.

"Not really," Monica said as she put a chunk of butter in the frying pan and turned on the burner. "I wish I knew what Dan and Betsy had been arguing about yesterday."

"There might not have been anything sinister about it," Greg said, fishing silverware out of the drawer. "I mean, she might have backed into his car while parking or made a rude comment about what he was wearing. It could have been anything—even something completely innocent." Greg put two forks down on the table. "I guess the first thing you'll want to do is to find out if Dan grew up in Cranberry Cove."

Monica smiled. "That should be easy. I'll ask the VanVelsen sisters. They know everything."

"That they do," Greg said with a wry smile.

• • •

The VanVelsen sisters, elderly identical twins, ran Gumdrops, the local candy store, where residents and tourists could buy bags of penny candy (now a dime or more thanks to inflation) and traditional Dutch confections like Droste chocolates and Wilhelmina Peppermints.

Monica had been planning to go into town to see the progress they were making on renovating Book 'Em. It would be easy enough to stop in to see the VanVelsens as well.

She spent a couple of hours with Kit in the farm kitchen, baking several batches of cranberry muffins and a number of loaves of cranberry bread.

"I'll be gone for a bit," she said to Kit as she put on her jacket. "I've got some things to do."

Monica first stopped at home to check Mittens's food and water bowls. Both needed refilling, and she smiled as Mittens meowed her thanks, rubbing against Monica's legs affectionately.

Monica grabbed her purse, dug out her car keys and went out the back door.

It was a bright day with blue skies dotted with fluffy white clouds that occasionally blotted out the bright sun, leaving patches of shadow on the road in front of Monica.

The scent of woodsmoke mixed with hay drifted through her partially opened window—two scents that Monica always associated with autumn. As she crested the hill by the abandoned Shell station, . Beach Hollow Road and Lake Michigan beyond came into view. The lake was relatively calm with only a bit of white froth topping the waves.

The few boats that had not been put in dry dock yet bobbed in the harbor by the Cranberry Cove Yacht Club and the blue-and-white club flag fluttered briskly out front in the breeze.

Gumdrops was on Beach Hollow Road, where all the shops were painted in various pastel hues. The Cranberry Cove Diner, favorite spot of the locals, was down the street, and next to it was Book 'Em.

Downtown Cranberry Cove was more crowded than usual, with tourists on trips to see the autumn leaves. Monica had to wait for a blue pickup truck to back out before she managed to get a parking space down the street from Book 'Em.

The scent of frying bacon and potatoes drifted out into the air from the Cranberry Cove Diner, where the door had been propped open to catch the breeze. The flowers in the baskets hanging from light poles meant to look like old-fashioned gas lamps were fading, but the yellow mums in the planters alongside the doors of Book 'Em were still bright with color.

The sound of hammering came from the upper floor, and when Monica opened the door, plaster dust was evident in the air. A loud bang from above made her jump and she noticed the overhead light fixture sway slightly.

Haley Bouma, the niece of Phyllis Bouma, Cranberry Cove's librarian, was behind the counter. Greg had hired her to help out occasionally. She was only in her teens and was already nearly six feet tall.

Several customers browsed the used book section, seemingly oblivious to the noise coming from the second floor.

Greg rushed forward to greet Monica, a feather duster in his hand. He glanced at it ruefully after kissing her on the cheek.

"It's a losing battle, I'm afraid," he said. "They're knocking down the wall between my former living room and the bedroom and it's been raining plaster all day."

Just then another loud crash made everyone jump. Monica was surprised to see that an older woman, sitting in one of the sagging armchairs scattered around the shop, hadn't even blinked at the noise. Nor did she seem to notice that the shoulders of her jacket were speckled with dust.

"It's hard working with that noise overhead." Greg pointed to the ceiling. "But I didn't want to close the shop any longer than necessary. Fortunately, the customers don't seem to mind." Greg brushed some dust off his trousers. "I will have to close though when they break through the ceiling to install the spiral staircase, but by then the renovations will nearly be done. The contractor said that is the last step before they paint."

"That's exciting," Monica said as she looked around the shop and tried to imagine an elegant wrought iron spiral staircase in the center.

"Would you like to see what the construction crew has done so far?"

"I'd love to."

Monica followed Greg through the stockroom and up the wooden stairs that creaked with every step. The noise from above got louder and louder as they approached the second floor and the air was thick with plaster dust. It stuck in Monica's throat and she began to cough.

Greg turned around. "Are you okay?"

"I'm fine," Monica managed to say.

Upstairs two men were hard at work, one wielding a sledgehammer against the partially collapsed wall and the other using a pry bar to remove flooring. Monica looked around the space, trying to envision the café when it was completed. She pictured tables and chairs against one wall and a coffee bar against the other. It was going to be lovely and would surely increase business at Book 'Em.

Suddenly she felt something cold and wet against her hand.

It was all she could do to stifle the scream that rose in her throat enough so that it came out as a rather pathetic squeak. She looked down not knowing what to expect.

A rather scruffy dog was staring at her, its pink tongue lolling out of the corner of its mouth and its tail wagging furiously. It had a shaggy brown coat desperately in need of brushing and one ear that stood up perkily while the other flopped over.

"What . . . ?" Monica managed to find her voice.

"Apparently he wandered in at some point when the men left the door open," Greg said, reaching down to scratch the dog behind the ears. "No one seems to know who he belongs to."

"How long has he been here?"

"A day or two." Greg stopped scratching and the dog nudged his hand gently.

"Where does he go at night?" Monica said, thinking of the temperature dropping now that they were into fall. Jeff was already on the alert for a frost, which could harm the cranberry crop.

"He's been staying here," Greg said. "I put down a bowl of water and Bart from the butcher shop gave me some scraps to feed him."

"What are you going to do about him?"

Greg shrugged. "I don't know. I thought of putting posters up around town. In the meantime, he seems to be fine here. I'll be sure to walk him before I leave."

Monica pulled her cell phone from her purse. "I'll show his picture to the VanVelsens and see if they know anything." She angled the camera and snapped a photo.

"Maybe we can keep him?" Greg said with a sheepish smile.

The dog tilted its head to the side and looked from Monica to Greg and then back again. He wagged his tail harder, as if trying to convince them.

"Maybe," Monica said. "But we first have to make sure someone isn't looking for him."

• • •

Monica left Book 'Em and headed down the street toward Gumdrops. She passed the diner, where Gus Amentas was behind the counter flipping burgers and frying eggs like a juggler. She waved to Tempest Storm, who was rearranging the crystals in the window of her new age shop Twilight, and finally paused in front of Danielle's, a pricey boutique frequented more by the tourists than the locals. There was a lovely sweater in the window — a chunky knit in autumn colors of rust and yellow. Monica sighed. There was no point in going inside. She knew without even checking that the price would be beyond her.

Finally, she reached Gumdrops. The shop smelled of sugar and chocolate mingled with the faint scent of cherries. The display case, filled with gumdrops, jelly beans, licorice, jawbreakers and other sweets, created a colorful backdrop against one wall.

The VanVelsen sisters were dressed in identical plum sweaters and plaid skirts. Gerda was flipping through a magazine at the counter while Hennie was unpacking a carton of Wilhelmina Peppermints. They both looked up when Monica walked in.

"Good morning, Monica," Gerda said.

Hennie glanced at her watch and then in her sister's direction. "It's after twelve so I suppose we should actually be saying good afternoon." She smiled at Monica "What can we get for you today?"

"Nothing today, I'm afraid, but I do have a question for you. Two questions, actually."

Monica pulled her phone out of her purse and brought up the picture of the dog that had adopted Book 'Em as its new home. "Do either of you recognize this dog? It got into Greg's shop when one of the workmen left the door open. It doesn't have any tags and we have no idea who he belongs to."

Gerda took the phone and peered at the photograph while Hennie looked over her shoulder. They shook their heads in unison.

"It doesn't look familiar to me," Gerda said, handing the phone back to Monica.

"Perhaps it's been chipped," Hennie said. "The vet would be able to tell you."

"Great idea." Monica dropped her phone back into her purse. "Now for my second question. Do you happen to know a Dan Polsky?"

"We knew his mother," Hennie said. "She used to run a hair salon out of her home. It was very convenient. She had a small room near the front door where she saw clients. It brought in a bit of cash. Her husband — he was a long-distance truck driver — was notoriously cheap with the housekeeping money."

"And rather a tyrant, I might add," Gerda said, her mouth pursing as if she had tasted something sour. "She couldn't take any appointments when he was home."

"That's right," Hennie said. "Apparently he complained about the smell of the permanent wave solution she used."

"We haven't been able to get a decent marcel wave since she passed away," Gerda said, touching her gray curls. "These young gals have never even heard of it," she sniffed.

"So Dan grew up in Cranberry Cove?"

"He certainly did," Hennie said, straightening a display of Venco licorice. "He was a quiet boy, as I recall. He spent most of his time with that girlfriend of his."

Gerda nodded. "Yes, he did. She's on the television now, you know."

Monica's breathing quickened. "She is? Do you happen to know her name?"

"Of course, dear. She hosts that program that comes on before the evening news. Gerda and I always enjoy it while we have our dinner."

"That's right," Gerda said. *"What's Up West Michigan."*

"Her name is Betsy DeJong," Hennie added.

Chapter 4

Monica was passing Twilight on her way back to her car when Tempest stepped out of the open door and motioned to her.

"I've just made some tea," she said. "Come have a cup. It's third eye chakra tea—meant to open the third eye energy center and provide intuition and focus."

"Okay," Monica said somewhat hesitantly. She wasn't at all sure she wanted her third eye opened. As a matter of fact, she wasn't even sure what her third eye was.

"Your third eye is located between the eyebrows," Tempest said, as if she had read Monica's mind. She tapped her forehead. "Here."

The shop was quiet with only the tinkling sound of a small tabletop water fountain filling the air.

Tempest pushed aside the beaded curtain and bustled into the back room, her blood red velvet caftan swirling around her ankles. Monica looked around the shop while she waited, admiring the jewelry in the display case—various amulets strung on leather cords and silver and quartz pendants, as well as crystals in various colors and shapes.

Tempest returned with two delicate porcelain cups on a small tray. She held one of them out to Monica.

"I heard about that young woman being murdered out near the farm," Tempest said after taking a sip of her tea. "You're not going to start investigating, are you?"

"Well . . ." Monica paused, trying to decide what to say. "It has made me curious."

Tempest fingered the amulet hanging on a silk cord around her neck.

"Don't," she said suddenly. "I sense danger." Tempest snapped her fingers. "I should do a tarot reading for you."

Monica wasn't sure how she felt about tarot cards, although she knew plenty of people did believe in them, and surely there was no harm in humoring Tempest.

Monica dutifully shuffled the deck Tempest handed her then gave it back with a slight feeling of trepidation. While she didn't entirely believe, she wasn't ready to hear any bad news.

Tempest pulled a card from the deck and frowned at it. She pulled another one and then another. Suddenly she gathered the cards together again and put them down on the counter. Monica noticed her hands were shaking slightly.

"What is it?" she said, reminding herself that no matter what Tempest said the cards revealed, she didn't necessarily have to believe it.

Tempest leaned both her elbows on the counter. The amulet around her neck swung forward and clanged against the glass case.

"I didn't like what I saw," she said. "I saw danger ahead—something dark."

"What does that mean?" Monica was half bemused and half anxious.

"The cards don't predict the future," Tempest said, tapping the deck with her finger. "They give insight into our current path. It looks as if the cards are saying you are on a possibly dangerous course."

Monica couldn't think of anything that she was doing that could be considered dangerous. Unless it was poking around gathering information that might lead to Betsy DeJong's killer? The thought sent a chill down her spine.

Tempest sighed and smoothed the folds of her caftan.

"The cards also give insight into the past. Investigating murder has gotten you in trouble before. Monica"—Tempest grabbed Monica's hands and held them between her own—"you've nearly been killed! Is it really wise to do it again?"

Monica felt a bit shaken when she left Twilight. She reminded herself that she didn't necessarily believe what Tempest had told her, but she had to admit that Tempest was right—investigating murders in the past had nearly gotten her killed. Maybe her luck had finally run out. Perhaps this time she should leave it up to Detective Stevens.

• • •

"What do you think?" she said to Kit when she got back to the farm kitchen and had explained about Tempest's tarot reading. "Maybe I should drop the whole thing."

Kit paused with his hands on his hips. "Darling, I'm quite sure that no matter what I say, you're going to go ahead and poke your nose into things anyway. But I do happen to believe in tarot cards. I had a reading done back when I lived in Florida and the cards told me I needed to move and that I would find happiness somewhere else." Kit paused dramatically. "So I came here, met Sean, got this job with you and voilà, I'm happy." He threw his hands into the air. "I think you should listen to your friend Tempest."

Monica laughed. "You're probably right."

Kit pointed a finger at her. "You know I'm right."

Kit went back to his dough and Monica got two pounds of butter out of the refrigerator and put them on the counter to soften.

And in spite of Tempest's and Kit's warnings, she started thinking about what she had learned from the VanVelsens about Dan Polsky and his relationship with Betsy DeJong. Soon she became lost in thought and went about mixing dough without even being fully aware of what she was doing.

"Earth to Monica," Kit said, snapping his fingers in front of her face.

Monica jumped. "Sorry, I was just thinking," she said. She hesitated for a moment.

"A penny for your thoughts."

Monica sighed. "Jeff told me that he heard Dan Polsky, one of his crew members, arguing with Betsy DeJong the day of the filming. I found it rather odd that they would know each other—after all, they moved in different circles—but according to the VanVelsen sisters, they both grew up in Cranberry Cove and actually dated when they were in school."

"Now that is interesting," Kit said. "What could have them arguing with each other after all these years? They're not still together—she's engaged to that guy running for the Senate, isn't she? The one with the professionally whitened teeth?"

Kit threw his hands in the air. "What am I doing? I shouldn't be encouraging you." He giggled. "But never mind what I said about not investigating. This is getting juicy!" He placed a finger on his chin. "Now, who do you think is guilty? Do you think Dan did it?"

"I don't know. There's not enough to go on at the moment. Jeff seems to think very highly of Dan. He's a good worker. Reliable, careful . . ."

Kit furrowed his brow. "Maybe it was the fiancé, the one who's a Senate candidate. He looks rather smarmy to me. Have you seen those campaign ads of his?" Kit shuddered. "Or perhaps it was that poor beleaguered camerawoman you told me about."

"Jasmine?" Monica began kneading the lump of dough on the counter, pushing it forward with the heels of her hands. "She certainly took enough abuse from Betsy, the poor thing. She's pretty laid-back though. She doesn't seem like the homicidal type."

"Well, neither did Ted Bundy, darling, or so they say. And he murdered dozens of women."

• • •

Monica knew Kit was right. She thought about it as she held her hands under the tap washing the flour off her hands. She wasn't going to be able to rest until she did a little more investigating. Surely asking a few questions here and there couldn't be all that dangerous.

She was turning out the lights in the kitchen when there was a tentative knock on the door.

Monica yelled, "Come in," and the door opened slowly.

"I hope I'm not disturbing you." Lauren stuck her head around the edge of the door.

"Not at all. I've finished for the day and Kit has taken all the goodies down to the farm store for me."

Lauren's normally bright face was drawn and even her blond hair looked lank. Something was obviously bothering her.

"Why don't I make us some coffee," Monica said, heading toward the coffee machine. "And I have some cookies that I snatched from the batch Kit was delivering."

Monica was quiet as the coffee machine gurgled and slowly dripped hot coffee into the carafe. She filled two mugs and put them on the table and then went back for a plate of cranberry walnut chocolate chunk cookies.

Monica took a sip of coffee and nibbled the end off one of the cookies and Lauren still hadn't spoken.

"Is something wrong?" she finally asked as gently as possible.

Lauren was looking down, her long blond hair creating a curtain around her face. Her head shot up suddenly.

"It's Mel. Melinda Leigh. I'm worried about her."

Monica cocked her head. "Okay," she said. "Is there a particular reason why?"

Lauren gave a long shuddering sigh. "Detective Stevens went

around to the apartment she's renting with some other girls. She's living over the pharmacy on Beach Hollow Road."

"I imagine Detective Stevens is talking to everyone who was at the filming that day."

"That's what I told her. She wasn't here when Stevens went around talking to everyone so Stevens went to her apartment. I told her not to worry but she wouldn't listen to me." Lauren ran her finger around the edge of her coffee mug. "I can't help but wonder if there isn't something that makes her think she might be a suspect. Something she doesn't want to tell me about."

"We probably all have a secret we'd be ashamed to admit to anyone. People cheat on their taxes, have affairs, hit a car in the parking lot and drive away. If Melinda is hiding something, it doesn't necessarily have anything to do with Betsy DeJong's murder. It could be as innocent as having shoplifted a pack of gum when she was in elementary school. Being questioned by the police sometimes has that effect on people."

Lauren picked a piece off her cookie and crumbled it between her fingers. "You're probably right. Still." She looked up at Monica. "Is there any chance you could . . ." Her voice trailed off.

"Investigate?" Monica said with a smile.

Lauren let out a relieved breath. "You've done it before."

And almost gotten myself killed, Monica said to herself.

She smiled at Lauren. "Sure. I can ask a few questions and see what I can find out."

Monica had been about to ask Lauren if everything else was okay—she kept picturing how Lauren had stomped off when Betsy began her rather flirtatious interview with Jeff—but she thought it best not to pry.

Whatever was wrong between them, they would have to work it out themselves.

• • •

WZZZ was located outside of Cranberry Cove, a short distance off the highway that led north to Grand Rapids. Monica spotted the building as soon as she exited the highway. It was painted the station's colors of red and white and had an enormous satellite dish out front.

Monica had told Greg that she was going to pick up a tape of the filming WZZZ had done at Sassamanash Farm so Lauren could put it on their website. He had rather dryly pointed out that everything was done digitally these days and surely they could simply email her the link to it. Monica had been forced to admit that she had an ulterior motive in visiting the station. Greg had merely smiled knowingly. Monica had to admit, it irritated her slightly that he found her so transparent.

Monica pulled into the station parking lot and found a spot next to one of the red-and-white WZZZ news vans.

She locked the car and walked to the entrance. The macadam in the parking lot was buckled and weeds grew in the cracks. The door squeaked as she pulled it open.

The reception area of the station had a black-and-white tile floor with several uncomfortable-looking red chairs scattered haphazardly about. Seated behind the curved particleboard reception desk was a young man in a blinding neon green shirt. His carrot red hair was shaved close to his scalp and he had a Bluetooth telephone headset wrapped around his ear.

Monica was walking toward him when a young woman with a clipboard whizzed past in front of her, nearly causing a collision.

Monica took a breath and continued toward the desk. She waited patiently until the receptionist had stopped talking into his headset then she asked to speak to Jasmine Talcott.

The young man pushed some buttons on his telephone console. "Visitor for Jasmine Talcott," he said and hung up. He looked at Monica. "It'll just be a minute. If you'd like to wait." He swept a hand toward the chairs.

"Thank you."

Monica chose one of the chairs and sat down. It was as uncomfortable as it looked. While she waited, she looked around. Framed portraits of station executives were lined up on one of the walls. One of them was slightly crooked and she itched to get up and straighten it but she managed to restrain herself.

A woman came through a door on the far side of the lobby and headed toward Monica. It wasn't Jasmine, but an older woman with long hair that was neither blond nor brown but something in between, a face etched with deep lines and a rumbling smoker's cough that forced her to stop briefly halfway across the floor. She was wearing a long paisley-print maxi skirt and ankle boots.

"I'm sorry," she said when she reached Monica. "Jasmine is off on a shoot and won't be back until this afternoon. Can I help you with something?" She paused. "I'm Patty, by the way."

"I'm Monica Albertson." Monica stood up. "I was hoping to get a copy of the segment you did on Sassamanash Farm the other day."

Patty smiled, revealing nicotine-stained teeth. "No problem. I can put it on a flash drive for you. Will that do?"

"Perfectly," Monica said.

She followed Patty across the tiled floor, through a door and into a warren of cramped cubicles. Patty's was at the end of a row. Unlike some of the others, her desk was very tidy—the piles of papers stacked on it perfectly aligned. She had a Beatles poster on the wall and a framed photograph of an older woman with tightly curled gray hair on her desk. Her mother? Monica wondered.

Patty shook her computer mouse and her computer sprang to life, her screen saver—a colorful shot of the Las Vegas strip—coming into view.

"Jasmine did a wonderful job filming the segment out at our cranberry farm," Monica began. "Although Betsy DeJong didn't seem too pleased with it for some reason."

Patty spun around in her chair. She rolled her eyes.

"Poor Jasmine. I feel sorry for her. Betsy was never pleased with anything she did. And Jasmine was a perfectly competent camerawoman. She's even won a couple of awards." Patty lowered her voice. "Betsy went so far as to try to get Jasmine fired."

"No! Really?" Monica feigned surprise.

Patty nodded her head. "She used to march upstairs to management at least once a week to insist that they get rid of Jasmine. Management had to walk a tightrope to keep Betsy happy while not giving in to all of her demands. Somehow they always seemed to find some way to humor her." Patty jiggled her mouse. "I think they should have gotten rid of Betsy. Frankly, I think she was more trouble than she was worth. Sue in human resources says she has a drawer completely full of applicants who would like to take Betsy's place and would be a sight more grateful for the opportunity."

"That must have made things really tough for Jasmine—having to work with someone who was creating such a hostile atmosphere."

Monica thought back to the day of the filming. She'd been

astonished at how well Jasmine had kept her cool. She wasn't at all sure she would have been able to do the same thing herself under those circumstances.

Patty pulled the flash drive out of the USB port on her computer and handed it to Monica.

"That should work for you." She reached for her mouse and clicked the file closed. "Jasmine usually took it in her stride, but the last time it happened I heard she really lost it."

Monica raised her eyebrows in inquiry. "Oh? She did?"

Patty nodded. "I heard one of the gals talking about it in the break room at lunch. Apparently Jasmine walked back to her desk as calmly as you please, picked up a pair of scissors and plunged them over and over again into her desk chair. They said that when she was done, half the stuffing was spilling out."

Monica thanked Patty, put the flash drive in her purse and wended her way back through the tightly packed cubicles. So Jasmine wasn't as unaffected by Betsy's taunting as she pretended to be. Monica couldn't imagine savagely attacking a chair with a pair of scissors, but then she couldn't imagine murdering someone either. There was obviously more to Jasmine than met the eye.

She opened the door that led to the lobby. As she crossed the lobby floor, she happened to glance to her right and once again she noticed the crooked picture on the wall. No one seemed to be looking so she headed over to it.

She was tapping the right corner of the ornate gilt frame to level it when another picture caught her eye—a blond woman in a dark blue suit and white silk blouse posed against the usual anonymous corporate background provided by the photographer. Out of curiosity, she checked the small gold nameplate attached to the frame. It read *Heidi DeJong, Senior Executive Producer.*

Any relation to Betsy DeJong? Monica wondered. The area was heavily populated by the Dutch, so DeJong was hardly an unusual surname.

Monica looked toward the reception desk. The receptionist was staring at his computer screen and didn't appear to be on the telephone. She went over to him and waited until he noticed her presence.

He looked up. "Can I help you?" He fiddled with the collar of his shirt.

"I was wondering . . ." Monica gestured toward the photographs on the wall. "Is Heidi DeJong any relation to the late Betsy DeJong, the host of *What's Up West Michigan*?"

He bobbed his head up and down repeatedly like a bobble head doll. "They most certainly were related. Heidi and Betsy were sisters," he said.

Monica was grateful he didn't ask why she was interested. "How nice that they could work together," she said.

"I don't know that I'd call it working together," he said and giggled. "Or nice, either, for that matter."

"Oh? Didn't they get along?"

He stood up and leaned his elbows on the desk. "My name's Josh, by the way."

"Monica."

"If there's one thing a television station reveres, it's the talent. But if you want to go into the whole corporate hierarchy thing, Heidi was technically Betsy's boss and should have had the upper hand. And that didn't go over very well with Betsy. She was the older sister and she felt that ought to give her some sort of privilege. When the two were together, fur would literally fly."

Well, that was interesting, Monica thought as she thanked Josh and headed out to her car. The wind had picked up, sending grit and loose gravel swirling across the parking lot. Monica quickly buttoned her jacket and turned up her collar.

So Betsy and Heidi didn't get along. Heidi might not have been at the filming at the farm, but if Monica remembered correctly, Bob Visser had said that Heidi had been the one to tell him where Betsy was that afternoon. And that meant that Heidi knew exactly where to find Betsy if she'd had murder on her mind.

What motive could Heidi have had for killing her sister? Monica wondered as she headed back toward Cranberry Cove. The fact that the sisters regularly squabbled didn't necessarily make Heidi a murderer. There had to be more to it than that.

Her trip certainly hadn't been in vain, Monica thought as she turned onto the road that led to Sassamanash Farm. She didn't have any answers yet, but she had plenty of new avenues to explore.

Chapter 5

Monica left her car at the cottage and was on her way to the farm kitchen when she ran into Jeff. He had been in one of the bogs helping with the boom and she noticed that his pants were wet up to the knees.

"Looks like your waders sprang a leak," Monica said when she caught up with him.

Jeff scowled. "No, it wasn't that. My foot caught on one of the vines, and when I tried to keep myself from falling, I managed to slosh water down my waders." He laughed briefly. "Occupational hazard, I guess."

"You look tired," Monica said. She knew that the harvest was always a lot of work and that Jeff and his crew would all need a rest when it was over, but Jeff looked even more tired than usual. The circles under his eyes had deepened until they looked like bruises and his face was slack with fatigue.

He ran a hand through his hair. "The frost alarms went off last night at three o'clock in the morning and I had to race down to the pump house to turn on the water to flood the last two bogs. I couldn't get back to sleep afterward." He smiled again. "All part of the job."

Monica still found it puzzling that the way to keep the berries from being ruined by the frost was to actually freeze them in water.

"I hope you can sleep tonight." She put a hand on Jeff's arm.

"It's not just that." Jeff frowned and looked off into the distance. "I'm worried about Dan and I don't know what to do. He said he didn't tell the police about his argument with Betsy DeJong the day she was killed. He won't even tell me what it was about or how he knows her." He looked at Monica and his scowl deepened. "I don't know whether I should go to the police and tell them myself or not." He kicked at a clod of dirt with the toe of his boot. "Dan's my buddy and a darn good crew member. I don't want to land him in it if it isn't necessary."

A loon spread its wings and took off from the banks of the bog, the sun reflecting off its glossy feathers. It gave a raucous cry that startled them both.

Jeff gave Monica a pleading look. "Is there any chance you could talk to Dan? You're good at that sort of stuff."

"You mean worm the truth out of him?" Monica asked with the hint of a smile.

Jeff nodded. "People talk to you. They tell you things. Maybe Dan will, too."

Monica wished she was as optimistic as Jeff about the possibility of Dan opening up to her. Jeff was putting too much stock in her capabilities. But she was willing to give it a try.

• • •

Monica hadn't expected to encounter Dan so quickly. She'd been hoping to spend some time thinking about her approach, but when she saw him sitting on a log by the side of the bog eating an apple, she decided she might as well get it over with. She really felt like turning tail and running, but she'd promised Jeff.

The ground was muddy where water from the bog had splashed up onto the surrounding area. Monica stepped carefully — it was slippery.

Dan stood up and threw the core of his apple into the field beyond. He was about to walk away when Monica caught up with him.

"Good throw," she said.

"The animals can feast on the core." Dan sat down again and Monica joined him on the log.

She thought he looked nervous. He was still wearing his waders and was fiddling with the buckles. He was clearly under some strain — it showed in the way the skin was stretched tight over his cheekbones and in the way the furrow between his brows had deepened.

"You must have been surprised when Betsy DeJong showed up the other day," Monica said. "I hear the two of you dated in high school."

Dan scowled and picked at a piece of loose bark on the log. "That was a long time ago."

"It must be strange seeing her on television now."

"I'm happy for her. I guess it's what she wanted." He shrugged.

Monica didn't think he *sounded* happy.

She took a deep breath. "Jeff is concerned about you."

Dan's hand jerked. "Why? What is he concerned about? If it's my work, then he'd better speak to me himself and not send someone else to do his dirty work."

"No, it's not that," Monica hastened to say. "He heard you arguing with Betsy. He's afraid the police will find that suspicious."

"He's not going to tell them, is he?" Dan's expression was resigned.

Monica avoided the question. "I guess he found it strange. You haven't seen Betsy in years and yet you found something to argue about immediately."

"It wasn't anything," Dan said, starting to get up. "And it's certainly none of your business."

He walked toward the bog and plunged into the water

• • •

Monica spent the afternoon at the farm kitchen working with Kit on a batch of cranberry salsa. Orders had increased and they had to work hard to keep up. Monica was also testing a recipe for cranberry compote that they hoped to sell in the farm store at Thanksgiving.

The pot with the cranberries, orange zest, sugar and spices was bubbling on the stove, filling the air with its delicious aroma.

Kit stopped and sniffed. "It smells like Christmas in here," he said as he filled containers with the first batch of salsa.

"It does, doesn't it?" Monica peered into the pot, where the cranberries were popping and bursting. "I think this is about ready."

She grabbed the handle of the pot and screamed, pulling her hand away as quickly as possible.

"What happened? Are you okay?" Kit rushed over to her.

"I've burned my hand," Monica admitted ruefully. "I forgot the handle was going to be hot."

"Let's get your hand under some cold water," Kit said as he led Monica over to the sink and turned on the tap. He gave her a suspicious look. "Are you feeling okay? You've been looking a little peaked lately."

"I am rather tired. I can't imagine why — I went to bed early enough last night and slept well."

"Everything is going fine here. Nurse Tanner prescribes a nap. Stat."

"I don't know . . ."

"I can handle things. The salsa is almost done and I'll put that compote in the refrigerator. We can do a taste test tomorrow."

Monica felt a wave of fatigue wash over her. "Maybe I will take your advice, nurse." She smiled.

"That's a good girl. Run along now." Kit made a shooing motion toward the door.

Monica couldn't imagine what was making her so tired — perhaps it was the stress of Betsy DeJong's murder and the subsequent investigation. One thing she did know, though, Kit was right—a good nap was probably all she needed.

Mittens was waiting by the back door of the cottage when Monica opened it. The cat meowed loudly and arched her back as Monica scratched under her chin and behind her ears.

Mittens was right on Monica's heels as she made her way upstairs. She paused briefly outside the spare bedroom and looked in. She and Greg had talked about its becoming a baby's room—possibly . . . maybe . . . eventually.

In her mind she'd sometimes imagined the room painted blue and sometimes pink with a crib all done up in Winnie-the-Pooh bedding. The idea filled her with longing at times and fear at other times.

The prospect was scary, but then she supposed everyone felt that way at first. Her own mother had been somewhat cold and distant, although Monica knew that she had done the best she could, especially after her father left her for another woman. Some good had come of that in the end—her half brother, Jeff. And Monica had subsequently become quite fond of Gina, the "other woman," especially since Gina had moved to Cranberry Cove to be near her son.

Monica took a last look at the spare room. Would they be using it eventually? There was no guarantee. They had to be patient.

• • •

Monica woke from her nap an hour later. She yawned and stretched. She definitely felt better, she decided, as she headed downstairs to start on dinner. She looked at her watch. Greg would be home soon.

She turned the television on in the living room and turned up the volume so she could hear the news in the kitchen.

She was scrubbing some of the last of the zucchini from the farmers market when the name Bob Visser caught her ear. She walked into the living room, rubbing her wet hands on her jeans to dry them.

Bob Visser was on the screen, smiling widely at the camera. He had taken off his suit jacket and had it slung over his shoulder. His tie was loosened and the sleeves of his shirt were rolled up.

It was a studied casualness that Monica had no doubt he had practiced many times in the mirror.

The reporter, Benjamin Dowd, was from a national network. His appearance was as calculated as Visser's with his carefully tailored suit, silk tie and expensive haircut.

He lowered his voice and expressed his sympathies over the death of Betsy DeJong, Visser's fiancée.

Visser assumed a suitably mournful expression and bowed his head briefly.

"It's been a terrible blow," he said. "A real tragedy. We had a wonderful life together planned out and now it's been snatched away by a vicious killer. But I want to thank everyone for their kind thoughts and prayers at this difficult time. Their kindness has been a ray of sunshine during this period of darkness." He bowed his head briefly.

Dowd then moved on to a few questions about Visser's Senate race and his proposal to fight for greater environmental protections, particularly for the Great Lakes. Visser answered the questions smoothly, but at the same time he managed to keep his replies from sounding slick or canned. Monica had to admit that he was good on camera.

Dowd's voice then took on a different tone — more challenging and almost menacing.

Visser must have noticed because his expression became less open and more guarded. His stance changed as well. It was almost as if he was bracing himself for a blow.

"You've certainly had your share of tragedy, Mr. Visser. I understand your first wife also died."

Visser scowled and gave a curt nod. It was clear he didn't like the turn the questioning had taken.

"Your first wife died under unusual circumstances, did she not?" Dowd said, looking straight at the camera.

Visser gave another curt nod. He looked around as if he hoped to be rescued.

"I understand it was a scuba diving accident that killed your wife?"

"That's right," Visser said, tight-lipped. "It happened while we were on vacation in Cozumel. A terrible tragedy."

"I also understand that there was some question at the time about the accident, isn't that right, Mr. Visser?"

Visser looked visibly startled. "I don't know what you mean. It was ruled an accident. There was no question about it."

"But weren't you detained by the authorities in Mexico and questioned in regard to the accident?" Dowd appeared to shove the microphone closer to Visser's face.

"Of course I was. Standard procedure. I was with her when the accident occurred. She had an unfortunate heart issue that hadn't been diagnosed. There was an opening—a flap—in her heart that should have closed up before birth but didn't."

"But didn't the authorities suspect her death wasn't an accident at all but was actually murder? And you were the prime suspect."

Dowd seemed to be taking great delight in provoking Visser. He held the microphone out to Visser, but instead of answering, Visser abruptly turned on his heel and walked away.

Dowd smirked. "I guess that's one question that Mr. Visser doesn't want to answer."

The cameraman then panned the crowd that had gathered to listen to the interview. Visser was walking away, with his back to the camera, when a woman went up to him and took his arm.

Monica recognized her from her picture. It was Heidi DeJong.

Was Heidi simply showing sisterly sympathy or was there more to it than that?

Chapter 6

Monica kept picturing Visser's interview on the news and how Heidi had taken his arm as he was walking away. There had been an air of possession about the gesture. Or was she simply imagining it?

Was there anything between the two of them—anything romantic? No one had mentioned it, Monica thought. Jasmine worked quite closely with Betsy and she hadn't said anything about it. Nor had Josh the receptionist.

Maybe someone at Visser Motors would know more? Heidi and Visser might have felt more confident meeting there, away from WZZZ and prying eyes. Monica decided she would pay them a visit soon. She could pretend she was in the market for a new car.

She had a sudden vision of herself, dressed in her faded jeans, stretched-out sweater and worn fleece, showing up at a luxury car dealership in her ancient Taurus with the muffler belching smoke and making rude noises. They wouldn't buy her story for a minute. She bit her lip. What to do?

The solution came to her as she was falling asleep that night. She'd take her stepmother, Gina, with her. Gina knew her way around an expensive car, having owned several Mercedes models herself. Besides, Gina would know how to look the part.

Monica would call her first thing in the morning and arrange it.

• • •

Kit seemed slightly miffed the next morning when Monica told him she had to leave to run an errand and she didn't know when she'd be back.

"Fine, darling," he said, his lower lip stuck out petulantly. "Leave it all to me, your almighty slave. I'll be fine."

Monica couldn't tell if he was kidding or not. Was he in one of his moods that would descend without warning and disappear as quickly as a passing cloud? She started to say something but bit her lip. She'd stay extra late tonight so she could give Kit the afternoon off tomorrow.

Gina had been more than enthusiastic when Monica had broached the idea of her plan to her. They'd agreed to meet that morning at Gina's aromatherapy shop, Making Scents. They would take Gina's car, which, although it wasn't the latest model Mercedes, would still give a much better impression than Monica's beat-up old Taurus.

Monica still felt slightly guilty about leaving Kit to do all the work as she headed into town, but the magnificent color of the changing leaves and the deep blue of Lake Michigan as the sun sparkled on it lifted her mood.

She parked along Beach Hollow Road and looked at her watch. She was a bit early — the part-time helper who was going to mind the shop while Gina was away wouldn't arrive for another twenty minutes. Plenty of time to pop into the Cranberry Cove Diner for a cup of coffee.

It was midmorning and the diner wasn't terribly busy. Gus, the owner and short-order cook, gave Monica a brief smile when she entered, which was a sign that she had truly been accepted as a resident of Cranberry Cove. It was a step up from a nod, which was what new residents got, and a scowl, which was intended to frighten tourists and summer visitors away.

Gus was flipping burgers with one hand and eggs with the other. Obviously the diner's patrons were mixed today — those just now eating breakfast and those who had already moved on to the lunch menu.

Monica stood at the counter and waited while a waitress poured her a cup of steaming coffee. She was about to perch on a stool when she saw someone waving her over to a booth. It was Detective Stevens.

She was nursing a cup of coffee and had pushed away a plate that was empty but for a couple of toast crusts and a smear of egg yolk.

"Good morning," she said when Monica took the seat opposite. "This is lucky. I was going to come and see you."

"Oh?"

Stevens nodded. "I have a few questions for you. How long have you known Melinda Leigh? She confirmed she'd been hired to take photographs of the farm for your Instagram account."

"Melinda? I met her for the first time the day of the film shoot. She seems like a nice girl. Why?"

Stevens shrugged but didn't answer.

Monica reached for the pitcher of cream and stirred some into her coffee.

"Has there been any progress on the case?" she asked as she stirred in the cream.

Stevens gave a bitter laugh. "Only that the killer was right-handed.

Not much to go on, I'm afraid. And no luck finding the rock the killer used so we could get a DNA sample. You'll no doubt hear about it on the news tonight."

Monica had a sudden vision of Jasmine stabbing her desk chair in fury. Had she used her right or her left hand?

Stevens glanced at her watch and began to gather her things together.

"Sorry, I've got to go," she said as she slid out of the booth.

"I wish I could have been more help."

Stevens smiled. "Don't worry about it."

Monica didn't stay much longer. She drained the last of her coffee, paid the check and left, heading down the street to Making Scents.

As soon as Monica opened the door of Gina's shop, the calming scents of lavender and bergamot drifted out. She immediately felt her shoulders relax and some of the tension leave her neck.

She had suggested that Gina dress to look rich enough to afford a Mercedes, and Gina had obviously taken that to heart. Monica stopped dead when she saw her.

She had enough initials on her to make up the alphabet, from the double *C* for Chanel on her necklace, the *G* for Gucci on her belt, a handbag printed with *LV* for Louis Vuitton, and sling-back pumps in leather embossed with *FF* for Fendi.

Her hair, which she went to Chicago regularly to have highlighted, was in an elaborate updo, and rings — both real and costume — graced several of her fingers.

"What do you think?" Gina did a spin in the middle of her shop. "Do I look expensive enough?"

Monica gulped. There were no words so she just nodded.

"Estelle can handle the shop while I'm away," Gina said, motioning to a dark-haired woman who was helping a customer. "Shall we go?"

Monica followed Gina out to her car, which might not have been the most current model Mercedes but was in excellent condition, with only a bit of wear on the edges of the leather seats showing its age.

It still felt luxurious to Monica when compared to her Taurus, with the chip in her windshield where a rock had been kicked up from the road and hit it, to the slight tear in the passenger seat fabric, which she'd temporarily mended with electrical tape, having promised herself she would get around to fixing it later.

Gina's driving made Monica especially thankful for the invention of seat belts. She clutched the door handle as they whizzed down the highway at fifteen miles an hour over the speed limit, and when Gina cut in front of an eighteen-wheeler hauling canned goods, she had to admit that she'd chickened out and briefly closed her eyes.

"I don't know how I'm going to broach the subject of Bob Visser and Heidi DeJong," Monica fretted as they neared the exit. "I don't know why I thought this was such a good idea." She stared glumly out the window.

"Leave it to me," Gina said as she flicked on her blinker. "I'll handle it."

Monica felt an overwhelming sense of relief when they pulled into the parking lot of Visser Motors without having had an accident or causing one. Colorful flags fluttered in the breeze outside the glass-and-steel building. Balloons tied to some of the vehicles in the lot whipped back and forth on their strings and sunlight bounced off the gleaming cars arranged in tidy rows.

Gina had barely put the car in Park before a salesman came out of the building and trotted over to greet them. He was wearing a natty navy blazer with gold buttons, a red tie and a matching silk pocket square. His fruity aftershave washed over them when they opened the car doors.

Monica noticed him admiring Gina's legs as she slid from the driver's seat. His eyes then glided over her outfit and finally her Mercedes. Monica could almost hear the calculator going in his head.

"Les Sullivan at your service, ladies." He held out a hand. "What can I do for you today?"

Gina ducked her head and batted her eyelashes. "I'm in the market for a new car." She motioned toward her Mercedes. "I'm embarrassed to be seen in that old thing." She giggled suggestively.

Monica had to hand it to her—she knew how to turn on the charm.

Les flashed his teeth. "You've come to the right place." He looked Gina up and down. "I think you're going to love the new models."

"I'm sure I will," Gina said in a throaty voice.

Monica trailed behind the two of them as Les led them over to a dark blue sedan. She might as well be invisible, Monica thought.

Les began extolling the virtues of the car, his gold and diamond pinkie ring flashing in the sun as he waved his hands around.

As they were talking, another car pulled into the lot. It was the latest model Mercedes and the most expensive one. Monica watched as a chauffeur jumped out of the driver's seat and went around to open the back passenger door.

The man who got out was wearing a suit that even Monica could tell was expensive. It had a faint sheen to it and was European-looking in cut. He was balding, with the rest of his hair slicked back. He began walking toward them.

He smiled — a grin that reminded Monica of a shark.

"Les, how are you?" He held out a hand.

He wasn't American, although Monica couldn't quite place his accent. She thought it was possibly Eastern European.

"Dimitri," Les said in an obsequious tone. He seemed nervous. "I wasn't expecting you."

Dimitri waved a hand. "No problem. I can wait." He walked back toward his Mercedes.

"Who was that?" Gina said, watching as Dimitri got in his car. The windows had a dark tint that made it impossible to see through them.

"A . . . a customer," Les said.

Monica noticed he was beginning to sweat.

"An old customer and friend of Mr. Visser's," Les said, wiping a hand across his brow.

"What a coincidence! I'm an old friend of Bob Visser's, too," Gina said. "How is he these days? I haven't seen him in ages."

The emphasis she put on the word *friend* made her meaning more than clear.

Les assumed a somber expression. "He's in mourning, as you can imagine. So tragic about that fiancée of his."

"Terrible," Gina agreed. "He must be devastated. After losing his first wife so tragically, too."

"She was — how shall I put it?" Les laughed. "Rather high-maintenance. The fiancée, that is. She kept Bob hopping." He shook his head. "She was useful though. She got that program she hosts on WZZZ to do a feature on Visser Motors when we celebrated our thirtieth anniversary. Money can't buy publicity like that."

"I never thought Bob would settle down," Gina said innocently, running a manicured finger over the shiny paint on the hood of one of the cars. "He didn't seem like the type." She looked at Les from under her eyelashes.

Les took the bait. He shook his head. "I'm not so sure Bob has settled down," he said in conspiratorial tones.

"Oh?" Gina said, tilting her head coquettishly. "That sounds more like the Bob I knew."

Monica held her breath. Was Les going to tell them what she already suspected? Had their trip been worth it after all?

"There was this other gal that began to come around regularly to see Bob. She was quite a looker too. Bob tried to tell me that she was his fiancée's sister, but come on, I told him — I wasn't born yesterday." Les whisked open the door of the Mercedes he was showing Gina and they were engulfed in that indescribable new car smell. "I got the impression this other gal had a pretty high-powered job. Bob once said that she was the sort who would make the perfect wife for a senator."

"Was Bob planning on breaking it off with the fiancée?"

Les shrugged. "I don't know. It kind of sounded like it."

"You don't know this other girl's name, do you?" Monica said.

Les looked startled, as if he'd forgotten that Monica was there.

He stroked his chin. "I know I heard it a couple of times. I recognized it as a name from a story — a children's story. But for the life of me, I can't remember it now."

• • •

"The woman had to have been Heidi DeJong," Monica said to Gina after they had disentangled themselves from a rather disappointed Les Sullivan and were on their way back to Cranberry Cove. "*Heidi* is a children's book."

"Is that what you were expecting to hear?" Gina said, negotiating a turn with one hand on the wheel and the other patting a stray hair into place.

"Yes," Monica said. "It gives Heidi a motive to kill her sister. With Betsy out of the way, she'd have Bob Visser all to herself. And that life Betsy had been planning in Washington would be hers instead."

"Couldn't Visser simply end his engagement to Betsy? People do that all the time these days."

"I don't know," Monica said. "It might not look good since he is running for office. Voters don't react well to that sort of thing."

Gina snorted. "That's true. Besides, who knows what secrets a jilted fiancée might decide to share with the press." She grinned. "If Visser does win his bid for senator, Heidi will be on her way to Washington, and like you said, the life Betsy had envisioned for herself."

They were quiet as Gina turned off the highway just outside of Cranberry Cove.

"Speaking of fiancés, you're still seeing Mickey Welch, aren't you?" Monica said.

Monica had been surprised to learn that Gina and Welch were dating. Welch owned the Pepper Pot restaurant in town, and while the restaurant was doing well, he was far from the rich playboy types that Gina usually went after.

"Yes," Gina said as she blared her horn at the car in front of her as it began a left turn without signaling. She buzzed down her window quickly. "Use your blinker," she shouted at the other driver.

"We've talked about moving in together," Gina said as she hit the gas and sped around the car in front of her. "Although I have to admit that the thought of settling down again scares me half to death."

"It's not so bad," Monica said with a smile. "Maybe you should give it another try."

Monica thought of Lauren and Jeff, whose wedding was scheduled for that spring. Was Lauren having second thoughts? She didn't know what Jeff would do if Lauren decided to leave him. She'd done so much to help him recover from the trauma he'd experienced while being stationed in Afghanistan.

Another thought crossed Monica's mind. What if Jeff was the one having second thoughts? But he wouldn't.

Would he?

Chapter 7

Kit was going to be even more annoyed, Monica thought as she headed to the library later that afternoon. She'd promised him that she would return to the farm kitchen to give him a hand when she returned from her trip to Visser Motors, but first she wanted to research a few things related to Bob Visser. She was going to have to give Kit a whole day off to make up for it.

She'd gone online as soon as she and Gina had returned to Cranberry Cove to see what she could find out about Visser's background—specifically his first marriage. *Michigan Today* magazine had done a piece on him when he first announced his candidacy for the Senate, which she'd managed to locate on their website. It included a brief biography that mentioned his first marriage and the subsequent death of his wife. Monica was pleased to see that the date had been mentioned—that would make her research a lot easier.

Monica made some notes, powered down her computer and headed out to her car.

Dark clouds were moving swiftly across Lake Michigan, and when Monica crested the hill into town, bloated raindrops began splattering against her windshield. By the time she reached the library's parking lot, the rain had turned into a drenching downpour.

Monica hadn't thought to bring her umbrella but managed to find a parking space fairly close to the entrance. Nonetheless, the shoulders of her jacket were soaked and water trickled down her face and dripped from her hair after her short jog to the door.

Phyllis Bouma, the head librarian, was at the circulation desk when Monica walked in, shaking the raindrops from her hair. Phyllis looked up from her computer as Monica approached the desk.

Phyllis had been a fixture at the library for more than thirty years. It had been suggested that she might like to retire, but she scoffed at the notion and said they'd have to drag her out by her feet kicking and screaming.

"My goodness, if you don't look like the proverbial drowned rat," she said. "Forgot your umbrella, did you?"

Monica nodded. "I hadn't noticed how dark it had gotten out until I was in the car and on my way. The sun had been out earlier."

Phyllis laughed. "That's Michigan for you. As the saying goes, if you don't like the weather, wait five minutes." Her tone became brisk. "Now, what can I do for you?" She gave Monica a shrewd look. "I bet you're investigating another case. I suppose it's the murder of that newswoman Betsy DeJong. It took place practically right under your nose."

Monica nodded. "I wondered if you had past issues of the *Cranberry Cove Courier* on microfilm? I need to look something up."

"We certainly do. Are you interested in a specific issue or time frame?"

"Yes." Monica pulled a piece of scrap paper from her pocket and glanced at it. "Anything you have from around April nineteenth, nineteen ninety-five."

Phyllis jotted the date down on a scrap of paper. "I've been meaning to thank Greg for giving my niece Haley a job at Book 'Em," she said as she led Monica toward the back of the library. "She needs some direction in her life—a purpose besides spending all her time on her phone texting with her friends and playing games." Phyllis turned around and glanced at Monica as they threaded their way through the stacks in the biography section. "How is she doing, by the way?"

"Just fine as far as I know. Greg is glad to have some help."

"Here you go," Phyllis said, holding the door open to a small room at the back of the library. She flicked on the light switch.

The room had two microfilm readers side by side on a long wooden table. The back wall was lined with metal storage cabinets.

"That was April nineteen ninety-five?" Phyllis glanced at the paper in her hand.

"Yes. On or around the nineteenth."

Phyllis pulled open one of the drawers and slid her glasses down from the top of her head. She scanned the contents of the drawer and finally removed a small box. She handed it to Monica. "Do you know how to work the machine?"

"Yes, thanks. I've used them before."

Phyllis smiled. "I'll leave you to it then."

Monica took the reel of microfilm from the box and placed it on the machine. She pressed a button and the film advanced until the front page of the *Cranberry Cove Courier* was visible on the screen. Monica turned the dial and scanned the pages as they went by.

Monica turned the dial again and the front page of the following issue of the newspaper came on the screen. Monica drew in her breath when she saw the headline: *Visser Motor's Owner's Wife Dies in Accident*.

Monica stopped scrolling. She fiddled with the focus button until the print became clear, then she began to read. The article was much shorter than she expected—it mentioned Mary Visser's death in a scuba diving accident in Cozumel, that the authorities questioning Visser was strictly routine, and that the death was ruled accidental. There was a very brief bio of Mary and a quote from Visser saying that without his wife's love and support, his success with Visser Motors would not have been possible. Monica was disappointed that there wasn't more. Why hadn't the reporter dug more deeply?

She sighed. There had been nothing much online either—April nineteenth had been the day of the Oklahoma City bombing and the papers were filled with stories about that. Besides, Visser was virtually unknown outside of Cranberry Cove, so why should his wife's accidental death in Mexico make a big splash?

But Monica would have expected the *Cranberry Cove Courier* to cover the story in more depth. Visser was a local man, and thanks to Visser Motors, she suspected he was quite well known in the community. She scanned through issues of the paper until she got to the one published at the end of April but found nothing further on Visser or his wife's death.

She reversed the film until she came back to the issue of the paper containing the original article on Mary Visser's accident. The byline under the headline indicated that the article had been written by a Brenda Croft. Monica wondered if she still worked for the *Cranberry Cove Courier*.

Monica removed the film from the reader, put it back in the box and took it up to Phyllis to be filed.

"Did you find what you were looking for?" Phyllis said.

Monica hesitated. "Sort of. Thanks for your help."

"Anytime," Phyllis said and turned to a patron who had approached the desk.

Monica went over to the shelves holding the local newspaper along with others from the area, as well as from large cities like New York City and Washington, DC.

The latest issue of the *Cranberry Cove Courier* was on the top of the stack. She carried it over to one of the chairs in front of the electric fire and opened it up. She found what she was looking for on the second page—an article on a new ruling by the Cranberry Cove school board written by one Brenda Croft.

So she was still writing for the local newspaper, Monica thought. She ought to be able to find her easily enough.

She glanced at her watch and felt a pang of guilt. Kit had been working all by himself for almost the whole day. She promised herself she'd make it up to him tomorrow.

Meanwhile she was going to pay a visit to the offices of the *Cranberry Cove Courier*, where she'd hopefully find Brenda Croft, or at the very least learn where she could locate her.

• • •

The *Cranberry Cove Courier* was housed in a squat cement building just outside of town. A bright blue Dumpster sat outside near the front door.

The rain had stopped but dark clouds still hung low in the sky and the air was heavy with dampness. Monica looked up. She wouldn't be surprised if it was going to rain again any minute. She quickened her step toward the entrance of the building.

The reception area was furnished with pieces that looked as if they came straight from the nineteen-seventies, and Monica suspected they had—mid-century modern chairs covered in orange and avocado fabric, sofas with wooden arms. When she peeked into the newsroom she half expected to see typewriters instead of modern-day computers.

A harassed-looking older woman with glasses slung around her neck on a chain sat at a desk out front.

Monica went up to her and asked if Brenda Croft was available.

The woman must not have heard Monica approach because she jumped and her elbow hit a mug sitting on her desk. Fortunately it was nearly empty and only a slow trickle of coffee dribbled out and onto the papers spread out in front of her.

"I didn't mean to scare you," Monica said.

"You're fine," the woman said as she dabbed at the liquid with a crumpled tissue. "Brenda's not in, but I can give you her cell phone number if you'd like."

"That would be great." Monica pulled a small notebook from her purse and jotted down the number the woman recited.

She thanked the woman, went back out to her car and quickly dialed the number and waited. She was about to hang up when Brenda finally answered.

Brenda suggested they meet at the Cranberry Cove Diner since she hadn't eaten since breakfast and was starved.

Monica stashed her phone, put the key in the ignition and started the car.

Once she reached Beach Hollow Road, she parked in front of Bart's Butcher and waved to Bart, who was putting up a poster in the window. He gave her a friendly salute in return. She passed Book 'Em where the whine of a drill came from the second floor, and finally reached the Cranberry Cove Diner just as the clouds overhead opened and rain began to fall again.

The diner wasn't terribly crowded, although soon the dinner crowd would begin arriving for the diner's early bird specials, like turkey and gravy on toast or meat loaf and mashed potatoes. Monica found a booth, slipped off her jacket, which was still damp from the deluge she'd been caught in earlier, and sat down to wait.

A few minutes later the door opened and a woman walked in. Monica didn't know what Brenda Croft looked like but she smiled in the woman's direction just in case. The woman approached Monica's table with raised eyebrows.

"Monica Albertson?" she said.

"Yes."

"Brenda Croft." She slid into the booth opposite Monica. The multitude of charms on her bracelet jingled as she slipped her trench coat off her shoulders.

She was an older woman with a fleshy face, an abundance of blush and yellowish hair done up in a French twist. There was a small stain near the shoulder of her sleeveless orange dress. She was wearing a musky perfume that barely disguised the scent of cigarette smoke that clung to her.

The waitress silently placed two menus on the table along with two glasses of ice water.

"I already know what I want," Brenda said in a gravelly voice. "How about you?" She glanced at Monica.

"Just a cup of coffee for me."

Brenda quickly scanned the menu. "I'll have the chicken fried steak and a bowl of chili on the side." She handed the menu to the waitress.

"Do you have a story for me?" she said to Monica as soon as the waitress left, pulling a notebook from her capacious purse.

"Not exactly." Monica took a sip of her water.

Brenda frowned. "Why did you want to meet me then?"

"I actually wanted to ask you about a story you did a number of years ago. Twenty-five years ago to be exact."

Brenda looked startled but also intrigued. "I can barely remember what I ate for dinner yesterday, but go on. Maybe you'll get lucky."

"It was on the death of Mary Visser—the first wife of Bob Visser, the man who's running for Congress."

Brenda nodded several times. "I know who he is. Yes, yes, as a matter of fact, I do remember that. I remember thinking at the time that it was quite curious."

"How so?" Monica stirred a spoonful of sugar into the coffee the waitress had set in front of her.

"In my mind it had the potential to be a big story. A very big story. It had legs, as they say." Brenda tucked a napkin into the neck of her dress as the waitress approached with her meal. "Local resident who owns a couple of big car dealerships and has a lot of money"—Brenda rubbed her thumb and index finger together—"goes on vacation in sunny Cozumel and his wife just happens to die while they're scuba diving?" She cut a piece of her steak and stabbed it with her fork. "And the authorities find the so-called accident fishy enough to detain the husband for questioning?" She waved her fork in the air.

"So what happened?"

Brenda put her fork down and leaned across the table.

"The editor told me to drop it. Drop the investigation. Stick with what we'd been told and basically do a fluff piece on the Vissers."

"Why would the editor do that? Like you said, it had the potential to be a front-page story."

Brenda rubbed her thumb and index finger together again. "Money. What else? Visser Motors is a huge advertiser. They place a couple of ads in every issue of the *Cranberry Cove Courier*. Obviously the editor didn't want to anger the golden goose. The paper runs on a shoestring as it is."

That wasn't all that surprising, Monica thought. The *Courier* was a small newspaper and obviously needed to keep their advertisers happy in order to stay afloat. Besides, Visser's wife's death might have been just what they said it was—an accident. Why risk losing all that advertising revenue if the story turned out to be a bust?"

"Did Visser inherit money from his wife?" Monica sipped her coffee.

Brenda's head shot up sharply. "No. See, that's the thing. What was the motive? Like you said, if he'd come into a bundle of money it would have made sense. But people want to get rid of their spouses for reasons other than money. That's what I told the editor but it fell on deaf ears."

Brenda pulled her bowl of chili closer and spooned some up.

"Maybe Visser had someone else tucked away, a new gal, and he didn't want the inconvenience of a divorce." Brenda lifted up the napkin tucked into her neck and swiped it across her lips.

"I don't know what the laws are in Michigan, but I imagine he would have had to pay the wife something. Possibly even half of everything he owned," Monica said. "I can see how he'd want to avoid that."

"Bingo." Brenda pointed her spoon at Monica. "I smelled a rat but they wouldn't let me out of the cage to go investigate, so nothing ever came of it."

• • •

Brenda wanted to pay for her meal, but Monica insisted on picking up the check. It was worth it—Brenda had given her some interesting information. Obviously, Monica hadn't been the only one wondering if Visser's wife's death was suspicious.

She hesitated outside the door of the diner and took a mental inventory of her refrigerator. Perhaps she'd better go to Bart's Butcher and pick up something for dinner—maybe some pork chops.

"Howdy," Bart called from the back of the shop when Monica walked in.

He had a whole chicken on the counter and was in the process of cutting it up.

"Are you in the mood for some chicken?" Bart flipped the bird over and patted it. "I'm spatchcocking this one for Mrs. Zuidema. It cooks faster that way. I could do one up for you too, if you'd like."

"Actually, I was thinking about some pork chops," Monica said, peering into the old-fashioned glass case, where meat was displayed in tidy rows.

"Excellent choice," Bart said as he wiped his hands on a towel. He removed two plump chops from the case. "These come from the Van Alst's farm." He pulled a sheet of butcher paper off the roll and placed the chops on them. "They don't get any fresher than that. Will two do you?"

"Perfect," Monica said.

She got out her wallet as Bart tied the bundle up with string.

"Heard about the murder out at Sassamanash Farm. Sad state of affairs when we have to worry about murders in Cranberry Cove."

Bart paused with his finger on the twine. "The wife and I watched Betsy DeJong read the news every evening. The wife also watches her other program—what's it called? *What's Up West Michigan?*" He shrugged. "I'm usually closing up the shop when it comes on, but I'll never forget that time on the evening news. It was earlier this year. They said it was a problem with the teleprompter, but I think someone decided to pull a prank on Miss DeJong."

Monica's ears perked up. "Oh? What happened? I'm afraid I wasn't watching."

Bart chuckled and shook his head. "The teleprompter speeded up and she began talking faster and faster until she had to stop reading just to catch her breath. Everyone thought it was quite funny. You could hear newsroom staff tittering in the background."

"What makes you think it was a prank?"

Bart ran a hand around the back of his neck. "It's never happened before, has it? And it hasn't happened since as far as I know. The wife and I thought it was downright funny, but judging by the look on Miss DeJong's face, she didn't find it half as amusing."

"I'm not sure I blame her," Monica said. "Appearance is everything in her profession. And I gather she was hoping to snag this job in Washington, DC. It would have put her on national television."

Bart handed Monica the package of pork chops. She thanked him and left the shop.

It began to rain again just as she reached her car. She ducked in quickly and put the package of pork chops on the passenger seat beside her.

Had someone pranked Betsy on purpose? she wondered as she started the car. Had Jasmine possibly done it? To get back at Betsy for trying to get her fired?

Or had Jasmine gone even further than a mere prank? All the way to murder to get her revenge?

Chapter 8

The rain continued to batter the car's windshield as Monica was on her way home. It was too late to go to the farm kitchen now—she'd have to trust that Kit was able to handle everything himself. She'd call him later and tell him to take tomorrow off.

She was putting the pork chops in the refrigerator when she heard someone banging on the back door. She pushed the curtain aside and peered out the window. Greg was standing on the doorstep, his hands full, holding a large cardboard box. Rain dripped from his nose.

"Thanks," he said when Monica opened the door.

"What do you have there?" Monica said as he put the box on the kitchen table.

"I stopped by an estate sale on my way home. It was take all or nothing so I've got to go through several of these boxes to see what's in them. But the price was right so I thought I'd take a chance there would be something good."

Greg hung up his jacket and sat down at the table. He looked at the clock. "Do I have time to go through these before dinner?"

"Sure."

Greg pulled the first of the boxes toward him and began unloading the books.

"Anything good?" Monica put two potatoes in the oven to bake. They would take at least an hour and Greg ought to be finished by then.

"Nothing special so far, but these can all go in the used book section. They're in good condition." He reached into another box and pulled out a volume. "Here's a blast from the past." He held the book up. "*All the President's Men* by Woodward and Bernstein."

"A bit before my time, I'm afraid."

Monica was peeling the apples she got at the Koetsier's farm stand when Greg suddenly shouted.

"Whoa!"

She put down her knife and turned around. "What is it?"

Greg held up a book, smoothing out its jacket reverently. "It's a first edition Harry Potter." He turned the book around to read the title. "*Harry Potter and the Prisoner of Azkaban.*"

"Is it worth anything?"

"I'll say. At least several hundred dollars." Greg put the book off to the side. "Let me see what else is here."

He stacked books on the table one by one as he continued going through the boxes and Monica mashed the cooked apples and fried the pork chops.

"Anything else?" she said when Greg had lifted a book out of the last carton.

"Nothing as spectacular as a first edition Harry Potter, but some good things for the used book section and a first edition Patricia Wentworth, *The Case of William Smith*." Greg brushed his hands together. "All in all, I'd have to say it's a good haul. Well worth driving a couple miles out of my way for." He looked thoughtful. "I wonder, though, if the person who was getting rid of the Harry Potter book knew what they were doing? A first edition!" Greg shook his head in wonder.

He put the books back in the cartons, which he placed on the floor near the back door. While Monica was finishing their dinner, he set the table and opened a bottle of white wine.

"I think a crisp Chardonnay will go nicely with the pork chops." He poured some in each of their wineglasses. "You haven't said—how was your day?"

Monica thought for a moment. "Productive. Gina and I paid a visit to Visser Motors and discovered that Visser apparently had a girlfriend on the side."

"Oh?" Greg paused with his glass halfway to his lips. "Do you know who?"

"It looks as if it's Betsy DeJong's sister, Heidi."

Greg's eyebrows shot up. "That gives them both a motive, don't you think? Visser and the sister?"

Monica nodded. "Yes. Betsy was certainly in their way. Visser could hardly dump her now that he's running for the Senate. That wouldn't make for very good optics." Monica served the dinner and joined Greg at the table. "You should have seen Gina working the salesman. The poor man was very disappointed when we left without plunking down nearly seventy thousand dollars for a new Mercedes."

Greg whistled. "I can't even fathom a car being worth that much."

Monica reached for her wineglass. "I also discovered that Visser's first wife died under somewhat mysterious circumstances."

Monica explained to Greg about the scuba diving accident in Cozumel between bites of her meal.

"If he did get rid of his wife, it wouldn't be surprising if he did the same thing with the fiancée he no longer wanted."

"True. But then there's also Jasmine Talcott," Monia said, pointing her fork at Greg. "Betsy treated her abominably. And despite her appearance, Jasmine has quite a temper according to a colleague at the station. Not to mention that someone played a nasty prank on Betsy while she was on the air. It could have been Jasmine trying to get revenge. Maybe she took her revenge too far in the end?"

Monica finished the last bite of her dinner and pushed her plate away. "There's also Dan Polsky, the fellow from Greg's crew. No one knows what he and Betsy argued about the day she was killed. It could have been nothing . . . or it could have been something."

Greg stood up and started taking the dishes to the sink. "It certainly is a puzzle," he said.

"How is the dog doing, by the way," Monica asked as she carried the wineglasses to the counter. "Any luck finding his owner?"

"No," Greg said. He opened the door to the dishwasher and began putting the plates in. "One of Book 'Em's patrons, Millie Barnes, offered to take the dog to the vet to get it checked over. Unfortunately it wasn't chipped, so no luck there."

"I guess we'll have to resort to posters around town then," Monica said.

Greg smiled. "We've given him a name, by the way."

"Really?"

He nodded. "Yes. We've decided to call him Hercule. What do you think?"

· · ·

Monica was at the farm kitchen early the next morning. She'd called Kit the night before and had told him to take the day off. He'd insisted he was fine but she'd managed to convince him. His partner, Sean, had agreed to take the day off as well and they were going to go hiking together.

Monica was relieved. She'd felt so guilty about abandoning Kit to do all the work. He'd done a wonderful job. He'd restocked the farm store with a lot of their product and had left the kitchen so clean it looked as if it had never been used.

Monica set to work making a batch of cranberry muffins for the patrons who would be stopping by on their way to work for coffee and something to eat for breakfast.

She was putting the first muffin tins in the oven when there was a timid-sounding knock on the door.

Monica brushed the tendrils of hair off her forehead that had been blown there by the blast of hot air from the oven and went to answer the door.

She thought perhaps she'd find Jeff or Lauren on the doorstep, but instead it was Melinda Leigh.

"Oh, Melinda," Monica said, opening the door wider. "Come in."

"I hope I'm not disturbing you," Melinda said, eyeing Monica's flour-covered apron.

"Not at all."

Melinda was wearing a small gold cross that nestled in the hollow of her throat and had her long blond hair held in a clasp at the nape of her neck. She reminded Monica of a pre-Raphaelite painting.

"I thought I would take some pictures of the kitchen and maybe some shots of some of the muffins and things before you bake them."

"Great idea. How is our Instagram account doing?"

Monica had no idea whether people followed those accounts or friended them or whatever other terminology might be used.

Mel gave a brief smile. "It's doing great. There's lots of engagement."

Monica assumed that was a good thing. At least it sounded positive.

Mel was silent for a moment, staring at a spot on the far wall.

"Is everything okay?" Monica asked.

Mel startled. "Yeah, sure." She bit her lower lip then blurted out, "Is it normal to be questioned by the police even when you had nothing to do with it? With the murder, I mean."

"They question everyone who might possibly have some information that would help them solve the case. It's not anything to be worried about. Besides, you didn't even know Betsy DeJong, did you?"

Monica looked at Melinda but Melinda's glance quickly slid away from hers.

That was odd, Monica thought. Melinda looked secretive—as if she was hiding something. But what?

"I'd better get started," Melinda said.

"I've got some muffins in the oven and I'm about to roll out some dough for cranberry scones. Would you like to photograph those?"

"Yes, perfect." Melinda fiddled with the settings on the camera slung around her neck. The strap caught on her ponytail briefly and she flipped her hair over it to free it.

"You have lovely hair," Monica said. "Are you Dutch like so many of the people here? I've noticed a lot of them are blond."

Melinda spun around. There was an odd look on her face.

"I don't know. I might be Dutch. I'm adopted. My adoptive parents both have dark hair and so do my siblings. People often come up to my adoptive mother and ask if I was really hers. It used to upset her." Melinda's mouth jerked to the side. "It was odd growing up and looking different from everyone else in my family."

"I can imagine," Monica said. "Have you ever thought about looking for your birth mother?"

"No. She gave me up so she probably wouldn't want to hear from me now. Besides, what if I don't like her? Or we don't get along. I don't think I could take the disappointment. I'm better off not knowing."

"I can understand that," Monica said. "I'd probably do the same in your circumstances."

Monica pulled the cranberry muffins from the oven and placed them on the counter. Melinda pulled Monica's red-and-white-checked dish towel from the rack and spread it under the tin of muffins and smoothed it out carefully. She then angled the tin just so before putting the camera to her eye.

Monica wondered if Melinda knew anything about what was going on between Jeff and Lauren.

"Something seems to be troubling Lauren," she said while Melinda snapped pictures. "Has she confided in you at all? Do you have any idea what's bothering her?"

The shutter clicked as Melinda snapped the photograph. She lowered the camera and looked at Monica.

"I think you'd better ask Lauren about it," she said before putting the camera to her eye again.

• • •

Monica spent the next several hours producing cranberry bread, cranberry walnut chocolate chunk cookies and several batches of cranberry scones. Suddenly she realized she was hungry — her stomach was actually growling in protest.

She still had some leftover soup in the refrigerator, which she heated up in the microwave and carried over to the table. She pulled out a chair and sat down with a sigh. Her back was beginning to ache.

She reached for her phone. She thought she ought to check out the farm's Instagram account and see what Melinda was doing.

It took her several minutes but she managed to download the Instagram app and log in. It didn't take long to find the farm account. Monica's breath caught in her throat — Melinda's pictures were lovely. She was truly a talented photographer. She scrolled through them — images of the bog, ruby red with the bobbing cranberries, water caught splashing up from the beater, a loon taking off from the water.

Monica realized she hadn't checked the farm's Facebook page in a long time — she left that up to Lauren. They used it to announce events at the farm like the cranberry harvesting tours and new products that they were introducing in the farm store. Lauren had tried to encourage Monica to write a blog, but so far she hadn't found the time to start. She did share recipes occasionally. That would have to do for the moment.

Monica brought up the farm's Facebook page. It had been several days since anything new had been posted. She wondered if Betsy DeJong had a Facebook page. It would probably be good publicity for someone in the media.

She glanced at the clock quickly — she could spare a few minutes to check. She typed Betsy DeJong's name in the search bar and hit Enter. There were several people with the same name but it was obvious from the profile pictures which one was the Betsy she was interested in.

Monica clicked on the name and was taken to Betsy's page. Her profile picture had obviously been taken professionally. Betsy's hair was perfectly coiffed, her makeup slightly exaggerated but carefully done, and her smile as wide and bright as ever. Monica felt a moment of sadness that her life had been cut short so horribly. It wasn't fair.

Betsy's page was filled with pictures of her smiling at the camera — photos of her interviewing people, sitting behind the news desk, spending her leisure time hiking or kayaking or playing tennis.

Monica scrolled through some of the entries, reading the various comments people had left. There was one picture of a younger Betsy in a cap and gown in front of a sign that read *Grand Valley State University.* One of the comments underneath the picture caught Monica's eye.

Hey girl, glad you made it at last. I thought we'd be starting our freshman year together and graduating together – what happened?

That was curious, Monica thought. What on earth did it mean? She checked the name on the comment – Kristen Huizinga. She clicked on the name and went to Kristen's page. There were wedding pictures, pictures of her daughter's first birthday, a photograph of Kristen at a staff Christmas party at the accounting firm where she worked, and pictures of Kristen when she was younger. Monica scrolled through them, stopping when she came to one of Kristen in a cap and gown standing with another girl in front of Cranberry Cove High School. The other girl was Betsy DeJong. It appeared as if Betsy and her friend Kristen had graduated high school at the same time but not college. Did that mean Betsy had taken a gap year, as they were calling it?

Was any of this even relevant? Monica wondered. But she realized that while she had learned a fair amount about Betsy's professional life, she knew next to nothing about her personal life. Maybe it was time to gather some more information. There might be a clue of some sort that would lead to solving the case.

Monica thought it would be helpful to talk to this Kristen Huizinga. Maybe she could shed some light on Betsy's life. Would she talk to Monica? Monica had no idea but she'd have to try.

• • •

Monica worked hard all afternoon. She missed Kit – not only his help but also his witty banter, which always cheered her up and made the day seem to fly by. By the time four o'clock rolled around, Monica's back was aching in earnest, her hands felt stiff from rolling out dough and even her feet, despite her comfortable sneakers, were starting to complain.

For once she was glad to turn the lights out, close the door on the kitchen and head back to her cottage.

The air felt fresh and cool against her face after the blasting heat from the kitchen oven. She made her way along the path, passing the bog Jeff had been working on the other day. The cranberries had all been harvested and the water drained and siphoned through canals to the next bog.

As she neared her cottage, Monica sensed some sort of activity in the distance—someone's voice carrying on the breeze, a car engine but no sign of a car. She continued walking, going past her cottage and down the road.

As she neared the site where Betsy had been murdered, she saw several people huddled in the road, cameras to their eyes. As Monica watched, another car came along and parked, disgorging several more people who had obviously also come to gawk at the murder site.

Monica felt her anger build and she was sure her face was turning red. The dirt road was private property. Residents of Cranberry Cove and even tourists had always respected that and Jeff had never found it necessary to put a chain across the entrance to the road. Monica didn't mind the occasional person who drove down it out of curiosity and a desire to see where the road led or in hopes of catching a glimpse of the bogs, but she resented all these people gawking at the site where a real, live person had been murdered. It was grotesque.

She decided she would head back to her cottage and call the local police department. Maybe they would send someone around to chase the voyeurs away, at least for the time being.

• • •

A policeman was standing near where Betsy DeJong had been killed when Monica left the cottage the next morning. She waved to him and he gave a brief salute. She was glad to see that the sightseers would be chased away. They'd soon tire of the story and move on to something else.

Kit looked quite rested when Monica arrived at the farm kitchen.

"You're looking good today," she said as she hung up her jacket.

"Nothing like a day off to put a person back together." Kit stretched, reaching his arms overhead. "By the way, what's that policeman doing on the road leading to your cottage?"

Monica explained about the people coming to see the murder scene.

"Did you unearth any delicious information yesterday?" Kit rubbed his hands together with relish.

Monica gave him a shortened version of everything she had learned.

"I'm trying to think of an excuse to talk to this Kristen Huizinga who was in school with Betsy," Monica said as she got some eggs out of the refrigerator.

Kit wagged a finger at Monica and then put his hands on his hips.

"Girl, you have to get creative." He put a finger on his chin. "Now, let me see . . . I suppose you could say you were with the police?" He regarded Monica critically. "Although I'm afraid you don't look tough enough for that role."

Monica laughed. "Thank goodness. I know I wouldn't be able to pull it off."

"How about you're with WZZZ and want to do an interview?"

"With what? A fake microphone? And looking like this?" Monica gestured to her curly brown hair, which was almost always in disarray.

"You have a point. Hmmm . . . how about saying you're a reporter then? For the local paper or that magazine *Michigan Today*. And you're writing a bio of the dearly departed Betsy DeJong."

"I'm afraid I'm not very good at lying. I tend to turn red, and that usually gives the show away."

"Who says you have to lie? All you have to do is *imply*." Kit clapped his hands together. "Goodness, that rhymes, doesn't it?" He twirled around in a circle. "I can see that embroidered on tea towels. What do you think? A new product for Sassamanash Farm?"

Monica laughed but she was thinking about what Kit said. He was right. She didn't have to actually come out and say she was a reporter. She only had to hint at it and hope that Kristen took the bait. With any luck she would be the talkative type.

Monica practiced various scenarios for approaching Kristen Huizinga in her head as she mixed dough and rolled it out. In the end, she had nearly talked herself into a bad case of stage fright. She'd have to pull up her socks, as her grandmother always used to say, and just do it.

She worked through the morning making cranberry salsa for another order from the Pepper Pot restaurant and several batches of cookies for their afternoon patrons who liked to take them home for dessert.

Kit turned to her suddenly, pointing his rolling pin at her.

"Well, aren't you going to go play reporter and interview that woman?"

"I hate to leave you alone again . . ."

Kit flapped a hand in the air. "Don't worry about it. I've got my mojo back and I can handle things just fine by myself."

Great, Monica thought. Now she had no excuse not to try to speak to Kristen.

She glanced at the clock. It was noon, so perhaps she'd catch Kristen coming or going from lunch.

Monica cleaned herself up as much as possible, basically brushing the flour off her clothes and running her fingers through her hair. She collected her jacket and her purse, said goodbye to Kit and headed out the door.

She walked back to her cottage for her car and then headed out. She'd looked up the accounting firm that Kristen worked for and was pleased to see it wasn't far. It was located in a small office park sandwiched between an insurance company and a nail salon. It didn't take her long to find it.

She parked as close to the front door as she could. The parking lot was nearly empty—she assumed everyone had gone out for lunch. She'd checked Kristen's Facebook page again to make sure she knew what Kristen looked like.

It wasn't long before cars began to trickle back into the lot. Most of the drivers and their passengers heading toward the front door of the building were carrying bags from various fast-food restaurants.

A yellow Volkswagen Beetle with flower decals on the front doors pulled into the lot and zipped into a parking space. A young woman got out carrying a bag from the Cranberry Cove Diner. She had blond hair, and from a distance she looked like the pictures of Kristen on Facebook.

Monica jumped out of her car and went over to her.

Kristen jumped and backed away. "Yes?" she said in a tremulous voice.

Monica held up a hand to show she meant no harm.

"Are you Kristen Huizinga?"

"Yes." She sounded hesitant.

"I wanted to talk to you about Betsy DeJong. I gather you were at school together?" Monica brandished the notebook she'd brought along with her.

"Oh! You're doing a story on Betsy. Of course I'd be glad to help. What do you want to know?"

That was easy, Monica thought. Kit was right. Kristen had just assumed Monica was a reporter.

"Is there somewhere we can talk?" Monica said.

"Sure." Kristen tilted her head toward the door of the building. "I'm on my lunch break." She held up the paper bag, where a grease stain was slowly spreading. "We can sit in the break room. No one goes in there except to get coffee."

Monica followed Kristen through the door, past the reception area and a large space filled with cubicles, into a windowless room lined with kitchen cupboards. A coffee maker sat on the chipped and scarred counter, the smell of burnt coffee wafting from it. Every couple of seconds it made a gurgling noise like someone gargling.

Folding chairs were pulled up to a long table. "Please, sit down," Kristen said. "Do you mind if I eat my lunch?"

"No, go ahead." Monica put her notebook down on the table next to her.

Kristen reached into the paper bag and pulled out a container of chili.

Chili wasn't actually on the diner's menu, but longtime Cranberry Cove residents knew that Gus kept a pot of it simmering on the stove at all times.

"So, what do you want to know?" Kristen said, spooning up a bite of chili.

"What was Betsy like?"

Kristen wrinkled her brow. "She was very determined. She knew what she wanted from the get-go." She put down her spoon. "I knew what I wanted, too, and I think that's why we became friends."

"What was it you wanted?" Monica said.

"To get out of the trailer park," Kristen said with a laugh. "I got my degree in accounting. I have a good job and my husband and I bought a nice house. And we go on vacations—all the things my parents didn't have."

"And Betsy? How did she grow up?"

"Her parents weren't at all like mine. They went to the Reformed Church over by the library every Sunday and Wednesday nights. Betsy was in the youth group there. She joined a sorority in college, too."

"Are her parents still alive?"

Kristen shrugged. "I don't know."

"Was Betsy popular?"

Kristen rolled her eyes. "With the boys for sure. Not so much with other girls, which is why I was surprised she joined a sorority. She was a cheerleader and was elected Snow Ball queen." Kristen frowned. "She didn't make prom queen though, and that really made her mad. She'd had her heart set on it."

"Did she get good grades?"

"Yeah, although she didn't work very hard. Not like me. I had to put in the hours to get even a B."

"So the two of you went on to college together?" Monica said, finally asking the real question she wanted an answer to.

Kristen frowned. "No, we didn't. It was really strange." She put her spoon down and looked at Monica. "She sort of disappeared over the summer. She'd already been accepted into college—Grand Valley State, where I was going—but when the first day of the semester came around, she wasn't there."

"Do you know where she went?"

Kristen shook her head. "No one does. I tried to talk to her parents but they refused to tell me anything. They all but shut the door in my face."

"Did she do drugs? Could she have been sent to rehab?"

Kristen shrugged. "It's possible. I don't know."

"Did you ever ask her where she went?"

"Yes, but she wouldn't say. Just acted all mysterious about it. We weren't close by then. She had her friends in the sorority and I'd made new friends of my own." Kristen took a bite of her chili. "Anyway, I ended up graduating before Betsy did. Although she did okay in the end, being on television and all. That was always her dream." She frowned. "She did okay. Except for being killed, of course."

Kristen wiped her lips with her napkin. "Am I going to be in the paper?" she said eagerly.

"Errrr, yes, probably," Monica fibbed.

"I'd better spell my last name for you then."

Monica was relieved when she said goodbye to Kristen and finally got back to her car. She was afraid her reporter act was beginning to wear a little thin. Hopefully Kristen wouldn't be too disappointed when an article never appeared in the paper with her name in it.

Well, she knew more about Betsy DeJong now, Monica thought as she started her car and headed out of the parking lot. She wondered if

Betsy's parents were still alive. If so, it might be worth talking to them.

Because she still didn't know the one thing she'd been after — why had Betsy disappeared for part of a year and what had she been doing?

Chapter 9

Somebody had to know where Betsy had disappeared to that summer after high school. Monica wondered if she'd confided in anyone at the station. Of course, Heidi probably knew, but Monica doubted that she would reveal anything about her sister.

She could drop by the station again and chat up Josh or Patty, but under what pretext? She could hardly pretend to be a reporter again. Anyone at the station who had seen the segment filmed at the farm would know that wasn't true.

Jasmine suddenly came to mind. Monica still wanted to know if Jasmine was right- or left-handed. She tried to remember which hand Jasmine had used to reach for the muffin Nora had given her when they were filming in the farm store, but she couldn't quite bring the picture to mind.

Muffins! That was an idea. She'd get together a couple of cranberry muffins, cookies and some scones and take them to Jasmine. It was a thin excuse but she thought it would work.

She headed back toward the farm and turned down the road that led to the farm store. She was pleased to see that the small parking lot was quite full. Hopefully Nora hadn't run out of anything.

Several people were sitting at the small café tables Monica had recently installed in the store, sipping coffee and nibbling on muffins and scones. A soft level of chatter filled the air.

Nora was putting cookies in a bag for a customer when Monica slipped behind the counter. She checked the display — they seemed to have an adequate amount of everything. Kit was going to be making several batches of cookies for the afternoon crowd.

"I need some muffins, scones and cookies," Monica said to Nora when the customer had departed. Nora handed her a paper bag and Monica began to fill it with half a dozen items. "I'm taking these to someone," she said when Nora looked at her questioningly.

"I'm sure they will enjoy them," Nora said as Monica closed the bag and went out the door.

• • •

Monica pulled into the parking lot of WZZZ. A brisk wind had stirred up some loose gravel and sent a piece of paper swirling past her feet. The temperature had dropped as well and Monica hurried toward the entrance to the station.

Josh, the receptionist, was behind his desk staring intently at his computer monitor. He jumped when Monica approached him.

"Sorry," he said, "I didn't hear you come in." He peered at her. "You've been here before, haven't you?"

"Yes," Monica said. "And I was wondering if I could speak to Jasmine Talcott?"

"Jasmine is in the editing suite. If you make a right after you go through the door and head down that hallway, the editing suite is right at the end. There's a sign on the door."

"Thanks."

Monica went through the door Josh had indicated and down the hall. She knocked on the door of the editing suite.

"Come in," a muffled voice came from inside.

The room was dimly lit with a large screen mounted to the wall and several smaller monitors on the table, where Jasmine was sitting with her fingers on the computer keys.

She turned around when she heard Monica.

"It's Monica, right?" She smiled.

"Yes." Monica held out the paper bag. "I've brought you some goodies from the Sassamanash farm store. We appreciate the great job you did filming us all in action the other day."

"How nice, thanks." Jasmine took the bag and opened it. She peered inside. "These smell heavenly. I haven't had any lunch yet." She waved a hand toward the screen on the wall. "I've been trying to get this project finished." She glanced toward the image that was temporarily frozen on the screen.

She took a scone out of the bag and took a bite. She closed her eyes.

"Heavenly," she said.

"How is everyone here at the station taking Betsy DeJong's death?"

Jasmine brushed some crumbs off her sweater. "They're horrified, of course. I mean . . . murder! On the other hand, I don't think anyone misses her." She took another bite of the scone.

"Not even her sister?"

Jasmine rolled her eyes. "I'm sure she's sorry that Betsy's been murdered but I don't think they got along all that well. I heard them arguing once. You could hear their voices even through the closed door."

"Something work-related maybe? I imagine it can be difficult for siblings to work together."

"Nah. It was something personal. Betsy was accusing Heidi of doing something."

"Do you know what?"

"No. I couldn't exactly loiter around outside their door listening."

Jasmine reached into the paper bag and pulled out one of the cookies. She took tiny bites, rather like a rabbit nibbling a carrot. Monica noticed that she held the cookie in her left hand. And she had reached for the bag with her left hand.

"I said nobody really misses Betsy but maybe not everybody. I forgot about Brittany Tyson. She's the WZZZ meteorologist. She and Betsy used to hang out together."

"Do you think I could talk to her?"

Jasmine looked at Monica curiously but didn't ask why. Monica was relieved.

"I suppose so. I don't know if she's here at the moment but I can check."

Just then Jasmine's telephone rang. She held up a hand, motioned for Monica to wait.

Jasmine listened for several minutes. "Let me write that down," she said, pulling a pad toward her and picking up a pencil. She took down a telephone number — with her left hand.

That ruled her out as a suspect, Monica thought as Jasmine pushed back her chair, got up and opened the door. Monica followed her down another hallway to an open door with a nameplate beside it reading *Brittany Tyson*.

Jasmine rapped on the doorframe. "Someone here to see you." She stepped aside.

Brittany was sitting behind a large desk that looked like real wood to Monica. Several tastefully framed photographs sat on top along with a delicate-looking orchid in a ceramic pot.

Brittany had dark hair in a perfectly sculpted pixie cut and was wearing bright red lipstick. There was a no-nonsense air about her heightened by the neatness of her desk.

She looked at Monica and raised an eyebrow.

Monica introduced herself. "Betsy DeJong was murdered near my brother's farm. I'm trying to get some information on her that might help find her killer."

Despite appearances, Brittany turned out to be warm and friendly and more than eager to talk.

"I was devastated when I heard the news," she said, straightening the stapler on her desk. "Betsy and I had become good friends. It's a great loss. We spent a lot of time together, even apart from the job."

"Girls nights?" Monica smiled.

"Yes, but other things, too. We went to Daytona Beach together on our vacation and we often went hiking on the weekend."

"So you must know a lot about her," Monica said

Brittany shrugged. "I guess."

"Did she ever mention taking time off between high school and college?"

Brittany drew her brows together. "No, she didn't." She picked up a pencil and began tapping it against the desk. "I do know that Betsy was older than her sister Heidi, although Heidi graduated before Betsy did. Heidi began working here right after graduation and worked her way up. Betsy started with the station a year later." She glanced at one of the photographs on her desk. "Betsy and Heidi were what they used to call Irish twins — both born in the same year."

"Do you have any idea why Betsy didn't start college right away?"

Brittany shook her head. "No. She never said and I'm afraid I never asked. Perhaps she wanted some time off."

"Maybe she was pursuing an interest or a hobby?" Monica said.

"I don't know. It's possible. She did want to take up scuba diving but that was later." She waved a hand in the air. "Her fiancé, Bob Visser, is an avid diver and Betsy wanted to be able to go with him. She even signed up for classes, but then she abandoned the idea. I don't know why." She shivered. "Maybe she got cold feet. You couldn't pay me to go scuba diving."

Brittany glanced at her watch. "Sorry. I'm afraid I can't tell you anything else. I have a meeting in five minutes. Can you find your own way out?"

"Yes." Monica thanked her and left the office. She was thinking as she walked back to the foyer. She didn't know all that much more about

Betsy except that she'd apparently abandoned her attempt to learn to scuba dive. And she and Heidi had been heard having it out over something. Were they arguing over Bob Visser?

But the trip wasn't a total waste. She now knew that Jasmine was left-handed and that there was something terribly mysterious about Betsy's disappearance from Cranberry Cove after high school. Why else would she have been keeping it a secret all these years? And why didn't anyone else know where she went?"

• • •

Monica hesitated at the exit of the WZZZ parking lot. Should she go into town or go directly to the farm kitchen? Her mother's birthday was coming up and she wanted to get her something. She thought perhaps she'd send a box of the Droste chocolates that her mother liked so much. She might as well do it now while she was in town and get it out of the way. Then she could hopefully get them in the mail on time.

Monica found a space right in front of Gumdrops. She parked and locked the car doors. As she was heading toward the entrance of the shop, she noticed a poster taped to a lamppost. The picture of the dog that had wandered into Greg's shop was on it with *Is This Your Dog?* in large bold type. The phone number of Book 'Em was printed underneath. She hoped the posters would soon lead to Hercule's owners. He was a sweetie, and they must be missing him.

When Monica opened the door to Gumdrops, a tinny-sounding bell tinkled inside the shop. Both of the VanVelsen sisters looked toward the entrance at once.

"We didn't think we'd see you again so soon," Hennie said. "This is a treat."

Both Hennie and Gerda were behind the counter leaning over a section of the newspaper.

"What's a six-letter word for dog?" Gerda said, her pencil poised over the paper.

Monica thought for a moment. "Canine?"

"Yes!" Gerda exclaimed. "That fits." She began penciling in the word.

"What can we do for you, dear?" Hennie said.

"I'd like a box of Droste chocolates. I'm sending them to my mother for her birthday."

Hennie turned around and took something off the shelf behind her.

"Droste does a lovely gift box." She shooed Gerda out of the way and put it down on the counter. "The chocolates are embossed with tulips and there's a selection of dark, milk, and white chocolate."

Monica looked at the box. There was a lovely pastel rendering of tulips on the cover.

"That's perfect," she said and reached into her purse for her wallet. "My mother will love it."

She noticed both VanVelsen sisters eyeing her figure intently. Monica smiled to herself. They hadn't given up on waiting for her to sprout a so-called baby bump. After the wedding, almost everyone in Cranberry Cove was waiting breathlessly for news of what they would have coyly called a bun in the oven. And now that she and Greg had been married for a while and Monica wasn't getting any younger, the scrutiny had intensified. Little did they know that she herself was wondering if it would ever happen.

She was content either way. She already felt as if she'd won the lottery meeting Greg and having him as her husband. Did she dare to hope for more? Would that be tempting fate?

Hennie looked at Monica with a sideways glance. "Any news about the murder out at Sassamanash Farm? There hasn't been much on the news lately."

"I'm afraid I don't know any more than you do," Monica said, aware of the fact that she was disappointing them. "Only what's been in the news."

"You were asking about Dan Polsky when you came in last. Did you have any luck finding the information you needed?" Hennie said with a sharp look in her eye.

"Sadly, not much," Monica said. "I'm hoping I'll have better luck tracking down some information on Betsy DeJong."

She knew she wasn't fooling the VanVelsen sisters. They knew perfectly well she was holding back some very interesting facts. She also knew they were quite confident about being able to worm the information out of her sooner or later—preferably before it was revealed to everyone else.

"I'm afraid we didn't know Betsy DeJong," Gerda said, looking up from her puzzle, pretending to be nonchalant.

Monica gave her credit card to Hennie, whose face was a study in disappointment. Obviously they'd expected Monica to have solved the case by now and shared the results with them. Hennie ran the card through the machine before handing it back to Monica.

Monica felt guilty. She knew they were dying of curiosity. She felt she owed them a little something. They had helped her numerous times in the past with their knowledge of the locals and Cranberry Cove history.

"I did learn that Betsy DeJong disappeared somewhere for a number of months after high school graduation and no one knows where she went. Or at least they're not saying. She ended up starting college late a year later. I thought that was odd for someone who was so keen to get ahead."

Both Hennie's and Gerda's eyebrows shot up in unison.

"I'm wondering where she went and what she was doing that was so important to her that she was willing to put her plans on hold." Monica sighed. "No one seems to know."

Hennie and Gerda exchanged a look that Monica couldn't quite decipher.

"In our day," Hennie said, "if a girl disappeared it meant only one thing."

Gerda nodded her agreement.

"What's that?"

Hennie and Gerda exchanged a glance again.

Hennie cleared her throat. "How can I put this delicately? It usually means that the girl is in the family way."

Of course! Monica thought as she left Gumdrops. Why didn't she think of that? She supposed it was because it didn't fit the image Betsy had crafted of herself as a dedicated, driven career woman. If what the VanVelsens said was true, then she must have put the baby up for adoption. Obviously she didn't want to be dragged down by a mistake made when she was in high school.

• • •

Monica stopped at Bart's Butcher on her way home for a roasting chicken for dinner and then headed to the farm kitchen feeling prickles of guilt at having left Kit to fend for himself again.

He was in good spirits though when Monica arrived, and she felt her shoulders and neck, which had been stiff with tension, relax.

She spent the rest of the afternoon measuring flour, rolling out dough and taking baking sheets in and out of the oven. It was after five o'clock by the time the last batch was finished.

Monica pulled on her fleece, locked the door and headed outside. The cool air felt good against her flushed face as she walked back to her cottage. A soft breeze whispered through the trees and sent dried leaves skittering along the path.

Mittens appeared as soon as Monica opened the back door. She was especially interested in the bag from Bart's Butcher that Monica was carrying and followed on Monica's heels as she went out to the kitchen and put the chicken on the counter.

Monica opened the refrigerator and peered inside wondering what to cook with the chicken. She had some carrots, which she could roast, and she had a bag of new potatoes in the pantry that would go nicely as well.

Monica washed her hands, tied on an apron and began peeling the carrots.

The chicken was in the oven and delicious smells were wafting from the kitchen when Greg's car pulled into the driveway. She heard the driver's-side door slam shut but then she heard the sound of another door opening and shutting. Had Greg brought someone home with him?

She was about to go peer out the window when she stopped short. She could have sworn she heard a dog bark. Had someone wandered down the path to their cottage while walking their dog? Monica groaned. She hoped it wasn't someone coming to gape at the site where Betsy had been killed.

She heard Greg fumbling with the knob to the back door and then the door opened, letting in a gust of cool air.

"How was your —" she said then stopped.

Standing in the middle of the kitchen was the roguish-looking dog Greg had named Hercule, his tail thumping against the table leg with each furious wag.

Monica was momentarily speechless.

Hercule was not shy and made himself right at home. He wandered over to Mittens's bowl and slurped up some water, then gave a shake, sending droplets spraying into the air.

Mittens, who had strolled into the kitchen to check out the

newcomer, voiced her displeasure at the dog's appearance with an aggrieved-sounding meow.

Greg had a sheepish expression on his face. He gestured toward Hercule.

"They're creating the opening between the two floors tonight and I didn't think it would be safe to leave Hercule there with all that going on. I hope you don't mind."

"I don't mind, but I think Mittens does." Monica laughed.

She felt a rush of warmth. Greg was so transparent. He looked as eager as a young boy with his first pet.

"Do we need to run and get dog food?" Monica glanced at Hercule doubtfully. "He looks hungry."

Greg held up a bag. "Bart had some scraps for me. Maybe we can pop them in the oven along with whatever you're cooking. It smells heavenly, by the way."

"Roast chicken with carrots and new potatoes," Monica said, taking the bag from Greg and reaching for a baking dish in the cupboard. She transferred the contents of the bag to the dish and slipped it in the oven.

"I hope you don't mind," Greg said. He took his jacket off and hung it on the hook by the back door. "His owner still hasn't come forward and I've put posters up all over town. I even contacted the nearest humane society but they didn't have any word of a missing dog answering Hercule's description."

While they were talking, Hercule had gone over to the oven and was sniffing around the edges of the door. He wagged his tail and licked his lips loudly.

Monica and Greg both laughed.

"It's almost ready," Monica told the dog, grabbing an oven mitt from the counter. She opened the oven door and took out the baking dish.

Hercule's tail wagged faster and he began to drool.

"It has to cool," Monica said to him as she put the baking dish on the counter.

He seemed to understand, sitting patiently and following her every movement with his eyes, his shaggy eyebrows bobbing up and down.

Monica took the roasting pan with the chicken, carrots and potatoes from the oven and put it on the stove while she got out serving dishes and Greg set the table. She found a ceramic bowl in the cupboard, checked that Hercule's food had cooled sufficiently and dished it out. He nearly knocked it out of her hand in his exuberance as she put it down on the floor next to the table.

By the time Monica finished carving the chicken and dishing out the vegetables, Hercule had licked his bowl clean and was standing by Monica's side watching her carefully.

She smiled at him. She had to admit he was a charmer.

"Maybe if no one claims Hercule, we can keep him," she said as she put a plate in front of Greg.

Greg's face broke into a slow smile. "I imagine we could."

"I could easily come back to the cottage to walk him midday," Monica said as she picked up her fork.

"And I could take him to work with me some days," Greg said. He speared a piece of chicken. "He could be a sort of store mascot." He leaned over and patted Hercule on the head. "He's friendly enough." He looked up at Monica and smiled. "Maybe I could get a painted wooden cutout of him made and hang it along with the Book 'Em sign out front."

Hercule, who had been lying at Greg's side, got to his feet and began pacing between the table and the back door.

"I think he wants to go out," Monica said.

"I'll get his leash."

"I'll come with you. I could do with some fresh air."

They pulled on their jackets, fastened Hercule's new leash to his brand-new collar and went out the back door.

Hercule seemed energized by the brisk air, his former torpor disappearing as he eagerly sniffed the terrain and scampered through the falling leaves.

Monica hooked her arm through Greg's. "It's rather nice having a dog." She smiled up at him.

There was a rustling sound in the long grass alongside the road, and Hercule waded through the weeds after whatever small creature was making its home in there. After a few minutes of poking around in the undergrowth, he gave up and plowed ahead, a couple of piece of dried grass clinging to his fur.

"Should we go back?" Greg asked a few minutes later after Hercule had finished his business. He turned up his collar and hunched his shoulders. "It's getting colder."

They turned around and began heading back toward the cottage. Hercule had lost none of his exuberance and continued to thrash back and forth through the weeds along the path. He darted into a clump of wild onion and came out with something in his mouth.

"Hercule, what do you have?" Monica said, squatting down to look. "It looks like a piece of paper," she said over her shoulder to Greg. "Possibly a letter of some sort, given the way it's folded."

Monica had to gently tease the paper out of Hercule's mouth. Hercule thought it was a great new game and wagged his tail enthusiastically. Finally, she managed to extricate the paper without too much damage—Hercule had only inflicted a couple of teeth marks and a slight tear.

"What is it?" Greg peered over Monica's shoulder as she unfolded the paper.

"It is a letter," Monica said, looking at the typed document. "The letterhead says Sheldon Armstrong MD."

"A doctor's note?"

Monica scanned the text. "It appears to be. A report on some tests a patient was given."

"It must have fallen out of someone's pocket," Greg said, reining in Hercule, who wanted to chase a squirrel. "Who is it addressed to?"

"That's the odd thing," Monica said, straightening up. "It's addressed to Mrs. Mary Visser."

Chapter 10

Hercule bounded at the end of his leash as Monica and Greg walked back to the cottage. As soon as they'd unclipped the dog's leash and hung up their jackets, Monica sat down at the kitchen table and read the letter.

"What's in it?" Greg said, motioning to the paper in Monica's hand.

"The letter is from a doctor who appears to be informing Mary Visser that recent medical tests revealed that she had a previously undiagnosed condition. Something called a patent foramen ovale in her heart."

"What on earth is that?" Greg said.

"I don't know." Monica frowned. "Visser did say something about his wife having a heart condition during that interview he gave on television. I suppose this is what he was referring to. According to Visser, it was some sort of cardiac ailment that led to her death during their scuba dive."

"This must be it then," Greg said, gesturing at the letter again. "I suppose that means Visser's wife's death really was an accident."

"I don't know," Monica said. "Visser got very agitated when that reporter asked him about his wife's scuba diving accident. Why? Why would he be upset if her death really was an accident?"

"You're not thinking that Visser murdered his first wife, are you?" Greg said.

"Yes. No. I don't know," Monica said. She was frustrated. She was convinced there was something she was missing — something she hadn't grasped.

She glanced at the date on the letter. "This letter is almost twenty-five years old. How did it get here, on the path to Sassamanash Farm?"

"Like I said, it must have fallen out of someone's pocket," Greg said.

Monica brandished the letter. "But whose? And why carry around a nearly twenty-five-year-old letter in their pocket?"

"You said Visser had been here to the farm. It must have been in his pocket."

Monica was shaking her head. "But why? Why would he have this letter with him? This whole thing occurred more than two decades ago.

Why put the letter in his pocket now? Why not leave it in a file somewhere?" Monica began clearing the dishes off the table.

"What if the letter wasn't in Visser's pocket?" Monica said as she ran water in the sink. "What if someone else brought it here?"

Greg raised his eyebrows. "Who else would have had access to Visser's personal papers?"

Monica brushed a curl off her forehead. "I can think of one person."

Greg raised his eyebrows again.

"Betsy DeJong."

"But why would she have that letter?" Greg said as he started the dishwasher.

Monica bit her lip. "I don't know. But I have the feeling it's important.

• • •

The doctor's letter to Mary Visser was sitting on the table when Monica went down for breakfast the next morning. She glanced at it. What should she do with it? Should she give it back to Visser? But what if it was a potential clue in Betsy's murder? Perhaps the best thing would be to give it to Detective Stevens and let her deal with it.

Monica was scrambling some eggs when Greg came back from walking Hercule. The dog bounded into the kitchen as if the chilly air had intensified his energy. He skidded across the floor toward Monica. She bent down and he gave her a good morning kiss as she ruffled the fur on his head and told him he was a good boy. Hercule wagged his tail enthusiastically.

Mittens strolled into the kitchen, glanced disdainfully at Hercule, raised her tail in the air and stalked over to the corner, where she began to groom herself.

"I've decided I'm going to take that letter about Mary Visser to Detective Stevens this morning," Monica said as she dished out some eggs for Greg.

"Wise idea," he said. He unfolded his napkin and placed it in his lap. "Let her deal with it. She'll know what to do."

They ate their eggs, trading sections of the morning paper back and forth across the table. Monica finished her breakfast, gathered up the newspaper and began carrying the plates to the sink. Greg already had his jacket on and was reaching for Hercule's leash.

"Do you mind if I take him to the store with me?" he asked, gesturing toward the dog.

"That's fine. It will save me having to come back to the cottage at lunchtime to walk him. I suppose you can leave Haley in charge while you take him out?"

Greg nodded and kissed Monica goodbye. He opened the back door and Hercule shot out of it so fast that Greg almost lost his grip on the leash.

Monica waved goodbye, put on her own jacket and headed out to her car.

The sun was out and the warmth felt good as it shone through her car windows. More of the leaves had turned color, Monica noticed as she drove down the road leading into town. Light sparkled on the tips of the waves that were slowly rolling in to shore on Lake Michigan. Soon there would be snow obscuring the beach and ice floes on the water. The thought made Monica shiver.

A few minutes later she was pulling into the parking lot of the police station. She hoped Stevens was in, but at the very least she would leave the letter for her along with a note.

Stevens was in and sitting behind her desk with a cup of steaming coffee in front of her and piles of folders next to her. A pair of blue-framed glasses were perched on her nose. Other pieces of paper were scattered across her desk.

She looked up when Monica walked in. "Monica." She stretched her arms over her head and groaned. "What's up? The desk sergeant said you had something for me?"

Her shoulders were slumped and she looked weary. She took a sip from the cup and grimaced.

"I should have stopped at the diner for some coffee. The stuff here is terrible. It tastes like motor oil."

"If I had known, I would have brought you some." Monica reached into her purse and pulled out the letter. "Greg and I found this on the path leading to the farm when we were walking the dog last night." She handed the piece of paper to Stevens. "I thought you might want to see it."

Stevens raised her eyebrows. "You've adopted a dog?" she said as she reached for the letter.

"It's more like he's adopted us. He wandered into Greg's store and so far we haven't found a clue as to his owner."

Stevens unfolded the letter and began to read it. "What on earth . . . ?" She brandished the paper. "This was at the farm?"

Monica nodded.

"We searched the entire area where the body was found. How did we miss this?" Stevens looked furious.

"I think the wind had blown it," Monica said. "Our dog found it in a clump of weeds alongside the path quite a ways from where Betsy's body had been lying."

Stevens blew out a puff of air. "Good to know we're not that incompetent." She glanced at the paper again. "This letter is twenty-five years old."

Monica pointed to it. "It's addressed to Mary Visser. She was Bob Visser's first wife. She died in a scuba diving accident when they were vacationing in Cozumel. According to Visser, the cause was some undetected heart ailment."

Stevens folded the letter up and put it on her desk. She sighed.

"Frankly, I have no idea what to do with this. But I'll put it in the file." She tapped the letter with her index finger. "It has nothing to do with Betsy DeJong though. It's just an old letter that someone must have dropped and not noticed."

Monica was glad Stevens was going to keep the letter. She still didn't know whether it was related to Betsy DeJong's death or was exactly what it looked like on the surface—a letter someone stuck in their pocket and then dropped. But her instincts told her it would come to be important eventually.

Whenever they managed to figure it out.

• • •

Monica headed straight back to the farm. She left her car at her cottage and walked toward the farm kitchen at such a brisk pace that she became quite warm and had to unzip her jacket.

One of the farm's trucks was parked outside the kitchen, *Sassamanash Farm* written in white on its cranberry red sides. The back doors of the truck were open and Monica could see wooden crates stamped with the farm's name piled inside.

The door to the kitchen was propped open and Mauricio, one of

Jeff's crew, was bringing in crates of cranberries and stacking them against the wall. He waved when he saw Monica.

Monica grabbed her apron and got to work on some dough for a batch of scones. Nora had called, sounding a bit frantic, to say they were nearly out. It had been a very busy morning.

That was good news, Monica thought as she measured flour into the mixer. Maybe Lauren's Instagram account was driving people to the farm store after all.

She was readying the scones for the oven with an egg wash and a sprinkle of sugar on their tops when there was a furious knocking on the door.

Someone sounded panicky, Monica thought as she made her way to the door. She opened it and Bob Visser nearly catapulted into the room.

He was wearing an impeccable suit, as always, with a red silk tie and matching pocket square. His face was as red as his tie. It was obvious that he was furious.

"How dare you," he said, stabbing a finger into Monica's shoulder.

She was taken aback. What did he mean? "I don't know what you're talking about."

"Yes, you do," Visser insisted, his face turning even more scarlet. "I've heard you're the town busybody, poking your nose into everything."

Monica was horrified. Were people really saying that about her?

"You had to go running to the police with that letter instead of bringing it to me, which would have been the appropriate thing to do." Visser was nearly spitting in his fury. "I had a visit from Detective Stevens again this morning. Do you know I'm running for the Senate?"

Monica nodded, still perplexed. "Yes."

He advanced on her, crowded her space, and she backed up quickly.

"I can't have the police banging on my door every other day. What if the papers pick up on it? Fritz Farrington, my opponent, would jump on that in a heartbeat and use it to his advantage. He'd have it in all his campaign ads before the day was over."

Monica was truly at a loss for words. "I thought the best thing to do was to take the letter to the police in case it had any bearing on Betsy's murder." She lifted her chin. "And if you don't like that, I'm sorry, but there's nothing I can do about it now. You've made your point and now I think it's time for you to leave."

Monica opened the door but Visser didn't budge. The look on his face was truly menacing. Suddenly Monica was scared. If he'd killed Betsy, what was to stop him from killing again? Was he really that mad all because of the letter?

Where was Kit? she wondered. He'd run some loaves of cranberry bread down to the farm store and should be along any minute.

Visser advanced again and Monica retreated so far that her back was now against the counter.

Suddenly the door opened and Kit strolled in. "Hello," he called as he took off his jacket and hung it up.

"Sorry. Didn't realize you had company."

He must have noticed the frightened look on Monica's face and sensed something was wrong because he stiffened and clenched his fists at his sides.

Kit was slender and not very tall, but for the first time Monica noticed how broad his shoulders were and how muscular his forearms looked.

"What's going on here?" he said. "I think maybe it's time for you to leave." He pointed at Visser.

Visser sneered at him. It reminded Monica of the bullies on the playground when she was young.

"I'm not finished here," Visser said and turned back toward Monica. He had begun shouting at her again when suddenly he was jerked backward.

Kit had grabbed hold of Visser's jacket and was dragging him toward the door.

"Let go of me," Visser yelled. "I'll call the police and have you arrested for assault."

"Yeah? Bring it on. I'll tell them you refused to leave the premises and that you were threatening this lady here."

By now Visser had wrenched free from Kit's grasp and had whirled around to face him, his fists at the ready. Monica reached for her cell phone to call 9-1-1.

There was a brief scuffle. Kit managed to grab Visser's jacket lapel. He dragged Visser to the door, shoved him out and slammed the door shut. Monica heard the click as he locked it.

He turned to face Monica, his hands on his hips, a worried expression on his face.

"Are you okay?"

Monica nodded.

"Now, tell me. What on earth was that all about?"

Monica took a deep shuddering breath. Her hands were shaking and the room appeared to be spinning. She put her hands to her head to try to stop it. Kit caught her just as she was about to hit the floor.

"Let's get you in a chair," he said. He propped Monica against the counter and went into the back room. He came out wheeling the office chair from Monica's desk.

"I'm fine," Monica insisted, but he made her sit and drink a glass of water. "It was the shock, that's all. He suddenly appeared at the door."

"Who is he? And what did he want?" Kit said, tucking in his shirt, which had come undone in the fracas.

"Bob Visser. He's running for senator and blames me for the police showing up at his door."

Kit snorted and tossed his head. "Remind me not to vote for him!"

• • •

Monica still felt a bit shaky as she rolled out dough for scones but she soon lost herself in the task and Visser's visit retreated to the back of her mind.

She took the last batch of scones from the oven.

"I'm going to run these down to Nora," she said to Kit as she reached for her jacket.

"Toodle-loo then."

Monica slung the basket over her arm and headed out.

She was pleased to see that business was still quite brisk when she arrived at the farm store. Nora was taking care of one customer while four others were waiting. Monica quickly arranged the scones in the display case and then jumped in to help.

"Thanks," Nora said, blowing a lock of hair off her forehead.

The last customers were gone except for a couple sitting at one of the café tables nursing their coffees and picking at the crumbs of their muffins.

"You've certainly been busy," Monica said, eyeing the empty spots in the display case.

"Yes. I think it's the publicity from that poor girl's murder. Everyone was asking me about it and they were quite disappointed that I wasn't able to share any gory details."

Monica gathered her things together. "Looks like you can handle things on your own now. I'm going to head back to start working on some cookies."

"Good. We'll need those this afternoon," Nora said, tidying a display of cranberry jam.

Monica was on her way back to the farm kitchen when she noticed someone coming in the opposite direction. As he got closer, she realized it was Dan Polsky.

Dan gave a strained smile as he neared Monica. His brown hair was lit with golden highlights from the sun and he still had the remnants of a summer tan. There was a sheepish look on his face as he approached.

He put out an arm and stopped Monica. "I'm sorry if I seemed a bit surly the last time we talked. I realized afterward that I'd been out of line." He squeezed the bridge of his nose. "It's just that there have been some things going on that have made me rather tense."

"Please, don't worry about it," Monica said.

Dan gave a curt nod.

"Several people have told me that Betsy left Cranberry Cove after high school graduation and didn't come back in time to start her first semester of college. No one seems to know where she went. Do you?"

Monica was fairly convinced that Betsy had gone off to give birth to a baby but she was hoping to get confirmation. There was still a chance that something else had been going on—rehab perhaps.

Dan's face closed down and he took a step away from Monica.

He shook his head. "No. No, I don't."

And with that he turned on his heel and stalked off.

That had touched a nerve, Monica thought. She also had the distinct impression that Dan knew exactly where Betsy had gone but didn't want to say.

And if Betsy had been pregnant, as the VanVelsen sisters had suggested, surely Dan knew about it. And why would that matter now?

He might have been angry at the time but surely that wouldn't drive him to murder some twenty-odd years later.

Chapter 11

Monica was still mulling over where Betsy might have gone during that gap between high school and college as she walked back toward the farm kitchen with her empty basket swinging from her arm. Surely Betsy DeJong's parents would know. If they were still alive.

Monica had barely walked in the door before she was pulling her cell phone from her pocket. She phoned the VanVelsens to see if they knew anything about Betsy's parents but came up empty-handed. They'd never known the DeJongs and had no information to give her.

She'd have to do some research herself. As soon as lunchtime rolled around, Monica grabbed her jacket and headed out to the library.

"More research?" Phyllis said when she saw Monica enter. She was organizing a stack of books on a trolley, ready to be reshelved.

"Yes," Monica said. "I need to go through some microfiche again."

"Tedious job," Phyllis said.

"You know the news anchor who was killed — Betsy DeJong?"

Phyllis nodded and adjusted the glasses perched on the end of her nose. "It's all everyone has been talking about since it happened."

"By any chance do you know if her parents are still alive?"

"The father passed away some time ago," Phyllis said, inserting a book into the row on her trolley. "Something to do with his liver." She put up a hand. "Although he didn't drink. It wasn't that. Some kind of cancer, I believe."

"And her mother?"

"She's still alive. She comes in the library occasionally. She's fond of biographies."

"You don't happen to know where she lives, do you?"

Phyllis hesitated. She fiddled with the gold chain around her neck. "I really shouldn't do this . . ."

Monica was silent, her fingers crossed.

"Her address will be on her library card application. It's all on the computer now." She motioned toward the desk. "I'm really not supposed to . . ." she said again.

Monica put out a hand. "I wouldn't want you to get in trouble."

Phyllis threw back her shoulders. "No one has to know. Let's go."

She waved Monica over to her desk. "I'll give you the address on one condition."

"Oh?"

"You fill me in on what you find out," Phyllis said with a twinkle in her eye.

Phyllis shook her mouse and the computer monitor sprang to life. Her fingers flew over the keys, then she reached for a piece of paper and a pencil. She wrote down the information and handed the paper to Monica.

"Good luck," she said.

Monica studied the address Phyllis had jotted down—227 Lakeview Street. She thought she knew where that was. She left the library and headed to her car.

The route took her past the harbor and the Cranberry Cove Yacht Club. She then turned down Lakeview Street, which stood on a slight rise above the town. The foliage was tangled and overgrown and partially obscured the view of the lake far below.

She found the DeJongs' house easily enough. It was part of a cluster of similar small houses, gathered close together as if for warmth. The houses had screened-in front porches and small, scrubby lawns overrun with crabgrass.

Monica found number 227 and parked her car at the curb. A tangle of juniper bushes lined the driveway, which had been eroded by the weather, leaving the macadam cracked and broken.

She walked up the worn flagstone path to the house. The screen on the porch door bulged outward and was coming off the frame near the bottom. Monica was going to knock, but when she tried the handle, it opened.

The porch was damp and sparsely furnished with a wooden rocker with peeling paint and a sagging wicker sofa covered in a faded and stained cabbage rose print.

Monica rang the bell but there was no sound echoing inside the house. She waited for a moment and then rapped on the door sharply.

After several minutes, a wraith-like older woman came to the door and opened it. She was wearing slippers and had a black cardigan over a plaid jumper.

"Can I help you?" Her mouth moved nervously.

Her skin was still youthful-looking and the remnants of beauty could be seen in her elegant bone structure. Monica thought that she must have looked like Betsy when she was young.

Monica introduced herself and said she wanted to talk about Betsy.

Mrs. DeJong didn't seem to find that unusual. Monica didn't know whether she was merely lonely or had mistaken Monica for a reporter or a member of the police, as other people had done.

She led Monica inside and into a small living room. It was shadowy with the windows looking out onto the darkened porch.

Mrs. DeJong was wearing a small gold cross around her neck and a large cross was hung prominently on the wall. A Bible with a worn leather cover sat out on the coffee table.

Monica sat on the sofa and Mrs. DeJong perched on a rush-seated wooden chair.

Mrs. DeJong gave a weary sigh. "So many people have been around wanting interviews," she said. "I suppose it's on account of Betsy's being on television and being engaged to Bob Visser who's running for the Senate. They want every detail about Betsy's life. A lot of people were interested in Betsy since she was on the television every day."

So she thought Monica was a reporter, Monica guessed.

"Some of them, I've sent away," Mrs. DeJong said. She smiled at Monica. "But you look like a nice girl." She cocked her head to the side. "Haven't I seen you in church?"

"It's possible," Monica said, although she went to the Episcopal church and not the Dutch Reformed one.

"I'm very sorry for your loss," Monica began.

Mrs. DeJong bowed her head and fingered the cross around her neck.

"Tell me about Betsy," Monica said, leaning forward with her elbows on her knees.

"She was very driven," Mrs. DeJong said. "From a young age she was determined to be a success." She smiled fondly. "She was very smart, you know. And a hard worker."

"She certainly was a success," Monica said gently. "Anchoring a news broadcast and having her own show."

"Yes. We were terribly proud of her. She knew what she wanted from life and she managed to get it." Mrs. DeJong brushed at an imaginary crumb on the front of her sweater. "We were so surprised when she became engaged to a senator." She ducked her head. "Well, he's not a senator yet, but he will be soon. Her father and I often wondered if she'd ever get married, but she waited until the right man came along — she wasn't going to settle for anything but the best." She reached out and picked up the Bible from the coffee table. She stroked the worn leather cover as if for comfort. "She almost ruined her chances at the life she wanted, but thank goodness our pastor stepped in and took care of things. But everyone makes mistakes, don't they?" She looked at Monica.

"Yes. Yes, of course." Monica couldn't help but think of some of her own mistakes.

"But Pastor Smit handled everything for us. Her father and I wouldn't have known what to do. But he took care of things and Betsy's future wasn't ruined."

"I understand that Betsy didn't start college right after graduating high school," Monica said as gently as possible. "Her friends said she disappeared for a while. Do you know where she went?"

Mrs. DeJong's face suddenly tightened. "I don't want to talk about it." She stood up abruptly. "I don't have anything else to say. I think it's time you left."

• • •

Monica sat in her car, undecided as to what to do. By now she was certain that Betsy had disappeared in order to give birth. She'd gotten pregnant — that was the mistake Mrs. DeJong had been referring to, it had to be. Did Mrs. DeJong really think people wouldn't guess?

Was Dan Polsky the father? He had been Betsy's boyfriend at the time. Or, had she taken up with someone else, unbeknownst to Dan?

Her return trip to the farm took Monica within a quarter of a mile of the Dutch Reformed church where the DeJongs had worshipped. She decided not to go home yet and instead turned down the street that the church was located on.

The church was set back from the street and was surrounded by large oak trees. Curling red leaves were scattered across the lawn. The exterior was fairly plain — painted white with two welcoming red doors. A paved stone walkway, bordered by a boxwood hedge in need of trimming, led to the entrance.

Monica made her way around to the side of the church, where she found another door that she hoped would lead to the church office. She pushed it open and made her way inside.

The air was musty, as if the windows hadn't been opened in a long time. It was quiet except for the muted sound of someone talking in the distance.

There were several heavy oak doors along the hallway but only one of them was open. Light spilled out of it, highlighting the worn carpeting. Monica looked inside.

A woman sat behind an old wooden desk with peeling veneer. She was probably in her thirties and had short, light brown hair with bangs that had been bleached blond. She was wearing a dark green crew neck sweater and had a plain gold wedding band on the ring finger of her left hand. There was a piece of wax paper spread out on the desk in front of her with a half-eaten sandwich on it.

Monica cleared her throat and the woman looked up. She smiled.

"Yes? Can I help you?"

"I hope so. Is Pastor Smit in?"

"I'm afraid he's out on a pastoral visit at the moment. Is there something I can help you with?"

Monica hesitated. "I was wondering if Pastor Smit still arranged adoptions. Someone told me that he did."

The woman looked Monica up and down.

"I'm asking for a friend," Monica said.

The woman gave her a conspiratorial smile. "Why don't you come in and sit down."

She closed the office door and led Monica into a small room furnished with a worn blue sofa and matching armchair.

"Have a seat." She motioned toward the sofa. "I'm Ruth, by the way."

"Monica."

"So, Monica, you asked about adoptions." Ruth folded her hands in her lap. "Pastor Smit does arrange private adoptions for members of our parish — both those who want to find a home for a baby they can't keep and those who would like to adopt. What is your friend's situation?"

Monica wet her lips. She hated having to lie.

"My friend . . . is quite young. It was a . . . mistake," Monica said, using Mrs. DeJong's words. "Can things be done quietly? She doesn't want anyone to know . . ."

Ruth smiled and reached out and patted Monica's knee.

"There's no need for anyone to know. The church has a lovely retreat on a lake where your friend can stay until after the baby is born. Then if she still chooses to put the infant up for adoption, a suitable home will be found. Rest assured we vet our adoptive families very carefully."

"That's most helpful," Monica said. "I'm sure my friend will be relieved to hear that."

"Have her give me a call when she decides." Ruth got up, smoothed down her skirt and went over to her desk. She handed Monica a card. Her name and contact information was on the front and there was a Bible verse on the back.

"Is there anything else we can do for you?"

"No, thank you. You've answered all my questions."

Ruth stood up. "Please tell your friend not to worry. Everything will be fine."

"Thank you," Monica said and left.

She couldn't prove it, Monica thought as she made her way back to her car, but it was highly likely that Betsy had been pregnant and had been whisked away to the church's retreat until she gave birth and a suitable adoption was arranged.

That answered one question. Whether it had anything to do with Betsy's murder or not, Monica had no idea.

• • •

Kit was out delivering an order of cranberry compote to the Pepper Pot restaurant when Monica got back to the farm kitchen. She quickly ate the ham and cheese sandwich she'd brought with her from home and then set to work.

The oven was going full blast and the kitchen was heating up. Monica took off her wool sweater and rolled up the sleeves of her shirt. Nevertheless, damp curls were plastered to her forehead by the time she pulled the first batch of cookies from the oven.

She transferred the cookies to a cooling rack and then went to the door and propped it open with an unopened bag of flour. A cool breeze drifted in and Monica stood basking in it for a moment before beginning on another batch of cookies.

She was dropping heaping tablespoons of the cranberry and chocolate-chip-studded dough onto a baking sheet when there was a tentative knock on the door. Monica looked up and saw Melinda peering around the edge.

"Come in," she called and motioned at Melinda with her hand.

"I don't mean to disturb you," Melinda said in her shy way. "But is it okay if I leave this here?" She held up a navy blue backpack.

"Of course," Monica said. "That's fine." She clapped her hands together and a cloud of flour formed in the air. "Your work on our Instagram account seems to be paying off," Monica said. "We're getting new customers. They seem to be responding to it."

A slow smile spread across Melinda's face. She ducked her head.

"Thanks. I'm glad you like what I've done." She gestured toward the door. "I'm off to get some more pictures. I'll be back in a bit."

Monica was getting the next batch of cookies in the oven when there was another knock on the door.

"Delivery," a man in a sweatshirt and jeans called out. He was wielding a handcart piled with boxes.

That must be the flour she ordered, Monica thought. She hurried over to the door and moved Melinda's backpack out of the way. She noticed some papers sticking out of the top. They looked like legal documents and had the seal of the State of Michigan stamped at the top. That was curious.

She put the backpack on the counter and led the deliveryman to the storage room, where he unloaded his cart and stacked the boxes.

As soon as he was gone, Monica glanced at Melinda's backpack. She couldn't help but wonder what those documents were about. She spent several minutes debating with herself before finally going over to the backpack.

She was only going to glance at the portion of the papers she could see sticking out, she told herself. There was no harm in that.

But when she saw the heading on one of the papers, she forgot all about her vow to herself. *Adoption Record* was written at the top in bold black print.

So Melinda had lied about finding her birth mother.

Monica eased the papers out far enough to read the rest of the information.

There was Melinda's date and place of birth and there were two lines underneath listing the names of the biological parents. Next to *Mother* the name Betsy DeJong had been filled in and next to *Father* was the name Dan Polsky.

Monica was so stunned she took a step backward. Betsy and Dan were Melinda's biological parents.

There was a letter that must have accompanied the adoption papers. Monica looked it over quickly. It was dated two days before Betsy was killed.

Melinda must have just found out who her biological parents were shortly before encountering them at the television shoot. *What a shock that must have been,* Monica thought. She couldn't begin to imagine how Melinda must have felt.

Monica tried to recall everything about that day. Had Melinda seemed upset or angry? Had she talked to Betsy or Dan? She couldn't remember.

Had Melinda confronted Betsy? Maybe they argued. Maybe Melinda resented the fact that Betsy had put her up for adoption.

But had Melinda been resentful enough to kill Betsy? Somehow Monica couldn't see her in that role, but it wouldn't be the first time she'd been wrong about someone.

The door opened, and Monica glanced in that direction.

"I've come for my backpack," Melinda said, picking it up and slinging the strap over one shoulder. "Thanks for letting me leave it here."

"Anytime," Monica said and waved as Melinda went out the door.

She was closing up the kitchen and walking back to the cottage when another thought occurred to her. Had Dan Polsky known about Betsy's pregnancy? Had he known about the adoption? He had been heard arguing with Betsy. Maybe Melinda had revealed the truth to both of them and Dan had become angry that he'd been left in the dark. No one knew where he really went that afternoon when Jeff couldn't find him.

It would have been easy enough for him to lie in wait for Betsy, argue with her and then hit her over the head with the rock.

Monica was still thinking about Melinda and Betsy as she opened the door to her cottage. Mittens greeted her with a plaintive meow and Monica bent down to pet her. The cat arched her back and purred loudly. Monica would have to show her some extra love and attention to make up for bringing a dog into the family.

Monica hung up her jacket, kicked off her shoes and poured herself a glass of iced tea. She took it into the living room and buzzed on the television. She spent an hour with her feet up watching a game show.

It was time to cook dinner when the program ended. That morning she had put some chicken breasts in the refrigerator to defrost. She planned to sauté them and top them with a balsamic glaze and a handful of dried cranberries.

She pulled open the refrigerator and checked the produce drawer. She had some fresh green beans from a local farm's late crop of vegetables that she thought would go nicely with the dish.

She had put a pot of water on the stove to boil and was cutting up the green beans when she heard a dog bark. She smiled. That must be Hercule heralding his and Greg's arrival home.

The back door opened and Hercule bounded into the kitchen, his leash trailing behind him. Monica bent down and he gave her an enthusiastic greeting, licking her face and wagging his tail furiously. She scratched under his chin and behind his ears.

Greg appeared in the doorway carrying a large carton.

Monica straightened up. "Another estate sale?" she said as Greg put the carton on the table.

"Not an estate sale exactly," he said, slipping off his jacket. "It was a moving sale. At Bob Visser's, as a matter of fact." Greg rubbed his hands together to warm them. "I have to say he's got a lot of confidence that he's going to win that Senate seat."

"But won't he keep his place here? Don't they usually do that?" Monica said, dumping the green beans into the pot of water boiling on the stove.

"His assistant, who was overseeing the sale, said he's planning to move to Grand Rapids to be closer to the airport. She said he's downsizing."

That was interesting, Monica thought. She remembered how Visser had so unceremoniously attacked her for giving that letter to the police. Were things getting too hot for him in Cranberry Cove?

"I suppose with his fiancée sadly murdered, he feels he doesn't need as large a home. You should see the place. It looks relatively new and is enormous. It's at the end of a long circular drive, and I thought I caught a glimpse of a pool and a tennis court out back."

"Car dealerships must pay well," Monica said as she checked on the green beans.

"How long till dinner?" Greg took a book out of the carton. "Time enough for me to go through these?"

"Yes. Go ahead. Hopefully you've got something good in there."

"The books are in excellent condition," Greg said as he flipped through one of them. "I doubt I'll find any first editions. They all look relatively new but they will definitely go on the used book shelf."

Monica retrieved a green bean from the boiling water, blew on it and nibbled on the end to check for doneness. She set the timer for another five minutes.

"What sorts of books are there? I'm curious to know what type of reading material Visser is drawn to."

"It looks like a mix. Fiction, political nonfiction, a couple of recent best sellers." Greg put his hand in the carton again and pulled out another book. "Here's an odd title. *Scuba Diving for Beginners.* This one isn't in the best of shape — not like the others."

Monica walked over to the table and took the book from Greg.

"Visser was an avid scuba diver," she said as she began to flip through it. "So I suppose it makes sense that he would have a book like this."

The cover was dog-eared and some of the pages were bent at the corner.

Monica had never been diving herself and she was quite certain she never would be. Being deep underwater and breathing air from a tank did not appeal to her. She shivered at the thought.

As she was paging through the book, it suddenly flopped open to a page bookmarked with an empty envelope addressed to Bob Visser. Several paragraphs on the page were underlined in black ink.

Monica glanced at the passages and was about to close the book and put it back in the carton when something caught her eye.

The heading of the paragraph was *Medical Conditions that Prohibit Diving.*

Monica started reading the text. One of the conditions listed was underlined. Monica read the description — patent foramen ovale, a heart defect where a hole or small flap-like opening in the heart fails to close before birth.

"*Oh my gosh!*" Monica said so suddenly that Greg jumped.

"What is it?" He raised an eyebrow and gestured at the book in her hand.

"I remember where I saw this before—patent foramen ovale. It was in that letter from the doctor to Mary Visser."

Greg looked confused. "Okay. Does that mean something?"

"Mary Visser apparently had this condition—a hole in her heart that failed to close before birth. People with that condition aren't supposed to scuba dive, according to this book." Monica waved the book in the air.

"But she went scuba diving in spite of it," Monica said. "In Cozumel on their vacation. Don't you see?" She looked at Greg. "Visser must have known that diving could be dangerous. He even underlined the relevant information in this book." Monica brandished the book again. "And he probably saw that letter from his wife's doctor."

"So you think . . ."

"I think Visser knew about his wife's condition and knew it was dangerous but took her scuba diving anyway."

"You can't just rent some gear and jump in the water," Greg said. "You have to go through training and pass a test."

"Maybe she did all that." Monica grabbed the pot with the green beans in it off the stove and drained the water. The steam wreathed her face and fogged the window over the kitchen sink. "Her first dives would be in a swimming pool, wouldn't they? And maybe Cozumel was her first real deep-water dive."

Greg whistled. "You think Visser killed his wife?"

"Yes. I think he knew it was dangerous for her to go diving but he didn't say anything. He was hoping this heart condition would kill her."

Monica finished cooking the dinner and she and Greg took their plates into the living room to eat off of tray tables in front of the television while they watched the news.

It wasn't until later, as she was washing and drying the last pan after dinner, that Monica had a sudden thought. She stopped dead, letting the pan sit in the soapy water in the sink while she contemplated the idea, turning it this way and that in her mind to see if it held up.

The more she thought about it, the more she was convinced she was right. She quickly dried her hands and went out to the living room, where Greg was sitting in an armchair, his feet up on an ottoman, reading the newspaper.

Greg must have sensed her presence because he looked up and raised his eyebrows.

"Is everything okay?"

Monica let out a gusty sigh. "I just had an idea about Betsy's murder."

Greg patted the ottoman and Monica perched on it.

"What is it?" he said, looking slightly bemused.

"What if Betsy found that book on scuba diving on Visser's bookshelf?"

"Why would she do that?" Greg stroked Monica's hand. "What would make her pick out that book?"

"She was planning on taking scuba diving lessons herself."

Greg's eyebrows shot up.

"Not only that, but according to her friend at the television station, she suddenly changed her mind and decided not to take up diving after all."

"She got cold feet?" Greg said.

Monica nodded. "Yes, and I think there was a reason why. She found that book on scuba diving on Visser's shelf and realized that he had used that information to kill his first wife."

"Why would he want to do that?" Greg massaged Monica's shoulders and neck. "Did he inherit money? Did she have a life insurance policy?"

"Apparently not," Monica said, stretching out her legs. Hercule was curled up right next to Greg's chair and she accidentally poked him with her foot. He grunted, lifted his head and then put it back down. He rolled onto his side and was soon fast asleep again.

"I don't know what Visser had to gain by killing his wife," Monica said. "I haven't figured that out yet. But I think Betsy found that book and it scared her. If Visser had no problem killing his first wife, what would keep him from murdering her?"

"Again," Greg said. "Why would he do that? What was his motive?"

"He was having an affair with Betsy's sister, Heidi."

"Whoa," Greg said, reeling back. "But why not simply break up with Betsy? People do it all the time."

"But those people aren't running for the Senate. He can't afford any negative press. His opponent would have a field day with it." Monica brushed a lock of hair off her forehead. "He was alarmed enough when that reporter brought up his first wife's death."

"But isn't Betsy's death sensational in itself?"

"Yes, but it makes Visser look like the victim in the whole thing. *The poor man,*" Monica said in an imitation of a newscaster, "*losing his fiancée just as they were about to get married and embark on a life together.*" She clasped her hands to her heart.

"So," Greg said. "Betsy figured out that he probably killed his first wife."

"Yes." Monica jumped to her feet and began pacing back and forth. "She's scared. She quits her scuba diving lessons, which makes Visser suspicious. Maybe he finds out that she found this book and put two and two together. I don't know how — perhaps she put it back on the shelf in the wrong place. Or perhaps she even forgot to put it back and left it lying out somewhere. He can't take any chances. Betsy has got to go."

"So he kills her?" Greg said.

"Yes. He knew she was at the farm filming that day. Heidi told him where to find her. So he shows up pretending he wants to say hello. He's acting like he's so crazy about her that he can't wait to see her. But in reality he had something very different in mind."

"That's chilling." Greg crossed his arms over his chest.

"It is. He pretends to leave but lies in wait for her. Jasmine said that when she left, Betsy was on her cell phone. What if he called her to delay her long enough for the rest of the film crew to leave?"

Greg lowered his eyebrows. "Pretty clever. Almost diabolical, I'd say."

"I know. He waits until everyone is gone and then approaches Betsy. She wouldn't suspect anything is amiss. She doesn't know that he knows she thinks he killed his first wife. He picks up a rock."

"And bam." Greg lifted his arm and dropped it.

"He kills her," Monica finished.

Chapter 12

It was raining lightly by the time Greg came in from walking Hercule later that night. The shoulders of his jacket were wet, and when Hercule shook, droplets of water sprayed into the air.

Mittens, who seemed to be accepting Hercule's presence, walked past him, her tail in the air.

Hercule bolted past them on the stairs, eliciting an annoyed meow from Mittens, as they made their way up to bed. He and Mittens each had a bed of their own and Hercule immediately jumped into his.

"Hercule certainly seems to feel at home," Monica said, bending down to scratch the dog's head.

"I already can't imagine what we did without him," Greg said, unbuttoning his shirt.

Monica pushed aside the curtain and peered out the window. The rain had stopped but clouds still covered the moon.

She was more tired than usual. She hoped she wasn't coming down with something. She got in bed, burrowed under the covers and within minutes was fast asleep.

• • •

At first Monica wasn't sure what it was that had awoken her, but then she clearly heard Hercule growling. He was standing at the window, sniffing, his ears up and alert, his tail stiff. She sat up in bed, her ears straining to hear.

She threw back the covers and went over to the window, her toes curling up against the cold floor. She looked out the window and shivered. Hercule was at her side, continuing his low growl.

Suddenly Hercule bolted down the stairs. Monica heard him race through the living room and into the kitchen, where he began scratching at the back door.

"What's that?" Greg said, rolling over, awake now. "What is Hercule barking at?"

"I don't know," Monica said. "Maybe he has to go out?"

"It doesn't sound like it." Greg swung his legs over the side of the bed. "He's growling, and he doesn't do that when he needs to go out."

He felt around on the floor for his slippers. "I'm going to check and make sure everything is okay."

"Do you think someone is out there?" Monica asked, reaching for her robe.

Greg saw her and held out a hand. "You stay here," he said. "Who knows what's going on. I'd feel better if you stayed here."

"It will be fine. I'll come with you," Monica said, buttoning her robe. "I'm not going to be able to go back to sleep anyway."

She followed Greg down the stairs, through the darkened living room and into the kitchen. She noticed that it had started raining again.

Greg took a flashlight from one of the cabinets. "I'm going to see if anyone's out there prowling around. Although what they think is worth stealing here I can't imagine."

He reached for Hercule's leash and snapped it on. Now that he had woken the humans, Hercule had stopped barking but was still giving low, menacing growls.

"Be careful," Monica said as Greg grabbed an umbrella from the stand by the door. "Do you want me to come with you?"

Greg smiled. "I want you to stay here," he said as he headed out.

Monica felt a flash of annoyance but then realized Greg was only thinking of her.

She went to the window and peered out, watching the beam of Greg's flashlight, blurred by the raindrops that continued to pelt the window, bob up and down as he walked down the driveway. Hercule was beside him, sniffing madly, his nose rarely ever lifting from the ground, obviously on the trail of something. But what? Had a deer or some other animal wandered close enough to the house for Hercule to pick up its scent? Or was it a human who was out there skulking around?

There was a nighttime chill in the kitchen. Monica shivered, tightened her robe around her and rubbed her hands together. What was taking Greg so long? She paced up and down, occasionally stopping to peer out the window. Finally she heard him at the back door, fumbling with the knob.

"What did you find?" Monica asked as Greg came in the door and unclipped Hercule's leash.

"I didn't see anything," Greg said, glancing toward the window. "But Hercule definitely smelled something. I did find a footprint right outside the back door—as if someone had stood there peering through the window. The rain had nearly washed it away, but I could definitely see it."

Monica shivered. "That's frightening." She ruffled the top of Hercule's head. "Good boy," she said. She turned to Greg. "Do you think we should call the police?"

"It wouldn't hurt to have them come out and take a look around. If it's someone who's up to mischief for some reason, there's no telling what damage they might do to Jeff's equipment."

Greg flopped into a kitchen chair and reached for his cell phone.

"Coffee?" Monica said, opening the cupboard and pulling out the can of coffee. "I can make some decaf. You must be freezing."

"A cup of hot coffee does sound good," Greg said, stifling a yawn. "I was chilled to the bone out there. The temperature has really dropped. It's a good thing Jeff has harvested nearly all of the bogs. I think we may be getting a frost tonight."

While Greg called the police station, Monica filled the carafe with water and poured it into the machine. In a few minutes there was a bubbling sound and the smell of freshly brewed coffee filled the kitchen.

She grabbed two pottery mugs from the cupboard, filled them and handed one to Greg.

"A patrol car is on its way. They'll look around and make sure no one is lurking out there."

"Good for Hercule for warning us," Monica said, wrapping her hands around her warm mug.

Hercule, who was curled up at Greg's feet, lifted his head at the mention of his name. He looked around and then slumped down again, his eyes blinking twice then closing.

Monica laughed. "I guess Hercule needs his beauty sleep."

Greg suddenly sat up straighter. "I think I hear the police." He pushed his chair back, got up and went over to the back door. He looked out the window. "The police are here."

Moments later there was a sharp rap on the door.

Greg opened it and a cold draft swept through the kitchen, fluttering the curtains and blowing a scrap of paper off the counter.

Two tall rather angular patrolmen stood on the doorstep. Monica recognized one of them as the officer who had showed up when Jeff had found Betsy's body. The lights of their patrol car were still on, illuminating several dozen yards of the driveway.

Greg explained that they thought someone had been prowling around outside.

The one patrolman, whose name Monica thought was Gil, touched his cap. "I'll check things out and we'll get back to you."

"Probably a couple of kids out on a lark," the other cop said, shaking his head. "I don't know what their parents are thinking letting them out this late at night."

They went off and Greg shut the door. The chill lingered in the room and Monica was glad for her cup of hot coffee.

She and Greg sat at the kitchen table, each lost in their own thoughts. Monica couldn't help but wonder if the person who had murdered Betsy had come to leave her a message. Or perhaps a threat as to what would happen if she continued to investigate? She shivered.

"Cold?" Greg said, a look of concern on his face.

"I'm okay." Monica took a sip of her coffee. It had become lukewarm.

Finally they heard a knock on the door. Greg jumped up and opened it.

One of the patrolman was standing there. His cheeks were red from the cold and he had turned his collar up.

"We checked all around but didn't see anyone." He pushed his hat back and scratched his forehead. "But we did find this." He held out a large rock. "It was right beside your door here. There don't seem to be any other stones around like it."

Greg inhaled sharply. "What the —"

"Looks like someone was going to use it to break your back door window."

Greg motioned to Hercule. "The dog must have scared them off." He reached down to pat Hercule on the head.

"We'll swing by again in a couple of hours to make sure everything is okay."

"Thanks," Greg said. "We'd appreciate that."

The patrolman touched his hat again. "Good night. Call us if you hear or see anything else suspicious."

"Do you really think someone was trying to get inside?" Monica wrapped her arms around herself. Suddenly she was shivering. The thought of someone breaking in was truly frightening.

Greg put the coffee mugs in the sink. "I don't know. I can't imagine what they thought they would find here. If they were after money, why not choose one of the houses in that exclusive development on the other side of town? That's what I would do."

Monica smiled. She couldn't picture Greg robbing anyone.

Greg was turning out the lights when Monica grabbed his arm.

"What if Visser realized he'd sold you that scuba diving book? And he was trying to break in and retrieve it?"

Greg made a face. "I can't picture someone like Visser skulking around in the dark and burglarizing a house in order to retrieve a book that may or may not be incriminating."

"He might have sent someone else to do it. He has the money for it." Monica tightened the belt on her robe.

Greg froze. "That could be." He sighed. "Good thing the police are going to be on the lookout. And good thing we have Hercule, right, boy?"

Hercule followed them up to bed, and before Monica had even taken off her robe and slippers, he was curled up on his bed fast asleep.

But Monica found that she couldn't sleep. Every nerve in her body seemed to be firing at once and she had to fight the urge to get up and pace around.

She couldn't stop wondering if Visser had been outside and had been chased away by Hercule's ferocious barking. Had she been right about the scuba accident that had killed his wife and was he feeling threatened?

Monica groaned. She ended up tossing and turning until she heard the birds beginning to sing outside the window, heralding the approaching dawn.

• • •

The rain had picked up again during the night, and by Sunday morning it was streaming down the windows and hammering on the roof.

Monica, who had finally fallen asleep near dawn, pulled the covers up, rolled over and didn't open her eyes again until nearly nine o'clock.

"I can't believe I slept so late," she said to Greg, who was sitting at the kitchen table nursing a cup of coffee when she came down.

He smiled at her. "You needed the rest." He gestured toward the oven. "I kept some eggs warm for you."

"Thanks."

Monica dug into the meal hungrily, and after she'd finished, she joined Greg in the living room, where a fire crackled and spit in the hearth. She curled up on the sofa with her cup of coffee and several sections of the newspaper that she'd picked up off the floor where Greg had scattered them.

Contentment washed over her as she listened to the rain pattering against the windows and the crackling of the logs in the fireplace. She finished reading the paper and picked up the book she'd left on the coffee table.

"Is Jeff still coming for Sunday dinner?" Greg said, glancing at his watch.

"Yes." Monica uncurled her legs and put down her book. "I should get the roast on."

"What's up with Lauren? Isn't she coming?" Greg said, retrieving the scattered sections of newspaper and stacking them neatly.

"She has an early meeting tomorrow in Chicago for that marketing company she's doing remote work for. She took the train there this morning and is spending the night with a friend in the city."

Monica went out to the kitchen and turned on the oven. The roast, which she'd gotten from Bart's, was in the refrigerator. She pulled it out, put it on her cutting board, seasoned it with salt, pepper and garlic and lifted it into the roasting pan.

She peeled several potatoes, cut them in chunks, scattered them around the pan and slipped it all into the preheated oven.

An hour later, delicious smells began to fill the kitchen as Monica set the table with place mats, napkins and tableware. She wished she had some flowers for a centerpiece, but as an alternative arranged some fruit in a crystal bowl.

She was taking the roast out of the oven when there was a knock on the back door. Hercule, who had been sleeping as close to the oven as he could get, suddenly jumped to his feet and began barking.

"A bit late, aren't you, buddy," Monica said, ruffling his head. "Come in," she called.

Jeff opened the door and dashed inside. "It's pouring again," he said as he wiped his feet on the mat. "I only had to run from the truck to the door and I'm already drenched." He brushed water off the sleeves and shoulders of his jacket and ran a hand through his dark hair. "It's getting colder, too. Just my luck the heater in the truck is malfunctioning."

"Go in the living room and get warm by the fire," Monica said. "I'll open a bottle of wine and get us some glasses."

While Jeff and Greg chatted in front of the fire, Monica took her glass of wine back to the kitchen to finish getting dinner ready. The timer dinged and Monica took out the roast, put it on the counter and slid the popovers she'd made into the oven. When they were puffed and golden brown, she pulled them out and put them in a napkin-lined basket.

Monica sliced the roast, arranged it on a platter and spooned the roasted potatoes around the edge. She put it on the table along with a bowl of peas and the popovers and then called everyone to dinner.

"I'm starved and this looks delicious," Jeff said as he slid into his place at the table.

They were quiet as they dug into the food, the only sound the scraping of forks against the plates.

"Everything was delicious," Jeff said, pushing back his chair when the meal was done. "Let me help you clean up."

"Excellent, dear," Greg said, kissing Monica on the cheek. "If it's okay with you, I'm going to go over the bookstore accounts." He raised his eyebrows. "Unless you need more help?"

"You go ahead. I've got it," Jeff said, carrying a stack of plates over to the sink.

They were quiet while Monica rinsed the dishes and Jeff stacked them in the dishwasher. They could hear the rain continue to lash the windows. Monica wondered if this would be a good time to ask Jeff about Lauren and whether or not there was any trouble between them. She didn't want to seem like the interfering older sister, but she was worried about them.

Their wedding was scheduled for that spring, when they could set up a tent alongside the cranberry bogs, which would be awash with pink flowers at that time of year. Jeff and Lauren had meant to be married the previous spring but Lauren's mother had been struggling through a bout of cancer and they'd decided to wait. Fortunately she was now finished with treatments and her cancer was in remission.

They were nearly done with the pots and pans when Monica finally decided to broach the subject. She put a hand over Jeff's as he was reaching for a towel.

"Is everything okay between you and Lauren?"

Jeff looked startled. "What do you mean?"

"I don't know. I've noticed that something seems to be bothering Lauren these days." Monica sprinkled some cleanser into the sink. "The way she overreacted when Betsy DeJong was interviewing you, for instance."

Jeff looked at his feet. "Oh, that," he said. He sighed. "Something did happen," he finally admitted. "But I'm sure I can fix it. Lauren is just a bit . . . touchy about it right now."

"She's not calling off the wedding," Monica said with a catch in her voice.

When Jeff returned from Afghanistan, his right arm injured, he had been angry and bitter. Lauren had played a big role in putting him back together again.

"No, nothing like that." Jeff hesitated. "At least I don't think so."

"Want to tell me what happened?" Monica tried to keep her tone casual.

"It's really stupid." Jeff poked at the throw rug in front of the sink with the toe of his boot. "It happened at Larry's bachelor party down at Flynn's."

Oh, dear, Monica thought. She knew men got up to all sorts of things at bachelor parties. Hopefully it wasn't anything that couldn't be put right.

"There were girls there," Jeff said. "Larry hired them. It was really goofy — one of them even jumped out of a large cardboard cake." He shook his head. "Real cheesy stuff."

"You didn't —" Monica began.

Jeff shook his head vigorously. "I'd had a few drinks but not that many. Besides, the women . . . well, let's just say they weren't my type."

"So what happened that upset Lauren so?"

"Everyone was having their picture taken with the girls. Larry had two of them sit on his lap. I really didn't want to do it but this blond came over and draped herself around my neck. Larry took a photo with his phone and texted it to me."

Monica could guess what was coming next.

"Lauren borrowed my phone to make a call and I guess she saw the picture. I told her that nothing had happened, but she's still mad."

"So that's why she overreacted to Betsy's flirting with you?"

"I guess so," Jeff said, his voice glum. "She's not normally like that."

"I'm sure she'll get over it," Monica said, flipping off the light over the stove.

"I hope so."

Chapter 13

Monica headed to the farm kitchen early the next morning. As soon as she had several batches of baked goods out of the oven and ready to go to the farm store, she left Kit to handle the rest.

She walked back to her cottage, picked up her car and drove downtown to the police station. Beach Hollow Road was quiet, although there were plenty of cars parked at the Cranberry Cove Inn, and even Primrose Cottage, the local bed-and-breakfast, looked to be full.

Monica had decided that since she'd given Stevens the letter from Mary Visser's doctor about her heart condition, she would show her the scuba diving book that Greg had picked up at Visser's moving sale.

She had no idea whether Stevens would take it seriously or not, but she at least wanted her to know about it. Hopefully Stevens would agree with her deductions and would look into it.

The desk sergeant informed Monica that Stevens was in a meeting when she got to the station. She hesitated but then decided to wait. She sat down in one of the molded plastic chairs, which were hideously uncomfortable and obviously designed to discourage people from lingering. Someone had left a copy of the *Washington Post* on one of them and she picked it up.

Monica flipped through the pages, reading an article here and there. One article in particular aroused her curiosity. It was on personal safety, with tips like what to do if you've been kidnapped and put in a car trunk, how to break a choke hold, and what to do if your hands have been bound with a zip tie. Monica read through the instructions and filed them away in the back of her mind. She certainly hoped she'd never have to test them out.

She continued turning the pages until a headline caught her eye. *Money Laundering Suspected in Sale of Condos.*

Monica folded the paper open and read the article. She knew next to nothing about money laundering, but the article explained it simply and clearly and slowly an idea began to form.

Suddenly she closed the newspaper and tossed it on the chair next to her. She jumped up, told the desk sergeant that she would come back later and headed out the door.

Within a couple of minutes, she was on the highway heading toward Visser Motors. The trip was considerably less hair-raising than it had been with Gina driving, and ten minutes later, Monica was pulling into the parking lot of the auto dealership.

Her beat-up old Taurus with its dented rear fender looked out of place amid all the shiny new cars, but she didn't care. She wasn't there to pretend to buy a car this time but to follow up on a hunch that was slowly taking shape.

This time, no one came running out of the building anxious to wait on her. Monica wasn't surprised. Not only was her car ancient but her jeans were faded and worn and her jacket was old and clearly out of style. She certainly didn't look as if she had the money to buy a used jalopy, let alone a brand-new Mercedes.

Monica didn't bother to lock her car—who would steal her old wreck when there was an entire lot full of brand-new luxury cars available? She said a silent prayer as she walked toward the building and pulled open the door to the dealership. Gleaming new-model Mercedes were displayed on the showroom floor and the air was redolent with that new car smell.

The salesman, Les, was perched on the edge of his desk, clipping his nails and swinging his leg back and forth. He looked startled when he heard Monica approach. He glanced at her and then looked around, as if expecting Gina to appear like a genie out of a bottle.

He quickly pocketed the nail clippers and plastered a smile on his face. "Can I help you?" he said with considerable less enthusiasm than he'd shown on Monica's previous visit.

"I'm not here to buy a car, I'm afraid."

Les snorted and crossed his arms over his chest.

He could at least *pretend*, Monica thought, feeling slightly irritated.

"I have a question for you." She lowered her voice conspiratorially.

Les looked bored. He began examining his fingernails.

"When I was here the last time, you had a customer come in while you were waiting on us. He was foreign—he spoke with an accent and was in a chauffeur-driven car."

Les frowned. "Dimitri, you mean? Yes, he's been a customer of Visser Motors for a long time. He buys a lot of cars," Les said with a smug smile.

"A lot of cars? What does he do with all of them? Does he rent them out? The one he was riding in looked brand new."

Les leaned closer to Monica and she was enveloped in his aftershave. She had to stifle a sneeze.

"I'll tell you one thing." Les winked. "He doesn't drive them," he said, and returned to examining his fingernails.

"Well, yes, I saw he had a chauffeur—"

Les shook his head. "That's not what I meant." He looked around and lowered his voice to a whisper. "Dimitri is just looking for something to do with his money. Get it?" He winked again.

Monica feigned surprise. "Oh," she said, widening her eyes.

"How do you think Visser made all his dough?" Les sneered. "Hint. It wasn't just by selling cars."

"And I imagine you make a nice commission on the sales," Monica said.

Les grinned and stuck his thumbs in the waistband of his trousers. "One of the perks of the job."

• • •

So Visser was laundering money, Monica thought as she drove away from the dealership. That would certainly impact his Senate run if anyone found out. Les obviously knew about it. She wondered if any of the other employees knew as well and were also turning a blind eye.

A thought was forming in her mind as she was about to turn off the highway. What if Visser's wife had found out about the money laundering and had threatened to expose Visser if he didn't stop. It would certainly give him a motive for killing her.

But who would know? Who knew Mary Visser at the time?

Monica had a sudden idea. She pulled off to the side of the road and rummaged in her handbag for her cell phone. She scrolled through her contacts and was relieved to see she had saved Brenda Croft's information.

Brenda's phone rang half a dozen times and Monica was about to hang up when Brenda's gravelly voice came across the line.

She agreed to meet Monica in half an hour at the Cranberry Cove Inn.

Monica called the Inn and reserved a table for two and then called Kit to see if everything was going okay. He sounded quite chipper and assured Monica that he had things under control. Monica breathed a sigh of relief as she hung up.

The parking lot of the Cranberry Cove Inn was quite full and she was glad she had called ahead. She squeezed her Taurus in between two SUVs and got out.

The Inn was the destination for Cranberry Cove residents when celebrating an occasion such as an anniversary, graduation or birthday, although it was now getting some healthy competition from the Pepper Pot farther down Beach Hollow Road.

Monica was five minutes early and gave the maître d' instructions to show Brenda to her table. She noticed the maître d's eyebrows rise almost high enough to meet his hairline when he saw Monica's casual attire but there'd been no time for her to go home and change.

Monica had barely sat down before she saw the maître d' weaving his way through the tables again with Brenda following.

"I have to say, you've aroused my curiosity," Brenda said as she took a seat opposite Monica. She glanced out the window. "The view is certainly spectacular."

Monica turned and looked. The Inn was set on a slight hill and the view of Lake Michigan beyond was magnificent. The water was rough today, the waves foaming and churning as they made their way toward shore, and dark clouds were massing on the horizon.

"So tell me what this is all about," Brenda said with obvious relish.

Before Monica could answer, the waiter appeared to take their drink orders.

"A martini." Brenda held up her hand. "Make it dirty," she said without hesitation. She rubbed her neck. "It's been a rough morning."

Monica ordered a glass of Chardonnay, although she normally didn't drink at lunch.

"It all revolves around Bob Visser," Monica said after the waiter had left. "Visser is using his car dealerships to launder money."

Brenda reached for her glass and the charms on her bracelet tinkled like wind chimes in a breeze. She was about to speak, but the waiter returned then with their drinks and took their lunch orders.

"I suspected something like that," she said after he left. "But I never got far enough to prove it."

"I know you started probing the death of Visser's wife."

"Yes, and I was called off," Brenda said. "I was furious but the editor insisted I drop it."

"I've discovered some things that might interest you." Monica took a sip of her wine. "Visser's wife had a heart condition that made scuba diving dangerous." Monica decided to keep the fact that she'd found that letter from Mary Visser's doctor to herself. "I discovered evidence that Visser knew about it but didn't bother to warn her. As a matter of fact, I suspect he encouraged her."

Brenda gave a rattling cough. "I knew it," she said triumphantly. "I always suspected there was something suspicious about his wife's death. Much too convenient if you ask me."

"Convenient?"

"It was well known that Visser had a roving eye. Different women all the time."

"Do you think that's why he killed his wife? If he killed his wife," Monica added, wanting to be fair.

Just then the waiter arrived with their meal—quiche for Monica and a Reuben sandwich for Brenda with a side of French fries.

Brenda reached for the saltshaker and liberally salted her fries, then grabbed one with her fingers and nibbled on the end.

"I think the wife knew about the other women. I don't think it was that. I do know that something was going on between them. I was going to interview their housekeeper—we had a brief conversation on the phone—but then the editor pulled me off the story and . . ." She shrugged. "But she did say that she heard Visser and his wife arguing before that trip to Cozumel."

"I wonder if there's any hope of contacting the housekeeper?"

"She might still be working for him. I've heard he pays well, which is at least one thing in his favor."

"Do you remember her name?"

"Consuelo. A nice girl." Brenda frowned. "Although I suppose she'd be middle-aged by now."

Monica took a bite of her quiche but she barely tasted it. She was itching to get going to see if Visser's housekeeper was still working for him.

"So what's your theory?" Brenda pointed her fork at Monica. "Not the other women, because you didn't even know about that."

"I think it was the money laundering. I think Mary Visser found out and objected. It forced his hand—he had to get rid of her because he had no intention of stopping."

"Interesting," Brenda said as she took a huge bite out of her sandwich. "You could be right." She shook her finger at Monica. "If you're right, I want an exclusive. I'm sure the story would get picked up by some of the national papers given that Visser is running for senator. Even my editor wouldn't be able to resist that." She sighed. "It's too late for my career. I'm almost ready to retire, but at least I'd go out in a blaze of glory." She grinned.

Chapter 14

Monica flicked on her radio as she waited to pull out from the parking lot of the Cranberry Cove Inn. The news was on. She wasn't paying too much attention until she heard Visser's name mentioned.

According to the announcer, Visser was making a campaign stop in Marquette in Michigan's Upper Peninsula, which meant he wouldn't currently be at home. It took six hours to drive to Marquette, making a total of twelve hours for the round trip.

Monica wondered if their housekeeper lived in. Would she even talk to Monica? She had no idea but she had to give it a try.

Monica pulled out her phone and put in the URL for the white pages. Someone behind her honked and she tossed her phone onto the passenger seat, quickly looked left and right to check for traffic and pulled out of the parking lot.

As soon as she could, she pulled over and grabbed her phone again. She brought up the white pages and put in Visser's name. Numerous other Vissers popped up but only one of them lived in Cranberry Cove. Monica recognized the street address that was listed. It was in a very exclusive neighborhood, where the houses were all enormous, the lawns and gardens perfectly manicured by a lawn service company and the cars in the driveway late-model foreign makes.

Monica felt out of place driving down the street in her crumbling Taurus. It was making an odd noise. She'd have to take it in to the garage to get it checked out.

There was an unnatural hush over the neighborhood, as if someone had put it inside of a bubble.

She found Visser's house easily enough. It was the enormous standard-issue brick Georgian with a huge circular drive and carriage house garage doors. The only car in the driveway was an older model Element. The housekeeper's? Monica wondered.

Suddenly she was overcome by an attack of nerves. What if Visser answered the door? What would she say?

She'd have to trust her subconscious to come up with something, she thought as she parked her car and got out.

The door knocker was a large, highly polished pineapple. Monica picked it up and let it fall. She heard it echo dully inside the house.

It wasn't long before the door was opened by a woman wearing jeans and a sweatshirt with the sleeves pushed up. She was in her fifties and still very attractive, with her lustrous black hair hanging loose around her shoulders.

"Consuelo?" Monica said.

"Yes," the woman replied with only the slightest trace of an accent.

"Could I come in? I wanted to ask you a few questions if you don't mind. It's about the murder of Mr. Visser's fiancée, Betsy DeJong."

Consuelo's expression turned solemn. "That was a terrible tragedy."

She led Monica past the living room and dining room and into the kitchen. It looked brand new, with stainless steel appliances, granite countertops, custom cabinets and an elaborately tiled backsplash.

Consuelo motioned toward one of the stools lined up along the island.

"Would you like a cup of tea or coffee?"

Monica shook her head. "No, thank you. I don't want you to go to all that trouble."

"No trouble," Consuelo said. "I was going to make some coffee for myself."

"Then I'll have a cup if you don't mind."

Consuelo put a pod in the coffee machine, pressed a button, and moments later hot brew was trickling out into a mug. She handed the cup to Monica.

"Cream and sugar?"

"No, thanks. Have you worked for Mr. Visser for a long time?" Monica said as Consuelo prepared a second cup of coffee for herself.

"Yes. It was my first job in the United States." She carried her mug over to the island and perched on a stool. "He has been very good to me."

"Did you know Mary Visser?"

Consuelo smiled. "Yes. She hired me. She was a lovely lady."

"Mr. Visser must have been devastated when she died."

A strange look came over Consuelo's face.

"Yes," she said simply and then looked away quickly.

"Did they often fight?" Monica said, blowing on her coffee. Steam was still rising from the cup.

"No, not really."

"I suppose all couples fight occasionally," Monica said. "It's only normal."

"True." Consuelo hesitated. "They did have an argument right before they left for their vacation in Cozumel. I wouldn't have remembered it except that it was the last time I saw Mrs. Visser."

"Oh?" Monica said. "What did they fight about? Weren't they excited to be going on vacation?"

"I don't know. I couldn't hear what they were saying," Consuelo said, pulling down the sleeves of her sweatshirt. "It was something about laundry. I heard that word clearly enough. Mrs. Visser said it several times. Maybe she forgot to pick up Mr. Visser's clothes from the cleaner or something." She shrugged. "I don't know."

On the contrary, Monica thought. It sounded as if Mary Visser had found out about her husband's money laundering operation and had brought it up to him right before they left on vacation.

Monica had done some research and had learned that Cozumel was known for its coral reefs, which attracted divers from all over. Had Visser chosen the spot on purpose?

There was no guarantee that Mary Visser's heart problem would cause her death on the first dive, or even on the fifth dive. But it must have seemed worth it to Visser to take that gamble. If it paid off, it would be an almost foolproof murder method.

And it certainly looked as if he'd gotten away with it.

Monica thanked Consuelo and headed to her car. Her next stop was going to be the police station. She thought she might have finally put the whole case together. She hadn't solved Betsy's murder yet, but she thought she might just have proved that Visser's wife's death wasn't an accident.

"You're back," the desk sergeant said when Monica approached him. "Have a seat." He gestured toward the row of plastic chairs. "Stevens is in another meeting." He glanced at his watch. "Should be ending soon if you want to wait."

Monica sat down but she was almost too jittery to stay still. She would have infinitely preferred pacing the floor to being seated but she managed to content herself with jiggling her leg.

The wait wasn't very long but it seemed like an eternity until the desk sergeant gestured her over.

"Stevens is in her office. She said to come on down."

"Thanks."

Stevens was behind her desk, which was piled, as usual, with file folders and stacks of loose paper. She had half a sandwich in one hand and a pen in the other. There was a smudge of mustard on her chin.

"Something new?" She looked up when Monica walked in.

Monica handed her the *Scuba Diving for Beginners* book.

Stevens frowned. "What is this? Are you taking up scuba diving? I didn't think you were the type."

"Hardly," Monica said as she sat down. "But I think it's the key to Bob Visser's first wife's death."

Stevens's eyebrows shot up and her eyes widened.

"You're serious," she said after several seconds.

Monica nodded.

"Do you want to explain? Because you've lost me." Stevens sat back in her chair and took a bite of her sandwich. "What does scuba diving have to do with anything?"

"Mary Visser had a heart condition. You saw the letter from her doctor."

"Yes."

"It's dangerous for someone to dive with that condition."

"Okay. I'm with you so far."

"My husband—Greg—runs Book 'Em in town. He sells used books as well as new. The other day he went to a moving sale that Bob Visser was holding and picked up a random carton of books. That scuba diving book was one of them." Monica gestured toward the book on Stevens's desk. "Visser had bookmarked a specific page. The bookmark is still there."

Stevens picked up the book and opened it. Once again, the book flopped open at the same page.

"See those passages underlined in ink?" Monica said.

Stevens was quiet, her brow furrowed as she read the paragraphs Visser had highlighted.

Stevens was shaking her head. "I don't know . . ." She put the book down. "If your theory is correct, based on this"—she tapped the book—"Visser intended to kill his wife and her death wasn't an accident." She rubbed the back of her neck. "But why? What was his motive? I've gone over the case files and he didn't inherit any money, which is one of the usual reasons. And he didn't remarry either, so it's doubtful there was another woman in the picture."

"No, he didn't inherit anything, but he stood to lose money if he didn't get rid of her."

Stevens tilted her head. "Sorry. You've lost me."

Monica leaned forward. "Visser is laundering money through his car dealerships. One of his salesmen all but admitted it. And when I was there a Russian came to buy a car when he already had a brand-new Mercedes."

Stevens looked amused. "Maybe he wanted two?"

"I talked to Visser's housekeeper. She's worked for him for years. Mary Visser was the one who hired her. She heard the two of them arguing right before they left for their trip to Cozumel. She couldn't hear the conversation but she did catch one word. *Laundry.* I think Mary Visser was on to her husband, had discovered he was laundering money and threatened to go to the authorities."

Stevens laughed. "I'm afraid I'm not following. I don't see how that proves anything."

Monica was frustrated. "But if you put it all together you get—"

"A lot of circumstantial evidence," Stevens said. "Which wouldn't hold up in court for a minute." She leaned back and put her clasped hands behind her head. "I suppose you're now going to tell me that this proves Visser killed his fiancée, Betsy DeJong."

Monica felt deflated. "Well, if he killed once, what's to stop him from killing again?"

"Assuming his first wife's death wasn't simply a tragic accident." Stevens glanced at the scuba diving book again. "But I suppose it warrants investigation. The pressure is really on to solve this latest case. I can't afford to ignore any leads that might help."

Suddenly she looked very tired and Monica felt sorry for her. She could imagine the stress she was under. Visser had always been a prominent figure in the community thanks to his car dealerships, but now his Senate run was making him a household name in other parts of the state as well. No doubt there was considerable pressure to solve this case as quickly as possible.

Stevens ran her fingers through her hair. "On top of everything else, I've got this custody dispute going with my ex. He walks out on us when Ethan is a couple of months old and now he thinks he can walk back in and take up where he left off." She shook her head. "Ethan doesn't even recognize him."

"Are you going to go to court?"

"I suppose I'll have to. What a waste of time and money." Stevens sighed. "Listen, I'll check into your theory and see if there's anything to it, okay? There is a certain logic to it."

"Thanks," Monica said as she got up.

Stevens leveled her gaze at Monica, her eyes narrowed. "But don't do anything to put yourself in any danger. Promise? That's my job."

"Promise." Monica smiled.

Certainly, asking a few questions wouldn't put her in danger, Monica thought as she got into her car.

Right?

Chapter 15

Monica thought about her talk with Stevens as she drove back to the farm. While Stevens had sounded quite lukewarm about Monica's theory, Monica saw there was a spark in her eyes nonetheless. She felt confident that Stevens would look into it even if it was only a cursory investigation.

The wind had died down and Monica noticed that the waves on Lake Michigan were less ferocious than they had been earlier. A sailboat bobbed up and down in the distance and a motorboat was pulling out of the harbor heading toward the open water.

There was little traffic until Monica got about a mile from the farm, where a tour bus with *Crestview Tours* written on the side was heading down the road. Monica supposed it was filled with people on a fall color tour.

The bus lumbered along at such a slow pace that Monica was tempted to pass it, but they were on a sharp curve and she couldn't see far enough ahead. She tried to contain her impatience as they made their plodding way down the road.

Finally she reached the lane that led to Sassamanash Farm. She was planning the rest of her afternoon and what jobs she would tackle first when she noticed something up ahead.

It was unusual to encounter another vehicle on this lane. It only led to her cottage and farther on to the farm itself. There was a separate road that led directly to the farm store and that was the one their customers used. As she got closer, she realized the vehicle was a red-and-white van, and when she got closer still she saw the WZZZ written on the side and the antenna on the roof.

What on earth was the news team from WZZZ doing back at the farm? Over the last few days, Betsy DeJong's murder had disappeared from the morning and evening news as well as the front pages of the newspaper. There was only an occasional brief update from a police spokesperson.

Had new information been discovered? Something that Stevens hadn't told her about?

Monica pulled off to the side of the road, turned off the engine and got out of her car. She walked over to the van. No one was in sight, but as she approached, the door to the van opened and Todd jumped out. He smiled at Monica.

"Howdy," he said when Monica reached him.

"Are you filming something?" Monica asked, looking around.

"We're doing an update on Betsy's murder," Todd said, cracking his knuckles.

"Has something new come to light?"

"Not really. But Detective Stevens is hoping that we can generate some renewed interest in the case and someone might remember something they hadn't come forward with before."

"But why here?" Monica said.

"Heidi thought it would add some interest to the segment. Heidi is WZZZ's senior executive producer." Todd made a face. "I don't know why she's stuck her nose into this. Normally she never leaves the rarified atmosphere of her corner office."

"Betsy was her sister," Monica reminded him.

Todd gave a short bark of laughter. "There was no love lost between them, believe me. I doubt Heidi's even given it a second thought."

That sounded awfully callous, Monica thought. Most likely Todd was exaggerating. There had to have been some sort of sisterly bond between the two women.

Then again, Monica thought, if Heidi was romantically involved with Visser and Betsy found out, that would be more than enough to sour their relationship.

Just then the van's driver's-side door opened and Jasmine jumped out. She waved to Monica and went around the back to begin unloading her equipment.

A rumble in the distance announced the arrival of another car. Monica recognized it as Stevens's. She didn't immediately get out and Monica could see she was talking on her cell phone.

"I should congratulate you on your new job as anchor of the evening news," Monica said to Todd.

He gave a self-deprecating shrug. "I never expected it. Frankly, I never wanted to be on the air. I liked pulling the strings in the background."

"You must miss Betsy," Monica said, probing.

Todd bowed his head. "It's been tough. Betsy and I were very close. We've worked together for several years now. You become like a family, you know?"

He dashed a finger under eyes that looked quite dry to Monica.

"Everyone at the station has been shaken up about the murder. We've reported on murders countless times, but for it to happen to one of our own . . ." Todd fished a handkerchief out of his pocket and blew his nose.

"Detective Stevens even came around to the station to put me and Jasmine on the hot seat again. Luckily for me I was at the Pepper Pot having lunch when the murder took place. I even have the receipt to prove it." He pulled a slip of paper out of his shirt pocket. "I've kept it in case I needed it." He grinned. "I even showed it to Detective Stevens when she started in with her questions. I have to say that sent her packing pretty quickly."

Todd turned around, nearly bumping into Jasmine, who was waiting with her camera perched on her shoulder.

"Where do you want to film?" she said.

Todd pointed toward the spot where Betsy's body had been found. "I think right at the murder scene, don't you?"

Monica thought that was a bit gruesome, but then again the public would probably eat it up. Enough people had wanted to come and see the scene for themselves.

Just then another car pulled up behind Stevens's. It was a late-model Mercedes with all the trimmings. The door opened and a woman got out.

For a second, Monica had a sense of déjà vu. The woman looked so much like Betsy that she immediately knew it was her sister, Heidi. Although Heidi was in a skirt suit with a silk blouse and low-heeled pumps and her makeup was subtler than Betsy's had been.

Todd all but clicked his heels when he saw her and hastened over to greet her.

By then Stevens had finished her call and gotten out of the car. She walked toward Jasmine.

"Are we ready?" she said, glancing at her watch. She looked stressed. "I only have a few minutes to spare."

Heidi must have overheard because she clapped her hands.

"Let's roll, people."

Jasmine handed Todd a microphone.

He walked over to Stevens. "Why don't you stand there." He pointed to a spot near where Betsy's body had lain.

"Too bad the crime scene tape has been taken down," Heidi said. "It would have added just the right touch."

Stevens scowled at her and motioned for Todd to get on with it.

Todd cleared his throat and tested his microphone.

"Ready?" Jasmine raised her eyebrows.

Todd nodded and then began speaking as the tape began to roll.

"We are here today at the site of the murder of WZZZ's beloved news anchor Betsy DeJong. With me today is Detective Tammy Stevens of the Cranberry Cove Police Department. She has agreed to update us on the case." He turned away from the camera, toward Stevens, and thrust the microphone in her face. "Can you tell us what's new, Detective Stevens?"

Stevens didn't look thrilled to be on camera. She gave a nervous half smile, cleared her throat and began to speak.

"There is nothing new that I can share with the public at this time, but I assure you we are making progress," she said.

Todd looked disappointed. "Are you following up on some leads?"

Stevens gave a coy smile. "Yes, we are. We have a lot of information to sift through." Her voice became more earnest. "If anyone thinks of anything that might be useful as we hunt for this killer, please call this number." She recited a telephone number.

Todd looked slightly worried. Monica supposed he wasn't used to having Heidi in the audience on a shoot. Plus, he was still quite new at his job. He was bound to be a bit nervous.

Finally the segment ended. Todd thanked Stevens, who immediately headed toward her car. She waved to Monica as she was opening the door.

Todd was already in the van with his cell phone to his ear. Jasmine went around the back of the van to stow her camera, then walked over to Monica.

"Listen, all that stuff Todd said —"

"Can we get a move on?" Todd called out the open window.

"Later," Jasmine whispered and trotted over to the van.

• • •

Monica flipped on the news the next morning while she was making breakfast. She could hear the television from the kitchen easily enough — the cottage wasn't that big.

Mittens was standing by her bowl waiting for her breakfast. Monica scratched her under the chin as she tipped out some cat food, and Mittens purred contentedly.

The weather came on as she was putting the bag of cat food away and the prediction was for a drop in temperature but plenty of blue skies and sun.

A commercial for dishwashing detergent followed and then the news came back on and she heard Todd Lipton's voice. She turned the gas off under the eggs and went into the living room.

Hercule, who had been standing right next to Monica at the stove, now followed her into the other room. Greg had come downstairs and he, too, stood in front of the television.

Mittens sauntered into the room and leapt onto the sofa, where she curled up on a pillow.

The television segment that had been filmed at the farm was on. Todd's questions were delivered smoothly and he looked remarkably good on camera.

"I'm surprised Todd has never been interested in being on camera before. He said he was content working behind the scenes."

"He's quite good," Greg said, putting his hands on Monica's shoulders. "But not everyone wants to be in the limelight. The limelight can so easily turn into a spotlight, and who wants to live like that?" He chuckled. "Although being on WZZZ in Cranberry Cove is unlikely to bring you international or even national attention."

The segment ended and the camera cut to the newsroom for the live portion of the show. Todd was behind the news desk and Monica immediately noticed a difference in his appearance.

His face was pale and he looked as if he was sweating. She knew the lights in the studio were probably quite hot but she'd never seen any of the other news anchors look like that.

"Good morning, this is Todd Lipton. I'll be anchoring the news this morning while Caroline Horst is on vacation."

"What on earth is wrong with that man?" Greg said. He pointed at the television. "He's sweating profusely, and look at his collar. It looks as if he got dressed in a hurry."

"Perhaps he's ill?"

"Could be," Greg said.

When Todd began delivering a piece on a controversial decision by the board of education, his usually smooth voice was notably shaky.

"Something is definitely wrong with him this morning," Greg said.

"He really must be ill. I'm surprised they didn't find someone else to read the news if he's that sick."

She looked at Todd again, trying to analyze the expression on his face. She realized with a shock what it was.

"He doesn't look ill," Monica said, spinning around to face Greg. "He looks frightened half to death."

"But this isn't his first time on camera," Greg said. "He's been anchoring the news and hosting *What's Up West Michigan* ever since Betsy died over a week ago. "It can't be first-time jitters. It must be something else."

It was very curious, Monica thought, but she quickly forgot about it as she finished cooking the eggs. Greg had brought in the paper and they traded sections as they ate their breakfast.

Monica cleared the table with Hercule dogging her every footstep in case there were any scraps for him, while Greg gathered the paper together and put it on the coffee table in the living room.

"Do you mind if I leave the rest of the cleanup to you?" he asked as he reached for his jacket. "I have to get to the shop early today to meet with the contractor. We need to go over a checklist of what still needs to be done."

"You go on. I'm almost finished anyway."

Monica put the last dish in the dishwasher as Greg clipped on Hercule's leash and led the dog out to the car.

Monica turned the dishwasher on, donned her jacket and headed out the door and toward the farm kitchen. She hoped to get a jump on some of the baking so that she could sneak out around lunchtime and head over to WZZZ. Ever since Jasmine had whispered "later" at her, she'd been dying to know what the young woman had been about to tell her.

The weather prediction had been correct. There was more of a bite to the wind than there had been yesterday and the skies were clear and cloudless. Monica buttoned the top button on her jacket and stuck her hands in her pockets.

The scent of cranberries and sugar lingered in the air in the kitchen and Monica sniffed deeply as she opened the door. This was her happy place—elbows deep in dough with the aroma of baking all around her.

She hung up her jacket and got to work. By the time Kit got there, she had a batch of cranberry muffins in the oven and another batch ready to go.

She'd barely finished the muffins before she was mixing dough for a couple of loaves of cranberry bread.

"You're working awfully fast this morning," Kit said as he poured himself a cup of coffee from the carafe on the counter.

Monica blew a strand of hair off her forehead. "I need to duck out later for a bit and I didn't want to stick you with all the work."

Kit waved a hand. "Oh, don't worry about that. I'll be fine. You go do what you have to do." He winked at her. "I'm assuming it has something to do with your investigation into that anchorwoman's death."

Monica felt her face get hot. "Yes, sort of."

Why was she equivocating? Monica thought. She probably wasn't fooling anyone.

"Well, yes, I have to admit it does have to do with Betsy's death." She rubbed her forehead. "It's all so confusing." Her face brightened. "But I may have solved the mystery of Bob Visser's first wife's death."

Kit whistled. "You're kidding." He grinned. "I should call you Nancy Drew from now on."

Monica laughed. "I shared my theory with Detective Stevens, but whether the police follow up on it or not is anybody's guess."

"They'd be foolish not to. Who do you have pegged as Betsy's killer?" Kit's tone was teasing.

"I'm stumped," Monica admitted. "So many people had a motive. Dan, Melinda, Visser, Heidi, Todd."

"Melinda? Isn't she that girl that's been going around taking pictures? She doesn't look as if she would hurt a fly."

"Yes. She's taking pictures for Instagram." Monica took some loaf pans off the shelf. "Melinda was adopted and I discovered quite by accident"—Monica felt her face color again—"that her biological parents are Betsy DeJong and Dan Polsky."

Kit's eyes widened. "Seriously? But why would she kill Betsy then?"

"She could have resented the fact that Betsy gave her up for adoption. I gather she feels as if she never really fit in with her adoptive family. They could have argued and things might have gotten out of hand." Monica shrugged. "Maybe she has a temper."

"That's quite the playing field." The timer dinged and Kit pulled open the oven door and peered inside. "A few more minutes and these should be done."

• • •

Shortly before noon, Monica took off her apron, ran her hands through her hair, put on her jacket and headed out to WZZZ to speak to Jasmine.

Today the waves on Lake Michigan were angry and lashed against the shore and the boats still in the harbor rocked with the motion. Monica headed through town and toward the outskirts of Cranberry Cove. She was a quarter of a mile from the television studio when she came to a halt.

The cars in front of her had stopped suddenly. Monica could see a police car up ahead. Its flashers were on, sending whirling red and blue lights against the landscape.

Monica tried to get a glimpse of what was up ahead but there was a blue pickup truck in front of her that dwarfed her Taurus and made it impossible to see.

Suddenly the red taillights of the pickup truck went off and it crawled forward slightly. Inch by inch the cars moved up until Monica was at the head of the line.

Two cars were blocking one lane and a tractor had pulled off the road just ahead of them. Monica suspected the car must have tried to pass the tractor and misjudged the timing. Fortunately it didn't look as if anyone was hurt. A policeman was standing in the middle of the road directing cars down the one available lane.

Finally it was Monica's turn to go. She crept forward past the two tangled cars to the open road ahead.

It was after twelve by the time she reached the television station. Several cars were pulling out of the parking lot as she pulled in. She hoped she hadn't missed Jasmine.

Josh had a paper bag sitting on the reception desk and a sandwich set out on a piece of wax paper. A large bite had been taken out of it.

Monica hurried over to him, slightly breathless.

"You're here again?" Josh said. "You should get a job here." He giggled.

Monica decided to ignore that. "Is Jasmine still here?"

"Let me buzz her and see if she's at her desk."

"She hasn't gone out?"

"I haven't seen her." Josh reached for the telephone.

Monica waited impatiently while he talked to someone on the other end of the line.

"She's away from her desk but apparently she has her coat on so I suspect she'll be coming this way any minute now."

Monica hoped Jasmine was just going to lunch and not out on a shoot.

"Do you want to sit down?" Josh waved a languid hand toward the chairs.

Monica was too jumpy to sit and instead paced back and forth in front of Josh's desk.

While Monica was waiting a young man in black pants and a black shirt buttoned up to his Adam's apple came up and began chatting with Josh. She heard the word *brawl* and hovered nearby, casually leaning an elbow on the reception desk and pretending not to listen.

"That was something," Josh said to his colleague. "It sure added a bit of excitement to this place."

Monica edged closer. "What happened?"

Josh dropped his tone to a conspiratorial whisper. "You should have seen it. It was epic. It's normally so dull around here." He pretended to stifle a yawn.

"What happened?" Monica said again.

"This man came in and boy, was he in a rage."

"His face was all red," the other young man piped up.

"He practically had the proverbial steam coming out of his ears." Josh giggled. He pointed to the young man. "This is Bert, by the way."

Monica nodded at Bert. "Why was he so mad? Did it have something to do with WZZZ?"

Josh shook his head. "No." He glanced at Bert as if for confirmation. "He asked for Betsy DeJong."

"But she's—" Monica began.

Josh waved a hand, halting her. "This was before Betsy was killed. Two or three days before. Right, Bert?"

"Yes." Bert fingered the top button on his shirt. "Fortunately Betsy wasn't here or I don't know what might have happened."

"Who was this man? Did he say?"

Josh and Bert looked at each other.

"It was Dan something-or-other," Josh said. "He wouldn't believe Betsy wasn't here and he tried to get into the offices to look for her."

"We had to call security," Bert said. He rolled his eyes. "Such as it is. Stan must be at least seventy years old."

"You don't know this man's last name?"

"I wish I could remember," Josh said, putting a finger on his chin. "Something with a *p* I think."

Dan Polsky, Monica thought. It had to be. "Did you tell Betsy about it when she came back?"

Both Josh and Bert shook their heads. "The powers that be decided it would be best not to tell her. They didn't want her upset right before she was due to go on the air."

So Dan Polsky must have known about Melinda before Betsy showed up that day at the farm. Had Betsy told him? Monica wondered. Or had it been Melinda who had told him the truth? Either way, had it pushed Dan into a murderous rage?

Finally the door opened and Jasmine walked out. She looked surprised to see Monica.

"Hey, how are things down on the farm?" She smiled.

"Fine," Monica said, hastening to get to the point of her visit. "I wanted to talk to you. Do you have a minute?"

Jasmine hesitated. "I was about to go out to get something to eat. I'm starving."

"I haven't had lunch either," Monica said, realizing she was getting hungry. "How about we meet at the Cranberry Cove Diner," she said as they began walking toward the door.

"Great. I'll see you there." Jasmine pushed open the door.

Monica pulled out of the parking lot behind Jasmine. She wondered if the accident she'd encountered earlier had been cleared up yet. As she passed the spot she noticed that the tractor had left and the two cars had been moved over to the shoulder, allowing traffic to pass in both directions. A tow truck was at the scene and a young man in overalls was hooking a chain to the bumper of one of the cars.

Monica continued on into town. Jasmine had snagged a parking spot in front of the diner. Monica wasn't as lucky. She went past the diner, pulled into a spot in front of the hardware store and walked back.

Gus nodded at Monica from his spot behind the counter, a pancake turner in one hand and an egg in the other. He deftly cracked the egg and it sizzled as it hit the hot grill.

Jasmine waved from a booth in the rear and Monica headed toward her.

"Thanks for meeting me here," Jasmine said. "I didn't eat any breakfast and I'm starved." She gave a shy smile. "I ran out of your delicious muffins."

The waitress slid two glasses of ice water on their table and slapped down two menus.

Jasmine scanned hers. "Someone told me they have great chili here but I don't see it on the menu."

Monica laughed. "You have to know to ask for it. It's a secret that separates the locals from the tourists."

"I see." Jasmine put down her menu. "That's what I'm having then." She grinned. "It will make me feel like an insider."

The waitress reappeared with a pad and pencil in her hand. They each ordered the chili. The waitress nodded and moved on to the next table.

Monica put her hands down on the table. "I wanted to speak to you about Todd Lipton. When we were filming yesterday you said that what he was saying wasn't true, but you couldn't finish because you had to leave."

"Yes." Jasmine leaned forward eagerly. "Todd is such a liar. He told you he never wanted the anchor job or to be host of *What's Up West Michigan*. That's not true."

"No?" Monica said, wiping some of the condensation off her water glass with her napkin. "He sounded very convincing."

"Don't let him fool you." Jasmine paused as the waitress slid steaming bowls of chili in front of them. "This looks delicious," she said, pulling a couple of napkins from the dispenser. "Todd had all but been told the job was his—Patty said he'd been angling for it for years—when it was announced that Betsy was going to be the new evening news anchor and host of *What's Up West Michigan*."

"Was Betsy a better fit for the job?"

Jasmine snorted. "Not exactly." She blew on her chili and scooped up a spoonful. "The president of WZZZ had a thing, shall we say, for Betsy." Jasmine tasted her chili. "This is good. Anyway, the rumor going around WZZZ was that Betsy slept with the president to get the job."

"Do you believe that?" Monica spooned up some of her own chili. "When a woman gets ahead there are always rumors like that."

Jasmine was already shaking her head. "No, this time they're true. One of the administrative assistants . . . caught them in the act." Jasmine blushed.

"Todd must have been furious." Monica wiped a bit of chili off her chin.

"You're not kidding. Furious isn't the word for it. Homicidal is more like it." Jasmine clapped a hand over her mouth. "I didn't mean that literally."

"Of course not," Monica said, but she was wondering. Had Todd been furious enough to murder Betsy? "But Todd said he and Betsy got along great. You'd think he'd have been happy for her once he got over his own disappointment."

Jasmine looked up, startled. "But they didn't get along. Not at all. They were always sniping at each other. It made the rest of us very uncomfortable." She shuddered.

• • •

Monica stood on the pavement for a moment lost in thought, still thinking about what Jasmine had said. A passerby accidentally bumped into her, bringing her back to the present. She glanced down the street. While she was in town, she'd visit Greg and check on the renovations.

A faint layer of plaster dust covered the window display of Book 'Em and the sound of a power drill was coming from the second floor. Monica opened the door and stepped inside.

Greg's book group was just finishing up, the members seated in a circle in the various chairs Greg had pulled together.

"Ooof," said Phyllis Bouma as she struggled to get up from the sagging armchair that was threatening to engulf her. She smiled at Monica. "Next time I'll choose one of the hard chairs instead. I should know better at my age."

"What are you reading?" Monica asked, glancing at the book in Phyllis's hand.

"*Strangers on a Train* by Patricia Highsmith. A real classic," Phyllis said appreciatively. "Have you read it?"

"No, but I saw the movie directed by Alfred Hitchcock."

"Did you know his daughter was in the movie?" Phyllis said.

"No. How interesting."

A woman was walking toward them and Phyllis waved her over. She had curly white hair and astonishingly blue eyes.

"Sally, this is Monica Albertson from Sassamanash Farm. Monica, this is Sally Bos."

Sally smiled at Monica. "Isn't that where that dreadful murder took place? That must have been horrifying for you." She clucked her tongue. "Poor Betsy. She didn't deserve that."

"You knew her?" Monica said.

"Yes, of course. I was her English teacher in high school. I had both of the DeJong sisters—first Betsy and then Heidi." She shook her head. "I felt sorry for Betsy."

"Why?"

"Heidi got everything she wanted—good grades, boyfriends, jobs. Even if it meant she had to take them from someone else. Even from her own sister."

Monica raised her eyebrows.

"Heidi graduated from college first and joined that television station and climbed the ladder while Betsy was held back because of—" She stopped. "I really shouldn't say." She pursed her lips. "Betsy had the worst luck but she had determination. I was so pleased when I saw she got that anchor job."

Sally glanced at Phyllis. "Ready to go?" She hooked her purse over her arm. "Lovely meeting you," she said to Monica as they turned to leave.

That was interesting, Monica thought. Heidi always got what she wanted even if it meant stealing something from her sister. Including her sister's fiancé.

"Want to see upstairs?" Greg said, walking toward Monica.

"I'd love to."

He led her over to the newly installed wrought iron spiral staircase that joined the two floors.

"What do you think?"

"It's perfect," Monica said as they climbed the steps.

Hercule was waiting at the top of the stairs. He butted his wet nose against Monica's hands and she bent down to scratch his head and tell him he was a good boy.

She straightened up and looked around. The transformation that had taken place in just a few days was amazing. Drywall was up and a roll of carpeting stood in the corner waiting to be installed.

Monica glanced at the area where the café would be located. She couldn't wait to decide on colors and order tables and chairs. Suddenly she had what she thought was a brilliant idea. She couldn't wait to share it with Greg later that evening after she'd thought it through.

Chapter 16

Monica got back to the farm shortly after two o'clock. As she walked from her cottage to the farm kitchen, she noticed Melanie taking pictures of a loon taking off from one of the bogs. She waved and smiled at Monica.

Kit was out making a delivery of cranberry salsa but had left a note saying they needed more cookies.

Monica gathered the ingredients together and measured out the chocolate chips, sneaking a couple for herself. She was dropping the dough onto a cookie sheet when there was a tentative knock on the door.

"Come in," Monica yelled, swiping an arm across her forehead to push back an errant strand of hair.

Melinda stuck her head around the edge of the door. "Is it okay if I come in?" She pushed the door wider. "I don't want to disturb you if you're busy."

"No problem," Monica said. "I'll finish getting these cookies in the oven and then I'll make us some tea."

"Please don't bother."

Monica smiled. "I could do with a cup myself. And a bit of a break."

She spooned the rest of the cookie dough onto the baking sheet and slid it into the oven. "How have you been?" she said to Melinda as she put two mugs of water in the microwave to heat.

"I'm okay, I guess," Melinda said, but the way she said it made it clear she was far from okay.

Monica finished preparing the tea and carried the mugs to the table. She looked at Melinda quizzically. Something was definitely wrong.

"You don't look as if everything is okay. Is something upsetting you?"

Melinda sighed loudly. "I guess you're right. I'm not okay." She ran her finger around the rim of her mug. "I know I told you I was adopted and didn't know who my biological parents were but that was a lie." Melinda ducked her head. "I did search for them and I found out a couple of weeks ago. It's Betsy DeJong and Dan Polsky."

Monica feigned surprise.

Melinda continued. "I was astonished when I found out they lived right here in Cranberry Cove. I'd seen Betsy on television, but what did

145

my father look like? Did I resemble him at all? Maybe I'd even passed him on the street or something, without knowing it."

"Did you try to visit either of them?"

Melinda shook her head and her long hair swished back and forth.

"No. I tried contacting Betsy at the television station but she would never return any of my calls. I met her and Dan for the first time at the film shoot."

"That must have been a very emotional experience for you," Monica said, picking up her mug. "To be confronted with both of them like that and so suddenly."

Melinda took a deep breath and exhaled. "It was. I didn't expect it so it really took me by surprise." She wrapped a strand of hair around her finger. "I'd always dreamed about meeting my parents." She looked up at Monica from under her eyelashes. "I realize now that the word *parent* refers to the person who took care of you and brought you up. Not the person who gave you up." She dashed a finger under her eyes. "It wasn't my adoptive parents' fault that I felt as if I didn't fit in. I did that to myself."

"I imagine it was a terrible shock to you, meeting your biological mother for the first time and then minutes later finding out that she'd been murdered," Monica said.

Melinda nodded. "It was. I realized that all my fantasies about having a relationship with her would never come true. And then the police came around asking me all these questions. I was scared they'd think I did it."

Monica felt a bit guilty knowing that she had thought the same thing herself.

"How did Betsy react when she met you?"

Melinda snorted. "She completely blew me off. Said she didn't know what I was talking about—she'd never had a baby. With all those people around I didn't get to talk to her again."

"I'm so sorry. I'm sure that wasn't the reaction you were hoping for when you decided to search for your birth mother."

"Here's the thing," Melinda said, putting her hands down flat on the table. "I did go up to Dan when you were filming that segment about the farm and I told him that I was his daughter. I'd called him after I got my adoption record. He'd been shocked—it seems he didn't know that Betsy had even been pregnant."

"She hadn't told him?" Monica said.

Melinda played with the handle of her mug. "Apparently not. I guess she didn't want anyone to know."

"She might have been afraid that Dan would want to get married and for Betsy to keep you. And that would have ruined everything. She had big plans for herself."

Melinda snorted. "And those plans didn't include being saddled with a husband and a baby." Melinda looked down and her hair drew a curtain over her face. "Dan was different, though. He asked me about myself — what were my adoptive parents like, was I happy?"

Monica couldn't even imagine how Dan must have felt, first finding out that he was a father and then meeting his daughter so unexpectedly.

"We went off together somewhere quiet to talk and that's why he wasn't here when that detective arrived. That means he couldn't have done it, right — murdered Betsy? She was already dead by the time we got back."

That gave both Dan and Melinda alibis, Monica thought. But was Melinda telling the truth? Was she possibly protecting Dan or herself? She had seemed sincere enough, but it wouldn't be the first time someone had fooled her, Monica thought.

• • •

Monica was washing out the mugs when Kit returned from his delivery.

"How did it go?" she said, running water into the sink.

"Just fine," Kit said, collapsing in a chair. "I am tired though from hauling all those boxes." He made a face. "I must be getting old."

Monica laughed. "You have a long ways to go before you can consider yourself old."

Kit shrugged. "I guess I'm out of shape then."

Monica went into the storage room and came out with another bag of flour, which she hefted onto the counter.

"I had an idea this afternoon," she said to Kit, who was washing the baking sheets now.

"Oh? Something good, I hope."

"I think so." Monica slit open the new bag of flour. "You know Greg is adding on to Book 'Em. He's turning the second floor into more sales space and is adding a small café."

"Where you'll be selling all things cranberry?" Kit said with a smile.

"Certainly some things, yes. But we'll probably branch out a bit."

"You're going to be spreading yourself terribly thin going between here and the café. It makes me tired just to think about it."

"That's what I wanted to talk to you about," Monica said, scooping some flour into a bowl. "How would you like to run the café?"

"Moi?" Kit pointed to himself.

"Yes. I think you'd be great at it."

For once Kit looked flabbergasted.

"I still have to run it by Greg but I'm sure he'll agree. So at least think about it."

"I'm really honored that you would consider me," Kit said, a catch in his voice.

"I can't think of anyone better." Monica smiled.

• • •

Monica was wiping down the counters when the door opened and Lauren walked in. She looked excited—her cheeks were pink and her eyes were dancing.

"I just talked to Nora," she said, plopping into a chair, "and she told me that several customers have come to the farm store because they saw our pictures on Instagram."

"That's great!" Monica draped the dishrag over the edge of the sink. "So you were right—it's paying off."

"Looks like it." Lauren jiggled her foot up and down. "I've had another idea as well." She leaned forward with her hands palms up on her knees. "I think the farm should advertise."

"Advertise?" Monica paused with two oven mitts in her hand. "You mean like in the newspaper?"

Lauren shook her head. "No. I'm thinking on television. The tourists will soon be arriving in droves on their autumn leaf tours. If we get in front of them on television, there's a good chance they'll stop in at the farm store."

"But won't it be expensive?" Monica furrowed her brow. "The budget is pretty tight as it is."

"A fifteen-second spot shouldn't cost that much. We'd run it on WZZZ during the local news, not on a national network." Lauren jumped to her feet. "I could go check for you and get the details."

"That's okay. I'll do it. I'll go tomorrow." That would give her another excuse to visit WZZZ, Monica thought

"Great." Lauren's face broke into a broad smile.

Monica took a deep breath. "Do you mind if I ask you something?"

Lauren's expression changed to one of wariness. "Sure."

"What is going on between you and Jeff? He told me about the photograph you found on his phone—the one that was taken at his friend's bachelor party. But it's not like you to get so upset over something like that."

Lauren deflated like a punctured balloon. She plopped back into her chair and appeared to be examining the wood grain on the table.

"If you don't want to talk about it, that's fine," Monica said. "But I care a great deal about both of you and you both appear to be unhappy." She shrugged. "Maybe there's something I can do?"

"It's not that picture that's bothering me. Not really," Lauren said, gripping the edge of the table.

Monica waited. Finally Lauren spoke again.

"I suppose I can tell you." Lauren looked off into the distance. "I went to the doctor because I was having this pain." She rubbed her stomach. "And it turns out I have endometriosis."

"Can something be done for that?" Monica said gently.

"There's medication." Lauren looked down at her hands. "The doctor said I have a relatively mild case." She tugged on the neck of her sweater. "But then I read online that it might mean I wouldn't be able to have a baby." She stifled a sob.

Monica reached out and put her hand over Lauren's.

Lauren looked up at Monica with tears glittering in her eyes.

"I know Jeff wants a family. It's really important to him. And I'm afraid I won't be able to give him one."

"What did Jeff say? Have you talked to him about this?"

Lauren nodded. "He said he doesn't care. That he wants to marry me no matter what. But how can I do that to him? It wouldn't be fair. He said he's always wanted to have his own family." She gave a brief smile. "We were talking about two—hopefully a boy and a girl."

"I think you should believe him when he says he doesn't care," Monica said. She squeezed Lauren's hand.

"But I've seen him looking at other women. Like he looked at Betsy DeJong when they were filming that segment. And that photo on his phone. I'm afraid he's having second thoughts. And that he's looking for someone else who can give him what he wants."

"I don't think you have to worry," Monica said. "One" — she ticked the items off on her fingers — "you said your case is mild. Two, it's only a possibility that it would affect your chances of having a baby. It's not a sure thing, and three, there's always adoption. Besides, I would talk to your doctor about it and not rely on something you'd read online."

"Do you really think Jeff isn't concerned about it?" Lauren's eyes were pleading.

"I do. I've spoken to him and all he wants is for things to go back to normal between the two of you and for the wedding to take place." Monica squeezed Lauren's hand again. "I think you and Jeff should have a serious talk so you can move past this."

Lauren sighed. "I suppose you're right." She lifted her chin. "That's what I'm going to do." She smiled. "Thanks so much." She touched Monica's shoulder. "I do feel better now. And I know I'll feel even better after I talk to Jeff."

• • •

The next morning Monica dressed with more care than usual — a pair of good black trousers and a rust-colored turtleneck sweater that while not new, had barely been worn. She glanced in the mirror. She thought she looked presentable enough to talk to the sales department at WZZZ and not as if she'd wandered in off the street.

No one needed to know that Monica's main reason for going to the television station was not to talk about advertising but to see if she could get any more gossip out of Josh. He seemed to relish talking about his coworkers.

Monica collected her keys, slipped on her jacket and headed out to her car. There was very little traffic and soon she could see the red WZZZ building in the distance.

As she approached the station parking lot she noticed several bright orange traffic cones blocking off the spaces in the front nearest the entrance. Men were clustered around a pothole, shovels in hand, and the smell of hot asphalt was in the air.

A sign directed Monica to the side of the building, where she found a space easily enough. She rounded the corner and was approaching the entrance when the door opened and Heidi DeJong walked out. She was dressed in a black pantsuit, a silk blouse and high heels. She walked briskly and Monica noticed a flicker of recognition in her eyes as she strode past, leaving behind the scent of her expensive perfume.

Josh was behind the reception desk nursing a cup of coffee and picking at a glazed doughnut. He licked his fingers and smiled when he saw Monica.

"You really should get a job here," he joked again. "You're becoming a regular."

Monica leaned on the desk. She rolled her eyes dramatically. "Did you see Todd doing the news yesterday? Was he ill? He seemed so rattled. It wasn't like him."

"Yes, I did. And no wonder he looked rattled," Josh said with relish. "The police had just been by to question him. A woman—Detective Stevens, she said her name was. I saw Todd after she came out of his office and his face was white and there was perspiration on his forehead."

"Do you think Todd had something to do with Betsy's death?"

Josh wrinkled his forehead and rubbed the back of his neck. "I suppose it is possible. He's got her job now so there's that. Plus, that other thing that happened would give him a motive."

"What other thing?"

Todd leaned forward. "Todd once asked Betsy out on a date."

Monica's eyebrows shot up. "He did?"

Josh nodded. " Yes, and you could say it didn't end well. Not well at all."

"Did Betsy turn him down?"

"Not only that, but a couple of the sales guys heard the whole thing and they ragged him about it for weeks. Punching above his weight, they called it." Josh pursed his lips. "I mean, you've seen Betsy. She's way out of Todd's league. And of course she became engaged to Bob Visser. That only rubbed salt into the wound." Josh took a sip of his coffee. "And Betsy told some of the women about it, so needless to say, it was all around the office in no time. I wouldn't be surprised if even the janitor knew about it.

"Anyway," Josh said and took a deep breath, "what can I do for you today? I assume you didn't come here to talk to me."

Yes, actually I did, Monica thought.

"I was thinking of advertising on WZZZ. Is there someone I can talk to about it?"

Josh pointed a finger at Monica. "You've got it. I'll get one of the salesmen on the line."

Josh made a call to someone and moments later the door opened and a young man walked out. He was dressed all in brown—suit, shirt, tie and shoes—and had dark slicked-back hair with a liberal application of gel.

He gave Monica a practiced smile. "You're interested in advertising, I understand."

"Yes. I'd like to get some more information about it. The cost and things like that."

"Come on back and we can talk."

He led her through the door and into the office area with its rows of cubicles. He turned toward Monica as they were rounding the corner and held out his hand.

"Brian Singer."

Monica shook his hand and introduced herself. "Monica Albertson."

"Well, Monica, so you are considering advertising with us. What kind of business are we talking about here?" Brian said, showing Monica into a room barely larger than a broom closet. There were no windows and the arm of Brian's desk chair was mended with black electrical tape.

"A cranberry farm, our farm store and our farm products."

Brian collapsed into his chair, leaned back, steepled his fingers and launched into a well-rehearsed spiel about the benefits of advertising with WZZZ.

Monica listened with only half an ear. She was thinking about what Josh had told her about Betsy and Todd. Todd must have felt quite humiliated. Maybe he killed Betsy for revenge? For making him look foolish? Maybe she teased him about it or threw it in his face?

"I think you can see why advertising on WZZZ should be part of your media plan," Brian was saying.

Monica blinked and tried to focus. She'd been daydreaming all during Brian's presentation and had barely heard a word. He was now handing her a glossy folder with a large picture of the WZZZ satellite dish on the front.

"Everything you need to know is right in there," he said, tapping the folder. "Rate sheets, testimonials, time slots."

"Thank you," Monica said and stood up.

"My card is at the front of the folder. Don't hesitate to call me if you have any further questions or would like to discuss signing on with us. We'd love to welcome you to the WZZZ family."

• • •

The sun hit Monica as soon as the door to WZZZ closed behind her. She stopped for a moment to savor the feeling of warmth on her face. She knew that soon enough the ground would be covered with snow and the temperatures would dip into the single digits.

Her visit to WZZZ had given her a lot to think about, and the information was swirling around in her mind as she opened her car door and got in.

She put the key in the ignition, turned it and started the car. She put it in reverse and began to back out of the parking space, but she quickly realized something was wrong. That was odd. The car had been running fine an hour ago. She let up on the brake, made sure the gear shift was firmly in reverse and tried backing out again. The car wasn't handling the way it normally did and there was an odd scraping sound coming from underneath.

Did she possibly have a flat tire? She groaned, turned the car off and got out. The left front tire was clearly flat. She looked around. So was the left rear tire. How could that be?

Monica circled her car. Both the right front and rear tires were also flat. This was no accident. She hadn't run over a nail or had a slow leak. Besides, all four tires wouldn't go flat at the same time. Someone had to have done this on purpose.

Who would do something like this? It could be hooligans out for some fun. But why choose her car? The more Monica thought about it, the more she became convinced that her car had been singled out on purpose.

Was it because she was asking questions about Betsy's murder? Was the killer trying to stop her from investigating?

She debated what to do. Should she call a tow truck? Or should she call the police?

She finally decided that Detective Stevens ought to know about this. She got back in the car, pulled her cell phone from her purse and dialed the Cranberry Cove police station. When the call went through, she asked for Stevens.

Luckily she'd caught Stevens in a quiet moment and the detective said she would be there in ten minutes.

Monica scrolled through her emails on her phone while she waited. The Pepper Pot restaurant was ordering more cranberry compote and the Cranberry Cove Inn was interested in possibly using her cranberry walnut chocolate chunk cookies in a welcome package for guests. They were asking if she could provide a sample for the owner.

That would mean increased revenue for the farm and Monica felt her spirits lift slightly.

Before she could reply to either email, she saw Stevens's car pull into the parking lot. Stevens stopped, got out and walked over to Monica's car.

Monica joined her. Stevens shook her head when she saw the flat tires. She squatted down and examined them carefully.

"It's not a flat. They didn't let the air out of your tires," she said as she stood up again. "Your tires have been slashed."

Monica felt her temper rise. She clenched her fists and felt like beating them against the side of the car. This was a deliberate act of vandalism. It would be one thing to have the car towed to a gas station and have more air put in the tires. Slashing them meant she would have to go to the expense of buying all new tires.

She felt tears pricking the back of her eyelids and blinked them away. It wasn't like her to get so emotional. She couldn't imagine what had gotten into her lately.

"Did you call a tow truck?" Stevens said.

"Not yet. I wanted to wait until you got here."

"You can go ahead. I'll give you a ride home if you like."

Monica arranged for the tow truck, and when her car was safely stowed on board, she and Stevens got in Stevens's car.

Stevens turned to Monica as they pulled out of the parking lot.

"Do you have any enemies?" Her tone indicated she was only half joking.

Monica wasn't sure how much to reveal. "No. At least I don't think so. Although I . . . I might have asked few questions about Betsy DeJong's murder."

"I don't think it has anything to do with that."

Monica was surprised. "Why not? Maybe I touched a nerve somehow and this was a warning for me to stop investigating."

Stevens shook her head as she turned on her blinker. "It can't be. It has to be something else."

"But why not?" Monica said again. "I can't imagine anyone else doing this to me on purpose."

"Then it must have been some troublemakers who thought it was fun to slash someone's tires," Stevens said as she looked in her rearview mirror.

"Why do you think it can't have anything to do with Betsy's murder? What if I got too close to someone and they were spooked. This is their way of warning me off. Besides, don't most vandals do their dirty work at night?"

"It can't be that. For the simple reason that we've already arrested the killer."

"What?" Monica swiveled in her seat to stare at Stevens. "Who?"

"I suppose it's okay to tell you. It will be on the news tonight. We've arrested Dan Polsky for Betsy DeJong's murder."

Chapter 17

Monica was still in shock when Stevens dropped her off at her cottage. The world felt as if it had tilted somehow. Stevens was wrong—she had to be. Monica was convinced now that Dan wasn't the killer, even though she had suspected him herself at one time.

Stevens had said that Dan showing up at WZZZ, ranting and raving about Betsy, was one of the things that had tipped her off. Had there been other evidence? Monica supposed there must have been but Stevens wasn't at liberty to reveal any of it.

If Dan really was the killer, then someone had slashed her tires for some other reason. Monica couldn't begin to fathom what that was. But what if Stevens was wrong and Dan wasn't the killer. A scene suddenly flashed through Monica's mind—Heidi leaving WZZZ just as Monica arrived.

Heidi had recognized Monica, she was sure of it. Was Heidi the one who had slashed her tires?

Monica was still pondering the idea when she arrived at the farm store. She was so lost in thought that she nearly collided with a customer who was leaving as Monica was about to enter.

"I'm so sorry," Monica said. She smiled an apology.

The woman stared at her for a second and then moved on without saying anything.

Nora was behind the counter when Monica walked in. She looked a bit flustered. A lock of hair had drooped onto her forehead but she seemed oblivious to it.

"I stopped by to see if you needed anything. Have you been busy?" Monica asked.

"We had one of those massive tour buses pull in. You know, the big ones that take senior citizens on their fall color tour. They all came in at once and wanted to be waited on immediately. It was pandemonium in here." Nora shook her head. "And of course the women all asked to use the restroom. I hope they haven't left it a mess."

"I'm sorry. If I had known, I would have come to help. You should have called me."

"No worries." Nora gave a tired smile. "It all worked out in the end.

Everyone got their muffins and cookies and I'm confident they left happy." She pointed to the display case. "You're going to have your work cut out for you though restocking. They nearly cleaned us out."

"Kit and I can manage it." Monica was already mentally preparing herself to get up extra early the next day.

She glanced at Nora. Nora looked tired and worn out like a faded version of her usual self. "Do you want to go home? I can stay and handle the store." She knew Nora had two children at home and a husband who would all be wanting dinner the minute Nora stepped in the door.

"I'm okay," Nora said, giving Monica a reassuring smile. "I'll be able to put my feet up for a bit when I get home. I've got beef stew in the slow cooker so no need to rush around getting dinner on the table." She glanced at Monica. "You might want to get going on the baking." Nora looked pointedly at the nearly empty display case.

Monica laughed. "Okay, I can take a hint."

Monica glanced at the display case again to see what was left. She made a mental note of what was needed, said goodbye to Nora, and was about to leave when the door opened and a customer came in, a woman in a flower-print maxi skirt who looked tantalizingly familiar. Monica was trying to remember where she'd seen her before when it came to her.

"You're Patty, aren't you?" Monica said. "You put the *What's Up West Michigan* segment on our farm on a flash drive for me."

"Yes, I remember. That's why I'm here." Patty smiled. "Ever since I learned about Sassamanash Farm, I've been curious about what you have here. My book club is meeting tonight and I thought I'd try some of your cookies. Jean over at the station said they're very good. She said they have cranberries in them and big chunks of chocolate. I'm a huge chocoholic myself." Patty scanned the contents of the display case.

"I'm glad she enjoyed them," Monica said. "Would you like to try one?"

Patty's face brightened. "Sure. Why not." She patted her stomach. "I can always start my diet tomorrow."

Monica stepped behind the counter, selected a cookie and handed it to her.

Patty took a bite and closed her eyes in rapture. "Delicious."

"How many would you like?" Monica said.

"I'll take a dozen, please. These are so rich, I'm sure two per person should be enough."

Monica smiled. "You may even have some left over for yourself."

Patty gave a laugh that turned into a rumbling cough. "I don't know about that. These gals love their sweets," she said when she'd caught her breath.

Monica picked up a sheet of glassine and began to fill a white paper bag with the cookies.

"So this is where Betsy DeJong was murdered," Patty said, looking around.

"No here exactly," Monica said. "It happened down the road past the bogs."

Patty pulled her wallet from her purse. "You'd think they would have caught the killer by now. Maybe they should call in the FBI. Who knows?" She shivered dramatically. "The killer might come after someone else at the station. Maybe it's a serial killer."

Monica didn't mention Dan's arrest, although that would probably have put Patty's mind at ease. Besides, Monica was convinced the police would end up letting him go. She was positive he didn't do it.

"I swear there were days when I thought that sister of Betsy's was going to kill her," Patty said, putting her wallet back in her purse.

"Who? Heidi?"

"Yes."

"What makes you think that?"

"The arguments. They were always arguing. Usually it was behind closed doors, but we could still hear them plain enough. Those walls are paper-thin. And sometimes they didn't even bother to close the door."

"What did they argue about?"

Patty threw her hands in the air. "Everything. Then when Betsy became engaged to Bob Visser, they started arguing about that." She frowned. "Things really blew up when Betsy became suspicious that her fiancé was cheating on her with Heidi."

Monica feigned surprise.

"That's when things got really rough. I heard Betsy tell Heidi that if she didn't stop seeing Visser—although she didn't call it that, she called it sneaking around—she would go to the press and tell them about it. That would scuttle Visser's chances of being elected to the Senate pretty quickly." Patty laughed. "We all remember what happened to John Edwards when his affair was leaked."

"Yes," Monica said. She remembered the scandal had ended Edwards's career.

Patty glanced at her watch. "I'd better get going," she said. "I have to straighten up before everyone arrives." She held up the paper bag. "Thank you."

Monica turned to Nora. "Are you sure you'll be okay if I leave?"

"You go ahead. I'll be fine. I doubt we're going to have another rush like that again."

So Betsy had threatened to tell the press that Visser was cheating on her, Monica thought as she walked back to the farm kitchen. There was a good chance that would ruin his Senate chances. At the very least it would create an uproar, which would drown out his campaign message. She could imagine his opponent painting him as the candidate who cheated.

If Heidi was determined that Visser would win the Senate race and that she'd be on his arm when the winner was announced, that gave her a good reason to murder her sister. Did Heidi really love Visser, Monica wondered, or was it the challenge of stealing him from her sister that she loved?

Monica heard the rattle of a truck coming down the road and recognized Jeff's pickup truck in the distance.

He pulled up alongside her and rolled down the window. His expression was grim.

"What's wrong?" Monica said.

"They've arrested Dan Polsky," Jeff said, rubbing a hand over his face. "I've known Dan for quite awhile and I'm convinced he didn't do it. But how can I prove it? I have no idea what else I can do to help him. He has a lawyer, he said. The guy's supposed to be good. Let's hope that's true."

"I don't think Dan did it either," Monica said. "At first I thought he might have. Melinda called him a couple of weeks ago and told him that he was her father. It must have come as a huge shock. He tried to see Betsy to talk to her about it but she refused to see him." Monica pushed her hair behind her ears. "Dan never even knew Betsy had had a baby — his baby — and had made the decision to put it up for adoption without even telling him."

Jeff grunted. "That doesn't make him a killer."

"Betsy did seem rather startled when she saw him working here that day they came to film that segment for WZZZ—the day she was killed," Monica said.

She brushed a piece of hair off her forehead. "I know the two argued, but Melinda said that she and Dan were together when Betsy was killed. At the time I wondered if she was telling the truth but now I think she was."

"That's the thing," Jeff said. He put his arm out the open window and let it hang against the side of the truck. "Dan told the detective that he was with his daughter but she said that didn't prove anything. That they could have agreed to alibi each other."

Jeff cracked his knuckles. "I wish there was something I could do to help the poor guy. He's frantic." He looked at Monica with pleading eyes. "Maybe you can do something? You've solved murders before." He hung his head. "I shouldn't even ask you. You've almost gotten yourself killed doing that. I wouldn't want anything to happen to you."

"I do have a few ideas about who might be the real killer," Monica said. "And don't worry. I'll be careful."

• • •

Monica spent the rest of the afternoon in the farm kitchen producing some of the product they would be needing at the farm store.

She sighed with relief as she slid the last sheet of cranberry scones into the oven. Her back was beginning to hurt as well as her feet. Her hair was stuck to her forehead where beads of perspiration had collected thanks to the blasts of heat from the oven. She brushed the strands away and dropped into a chair.

It had been a stroke of luck running into Patty at the farm store. Betsy threatening to tell the press about Visser's affair with her sister certainly gave Heidi more incentive to murder her. But to murder your own sister? Surely there was at least some love between them. Did Heidi really want Visser that badly?

Maybe there was more to it than just that. Monica pulled out her phone and brought up her Facebook account. She typed in Heidi's name and waited. Heidi's page popped up almost immediately. There wasn't very much on it—a profile picture of Heidi, the same photograph that hung on the wall at WZZZ—the date she joined Facebook and birthday wishes that other people had left on her timeline almost a year ago.

Monica scrolled through them quickly and was about to close the page when an entry caught her eye.

Hey girl, happy birthday. Guess what? I'm managing Bob Visser's campaign office. Isn't he the guy your sister is engaged to? Small world, right?

It was signed Zoe Jones.

That was interesting, Monica thought. Maybe this Zoe would be able to tell her some things about Heidi.

Monica glanced at the clock. She'd be late getting home, but it might be worth tracking Zoe down now and talking to her. Visser's campaign office was above the hardware store downtown. Monica had noticed the banner hanging in the window. It would only take her a few minutes to get there.

Monica pulled the baking sheet of scones from the oven and transferred them to a rack. While they cooled, she tidied up the kitchen then washed and dried her hands. She put the scones into airtight containers, grabbed her jacket and turned out the lights.

The cool autumn air felt good against her face and she felt her energy renewing. She walked briskly down the road toward her cottage, picked up her car and headed into town.

Downtown Cranberry Cove was quiet with that hush that descends on small towns after five o'clock. Cars were parked sporadically along Beach Hollow Road, several in front of the diner and one or two in front of the drugstore. Some of the shops were already shuttered, like Danielle's and Gina's Making Scents, but the lights were still on in the hardware store when Monica pulled into a parking space.

She got out of her car and then stepped back so she would have a view of the second floor. A faint light showed through the dusty windows. Someone was still there. She just hoped it was Zoe Jones.

The door to the upper level was to the side of the main entrance to the hardware store. Monica tried the handle and was relieved when the knob turned.

The wooden stairs creaked and groaned under her weight as she climbed to the second floor. There was a small landing at the top and a frosted glass door with *Bob Visser Campaign* on it in gold lettering.

Monica knocked, waited and then tried the door. It was unlocked.

The door led to a large and open room with several beat-up metal desks spaced a couple of feet apart. Cardboard boxes overflowing with campaign materials were shoved against the wall opposite the windows and a stack of yard signs was leaning against the leg of a chair.

A young woman sat at one of the desks in front. She was wearing jeans and a sweatshirt with *Bob Visser for Senate* on the front. Her dark hair was gathered into a loose bun on top of her head that wobbled when she moved. Her eyes were on her computer monitor and her hand was resting lightly on the mouse. She looked up when she heard Monica open the door.

"Can I help you?" she said with a cheerful smile. "Are you looking for a yard sign or a bumper sticker?" She motioned toward the cartons along the wall.

Monica shook her head. "I'm afraid not. Are you Zoe Jones by any chance?" Monica asked.

"Yes." Her tone was wary.

"I know this is out of the ordinary," Monica began. "But you're a friend of Heidi DeJong's, aren't you?"

"We were sorority sisters in college." Zoe looked alarmed. "Why? Has something happened to her?" She put a hand to her chest. "I heard her poor sister was killed."

"No, no, it's nothing like that. Have you two stayed in touch since then?"

"Yes, we have. We get together for a girls' night every once in a while with some of our other sisters who live near here." She shuddered. "I was horrified when I learned that Betsy had been killed. I called Heidi as soon as I heard."

"Poor Heidi," Monica said, hoping Zoe wouldn't detect the note of insincerity in her voice. "It must have been devastating for her to lose her sister like that. And in such a gruesome manner."

Zoe snorted. "Heidi's not exactly broken up about it. She and her sister weren't close. As a matter of fact, they didn't get along."

"Oh?" Monica feigned surprise.

"Heidi was very envious of Betsy and her engagement to Bob Visser. Betsy was really obnoxious about it, always going on and on about the glamorous life she was going to lead in Washington married to a senator. She said who knows, they might even be invited to the White House someday."

"I can understand Heidi being jealous," Monica said. "I probably would have been too. It sounds like an exciting and terribly glamorous life."

Zoe dropped her voice to a whisper. "Can I tell you something? No one knows this, but frankly, Bob was planning to break it off with Betsy as soon as the election was over."

"Really?" Monica said.

Zoe nodded and her untidy bun wobbled precariously. "Bob met Heidi at a charity function and, well, they fell for each other right off the bat. Love at first sight, like in one of those romantic movies. After he met Heidi, Bob realized his engagement to Betsy was a mistake, but he couldn't do anything that would jeopardize his chances of winning the race." She made a face. "It wouldn't look good if he broke it off. Voters don't like that sort of thing."

Zoe picked up a water bottle that was sitting on her desk, unscrewed the cap and took a big glug. A few drops of water dribbled onto her sweatshirt.

"Heidi was so excited about meeting Bob. She'd spent so much time on her career—she's got a great job at that television station WZZZ—that she rarely ever dated."

"So Heidi is willing to give up her job and move to Washington with Bob Visser?"

"Oh, yes. They're going to be the golden couple." Zoe's expression turned dreamy. "They'll give parties and serve champagne and all the important people will be invited. Heidi has it all planned. She said it's time she got out of pokey old Cranberry Cove."

"Didn't she feel sorry for stealing her sister's fiancé?"

Zoe looked momentarily uncomfortable. "You never know when love is going to strike, do you?" she said somewhat defensively. "Besides, she said it was better that Betsy find out Bob wasn't in love with her before the marriage. She said she was doing her sister a favor—saving her from a divorce."

That was one way of looking at it, Monica thought. Heidi was obviously one of those people who didn't care what it cost to get what she wanted and who didn't lose any sleep over it either.

Maybe Heidi hadn't wanted to wait until after the election for Visser to break up with Betsy. And maybe she decided to take matters into her own hands to hurry things along.

"Zoe—that's an unusual name," Monica said, thinking it best to change the subject before Zoe began to wonder why she was asking so many questions.

Zoe smiled. "With a last name like Jones, my parents thought I deserved a more unique first name."

"It was nice meeting you, Zoe. I should be going."

"Wait." Zoe jumped up. "Would you like a bumper sticker or a yard sign? We also have T-shirts and bandannas."

Monica hesitated. "I'll take a bumper sticker," she said.

Zoe was going to be devastated when Visser's Senate chances went down the drain, Monica thought as she headed back down the stairs and out to her car. Even if Heidi hadn't murdered her sister, it was bound to leak out sooner or later that she and Visser had been sneaking around as Betsy had put it.

And Monica was quite sure that wouldn't go over very well with the voters. The sun was hovering low on the horizon when Monica left Visser's campaign office. It looked as if it was about to dip into Lake Michigan. The light was fading too and dusk was settling over Cranberry Cove as she headed back to Sassamanash Farm. The lights had been out at Book 'Em, Monica had noticed as she drove past the shop. Greg would be home by now. He stayed open longer in the summer months when the tourists would often come in late to pick out a book to read on the beach the next day.

She was mentally going through the contents of her refrigerator and wondering what she could throw together for dinner, but she needn't have bothered. Delicious smells greeted her when she opened the door to the cottage.

Greg was at the stove, an apron tied around his waist, stirring something in a pot. Both Hercule and Mittens were watching him intently.

"What smells so good?" Monica asked as she took off her jacket and hung it up.

"I rummaged in the fridge and managed to throw together some vegetable soup."

Monica peered into the pot. "It looks heavenly."

"I'm going to turn on the news while this simmers," Greg said, kissing Monica on the cheek. "Come put your feet up for a bit. You look tired."

"I am, rather."

Monica followed Greg out to the living room, Hercule right on their heels.

Greg switched on the television and Monica settled on the couch, her feet tucked under her.

The television sprang to life. It was tuned to WZZZ's local evening news. There were the usual reports about school board decisions, car accidents, road closures and of course the weather. Monica was about to check on the soup when the scene switched to an outdoor shot and Todd Lipton holding a microphone.

He was standing in front of Visser Motors.

Monica sat back down abruptly. What was going on? Had Visser been arrested for Betsy's murder? But that couldn't be, Monica thought. They already had Dan in custody.

Todd began speaking and Monica listened openmouthed. The FBI had raided Visser Motors on a tip that the business was laundering money. As Todd reported the story, the camera panned the scene, showing several men coming in and out of the dealership carrying boxes and computer hard drives.

"I can't believe it," Monica said. She turned to Greg. "I'm the one who told Detective Stevens that I suspected Visser was laundering money. She must have alerted the FBI."

"Maybe you'll get a reward," Greg teased.

"I wonder if this will motivate them to look into Visser's first wife's death again?"

"It might," Greg said, picking up the newspaper that was alongside his chair. "But that was an awfully long time ago. I don't see how they could prove anything at this late date."

"There's no statute of limitations on murder," Monica said.

"True." Greg put the newspaper on the coffee table. "Do you think Visser murdered his fiancée as well?"

"I don't know." Monica frowned. "But if either he or Heidi did kill Betsy, it was in vain. Visser's certainly not going to be elected to the Senate now."

Chapter 18

Monica felt leaves crunch under her feet as she headed toward the farm kitchen the next morning. The trees had all turned glorious colors of red and yellow in nature's annual miracle that was autumn.

She unlocked the door to the farm kitchen, opened it and flicked on the lights. She felt a wave of fatigue settle over her but she shook it off. She reminded herself of Newton's law that a body in motion stays in motion and forced herself to get busy.

First, more compote. She put a pan on the stove, added cranberries, orange juice, orange zest and some sugar. She gave the mixture a good stir and turned the flame to low. Within minutes, the compote was bubbling and the cranberries were popping. Monica stirred the pot and used a wooden spoon to muddle the cranberries.

While that cooked, she thought she would start on some scones. They were always in demand in the morning, although Monica often enjoyed one in the afternoon with a cup of tea.

She was rolling out the dough when she smelled something off. She glanced at the pot on the stove and discovered one of her oven mitts in flames. It had obviously been too close to the burner and had caught fire.

Monica gasped. She wasn't usually so careless. She picked up the mitt with a pair of tongs, dropped it into the sink and ran water on it. It sizzled and the flames went out.

Monica was turning the gas off under the compote when Kit arrived.

He looked around and sniffed. "What's that funny smell? It smells like . . . smoke."

"I'm embarrassed to admit that I set my oven mitt on fire. Fortunately I was able to drop it into the sink and put the flames out."

"Tell me you weren't hurt!"

Monica held up her hands. "No casualties. Other than my feeling incredibly stupid for having left the mitt so close to the burner."

"No worries. It happens to the best of us."

Kit peered into the sink. He picked up the mitt and held it in the air.

"Lovey, I fear this is for the garbage." He dropped it into the can, where it landed with a thud.

Kit reached for his apron and tied it on. "What's up this morning?"

Monica brushed a strand of hair back from her face. "I'm working on some scones, so why don't you get started on a batch of muffins."

"Right-o." Kit reached for the flour. "By the way, I saw on the news that that Visser fellow is being investigated for money laundering. Didn't you tell me you thought he might have killed his fiancée?"

"Yes," Monica said, brushing the tops of the scones with an egg wash. "But the police have arrested Dan Polsky. He's one of Jeff's crew. One of his best men, as a matter of fact."

"So it wasn't Visser then?"

"I don't know if Visser did it or not, but I'm positive Dan didn't."

"You know, I just remembered something," Kit said, turning off the mixer. "I don't know whether or not it's important, but as I was heading out on my errands that day you were filming, I saw a car parked some ways down the dirt road that leads out to the main road, probably about a quarter of a mile from your cottage. A man got out of the car and began walking toward the farm."

"Did you tell Detective Stevens that?"

"No. I never talked to her. I wasn't here when the murder took place and I didn't get back until after she'd already left." Kit took a spatula and wiped down the sides of the mixer bowl. "And frankly, I'd totally forgotten about it until now."

"Did you see what kind of car it was?"

Kit sighed. "Sorry, darling, but no. I'm not one of those men who drool over anything with four wheels and throw around phrases like *catalytic convertor, camshaft and drive train.* I leave that to Sean. I don't know a make from a model, to be honest with you."

"Well, did you see what the man looked like?"

"Now that's the kind of thing I do notice." Kit posed with his hands on his hips. "He had on a baseball cap—a ratty-looking thing—so I didn't get a good look at his face. But I did notice what he was wearing. He had on jeans with a button-down shirt that wasn't tucked in—it was pulled out and left loose. But here's the funny part. He had on a pair of dress shoes."

"Dress shoes?" Monica raised her eyebrows.

"Yes. Odd, right? Cordovan wingtips, no less. They looked expensive. Definitely real leather." Kit tapped his chin with his index finger. "Now, why would someone dress in jeans and a baseball cap but then put on a pair of fancy shoes?"

"And walk down a dirt road in them," Monica said. "My sneakers are always dusty by the time I get here." She paused. "Besides, that road only leads to the farm. And it's the long way around. Much easier to take the road farther down, which takes you right to the farm store. We almost never see any cars other than mine, Greg's and Jeff's on that stretch."

"It doesn't make sense." Kit shook his head. "It's not like he was making some kind of fashion statement."

"Was he tall?" Monica asked, thinking of Visser's six-foot-plus frame.

"No. He was rather short actually." Kit waved his hands around. "And a bit on the stocky side." He giggled. "Just the type I go for." Kit suddenly gasped and clapped a hand to his mouth. "Do you think he was the murderer?"

"I don't know. But I do know that wasn't Dan. He was wearing boots that day. And a sweatshirt. He was helping Jeff with the cranberry harvest. And Visser is tall and lean, not short and stocky."

"Who does that leave?" Kit cocked his head to the side.

"Not Heidi, obviously. Although I think she had a strong motive." Monica shook her head. "No, the only one left who was at the filming that day was Todd Lipton, the producer."

"Turned anchorman," Kit said, flapping his hand. "Now that I think of it, he's about the right size and build. He definitely could have been the man I saw."

"He left the filming early." Monica sliced open a carton of glass jars and lined them up on the counter, ready for the compote. "He could have changed his clothes and come back."

"And obviously forgot to bring another pair of shoes," Kit said. "Very poor planning if he's our killer."

"Yes." Monica paused. "But he said he was having lunch at the Pepper Pot when the murder occurred. He even had the receipt."

"He could easily be lying. Did you actually see the receipt?"

"No, but he said he showed it to Detective Stevens. The date and time are stamped on it."

Kit shrugged. "Maybe he picked it up out of the garbage or found it lying on the floor and figured it would come in handy."

"I know the owner of the Pepper Pot. He's dating my stepmother, Gina. I can ask him if he remembers seeing Todd that day."

"There you go," Kit said with satisfaction. "Case solved."

• • •

Monica filled the last jar with cranberry compote and screwed on the lid just before the noon whistle blew.

"I'm going to run out for a bit," she said to Kit, who was prying open a crate of cranberries.

"See you later."

Monica took a moment to brush the flour off her jeans and run her fingers through her hair. She really ought to powder her nose but she didn't want to waste time.

It only took her a few minutes to walk back to her cottage and get her car. As she drove down the dirt road she tried to picture where Todd's car might have been parked. She noticed some flattened grass as she rounded a curve and she imagined that was where he had lain in wait for Betsy.

Betsy had been sitting in her car talking on her cell phone. Had Todd called her on some pretext to delay her until after Jasmine left in the news van and the coast was clear?

The drive into town didn't take long and soon Monica was pulling into the parking lot of the Pepper Pot. The lot was full and they appeared to be doing a brisk business. The Pepper Pot was the newest restaurant in town and its atmosphere was more casual than the Cranberry Cove Inn. It attracted quite a crowd at lunchtime—people who had expense accounts or who could afford a lunch that didn't come from the Cranberry Cove Diner or a fast-food restaurant.

The sound of clattering dishes and enthusiastic chatter greeted Monica when she pushed open the door. The hostess was behind the desk, a telephone receiver clamped to her ear and a pencil in her hand hovering over a reservation book. A couple in expensive casual attire was trying to get her attention.

"We've been waiting for five minutes," the woman said, her tone accusatory, as she fingered the gold necklace around her neck.

The hostess put a hand over the telephone receiver. "I'll be right with you." She gave them a bright, insincere smile. Finally she put down the phone and turned to the couple who had been standing there impatiently.

Monica let her eyes wander around the restaurant at the lunch crowd until the hostess returned to her position at the front of the restaurant.

"Hello. Can I help you?" she said. "Do you have a reservation?" She glanced down at her book.

"No. I'm not planning on eating. I'm here to see Mickey Welch. Is he in?"

"I'll check." She picked up the telephone, spoke briefly and then turned to Monica. "He's in his office. Go through the door at the back of the dining room, then take a left. Second door on your right."

"Thanks."

Monica made her way through the crowded restaurant to the door the hostess had indicated. She turned left and headed down the hall. The walls were lined with framed photographs from the annual Cranberry Cove yacht race from Michigan to Chicago. She found Welch's office easily enough, knocked briefly on the doorjamb and walked in.

He was sitting behind his desk, which, although good-sized, appeared dwarfed by his bulk. He looked up and smiled, revealing a gap between his two front teeth.

"Monica! What can I do for you?" He ran his hands through his shock of silver hair. "I have to tell you that my customers are eating up our new dessert featuring your cranberry compote. Pun intended," he added with a laugh.

"I'm glad to hear that." Monica cleared her throat, which had suddenly gone dry. "I have a question for you."

Welch leaned back in his chair and put his arms behind his head. "Go ahead. Shoot."

"Do you know the new anchor of the evening news on WZZZ? Todd Lipton. He also hosts that program *What's Up West Michigan*."

"I don't really know him, but I do know who he is. Back when I first opened the Pepper Pot, he produced a feature on the restaurant. Seemed like a nice enough guy."

"Monday, the day Betsy DeJong was killed, he claims to have been here at the restaurant having lunch. I wondered if you remembered seeing him?"

"Monday?" Welch's chair shot upright and he put his hands down on the desk. "He couldn't have been. He must be mistaken. We're closed on Mondays. Ever since the summer season ended." Welch frowned. "What's your interest in this?"

"A member of Jeff's crew has been accused of the murder. Neither of us believes he did it. I'm trying to prove that he's innocent."

"And you think this news guy might have done it?"

Monica shrugged. "Just tying up loose ends."

"Ah. Good luck." Mickey shook his finger at her. "And do be careful."

Monica smiled. "Believe me, I will."

So Todd's alibi had been false, Monica thought as she walked back through the crowded restaurant. Had Stevens also checked with the Pepper Pot? Or had it been put on the back burner while she chased other leads?

Monica was mulling over the possibilities as she left the restaurant. She wasn't looking and suddenly found herself face-to-face with Todd Lipton, who was on his way into the restaurant.

She could feel her face coloring and she felt as if the word *guilty* was stamped on her forehead. She tried to smile but knew it probably looked strained.

Todd frowned and was studying her face intently, making Monica feel even more uncomfortable.

"Did you have a good lunch?" he said.

The tone of his voice was menacing and Monica felt a chill, as if a cold breeze had suddenly blown past.

"Y-yes," she said quickly, trying to walk around him.

He blocked her way. "What do you recommend?"

Monica knew he was playing with her. Like a cat toying with its prey. And he was obviously enjoying her discomfort.

Monica wracked her brain for a dish that was likely to be on the Pepper Pot's menu at lunchtime. She remembered smelling the aroma of sizzling meat and frying potatoes when she'd walked into the restaurant.

"I had the hamburger and fries," she said, trying to make her voice sound normal. "It was excellent."

"I'll keep that in mind." Todd sneered at her.

Monica started to walk past him when her stomach suddenly growled. She prayed Todd hadn't heard it. Far from having just eaten, she was actually starving.

• • •

Monica was planning to spend the afternoon at home balancing the farm's books. She had a better head for numbers than Jeff and had agreed to take on that task. She rather enjoyed the challenge. So far she had managed to pull the farm out of a hole and into the black, if just barely.

She was unlocking the back door when she heard scratching noises. Hercule? She opened the door and the dog bounded at her, its tail wagging furiously.

"What are you doing here, boy?" she said, reaching down to scratch his head. "Why aren't you with Greg at the bookstore?"

Hercule was so excited to see her that he began to race around the kitchen in circles while Mittens looked on disdainfully, daintily grooming her paws.

A note was propped against the saltshaker on the counter. It was from Greg, saying that he was going to an estate sale and had dropped Hercule off at home in the meantime. He had added a string of Xs for kisses and Monica smiled.

She checked the animals' food and water bowls and then began to think about her own lunch. She pulled some sliced turkey from the refrigerator along with the remains of some cranberry sauce and made herself a sandwich.

Hercule stood by her side the entire time she was eating, staring at her with his big brown eyes and sweeping the floor with his tail. Monica saved him a tiny corner of her sandwich, which she put in his dish. He swallowed it in one bite.

She took care of the dishes and then set up her laptop on the kitchen table. She powered it on and brought up the financial program she was using for the farm's accounts.

She was checking the balances on her books against the bank's when she thought she heard a car in the distance. Maybe Greg had finished early and was coming home? But half an hour went by and there was no sign of him. It must have been someone else. She hadn't heard the car pass the cottage, so perhaps the driver had realized they'd made a wrong turn and had gone back the way they'd come.

She was adding up some figures when Hercule, who had been sleeping peacefully by her side, suddenly jumped to his feet. He trotted over to the back door and began sniffing it while emitting a low growl.

"What is it, boy?"

Monica got up and looked out the window. She didn't see anyone. It was probably a small animal—a mouse or a chipmunk—attracted by the warmth that the cottage emitted that had set him growling.

She sat back down and forced herself to concentrate but it was hard to focus. She yawned and her eyes watered, blurring the figures on the computer screen in front of her.

She couldn't shake the feeling of unease that had settled over her. Hercule was now lying down by the back door, occasionally sniffing or growling softly.

She wished that whatever small creature had taken up residence outside would go away. Hercule was making her nervous. She forced herself to go back to the task at hand. She got up from the table, retrieved a stack of bills from a basket on the kitchen counter and began sorting through them, putting them in separate piles.

She had finally immersed herself in the farm's accounts again when she thought she heard a noise outside the window. It was just nerves, she reassured herself. She had no idea why she was feeling so on edge. It wasn't like her.

Maybe it had been her encounter with Todd that afternoon that had set her off. She had had the distinct feeling that he had known exactly what she was up to when she visited the Pepper Pot.

She got up and peered out the window again, trying to convince herself that she was imagining things. As she suspected, there was no one there. Hercule, meanwhile, had stopped growling and sniffing and was asleep in front of the back door.

It was only a few minutes later when Monica heard a noise by the door. This time she was positive it wasn't her imagination and that she'd actually heard something. There had been a shuffling sound, although perhaps that had simply been some dried leaves being blown across the mat by the wind? But what if someone *was* out there? She felt goose bumps pricking the skin on her arms and legs.

She would call Greg, she decided. She wasn't normally so needy and dependent but today her anxiety was getting the best of her. She picked up her cell phone and was about to ring him to find out how much longer he'd be when Hercule opened his eyes, jumped to his feet and began barking in earnest.

It had to be Greg, Monica thought. Relief washed over her. But why was Hercule barking at him? His normal greeting was to whine and scratch frantically at the back door until it was opened.

There was a knock on the door and Hercule's barking intensified.

Monica pushed the curtain aside and looked out the window but didn't see anyone. Had she imagined the knock? Was she losing her mind?

She let the curtain drop back into place. She was about to sit down when someone knocked again. Monica jumped up from her seat, banging her knee against the table in the process.

She went to the door and hesitated but then reached for the knob. Her hands were shaking as she turned it and finally opened the door.

Chapter 19

"What do you want?" Monica said, trying to keep her voice from shaking.

Todd Lipton put the flat of his hand against the door and pushed it roughly. It sent Monica reeling backward. She hit her hip against the edge of the kitchen table and winced. Before she could regain her balance, Todd had stepped over the threshold and into her kitchen.

She felt her heartbeat ratchet up like a plane's engine revving for takeoff. She told herself she could talk her way out of this but her mind suspected that wasn't going to be possible.

Hercule had stopped barking, but he must have sensed Monica's fear because he kept up a low, guttural growl, his eyes focused on Todd.

"What do you want?" Monica said again, the words sticking in her dry throat. "Do you want to film at the farm?"

Todd's upper lip lifted at the corner, curling into a sneer. "I think you know why I'm here. You've been asking questions about me. I heard that you've done that before. I can't take the chance that you'll go running to your pal Detective Stevens with the information."

"But I wouldn't," Monica said. She knew Todd wouldn't believe her, but if she managed to stall Todd long enough, perhaps Greg would get home. "Detective Stevens wouldn't take me seriously anyway."

"I can't take that chance," Todd said. He seemed nervous, his eyes darting around the kitchen and his hands moving restlessly.

Monica wet her lips and looked at the clock. "My husband will be home soon." Despite her efforts her voice shook and she knew she sounded far from convincing.

Todd laughed. "So what? This will all be finished by then." He looked around the kitchen.

"Would you like a cup of tea?" Monica said, hoping to stall as long as possible.

Todd grinned. "Sure. Why not."

Monica put the kettle on the stove and turned the gas on low so that it would take an eternity for the water to boil. She grabbed a mug from the cupboard. Her hands shook and it clanged against another cup. The sound made her flinch.

Finally, she could delay no longer. The kettle whistled and steam streamed from its spout. She poured the water into the mug, added a tea bag and plunked it down on the table in front of Todd, who had taken a seat.

"Have a seat," he said, motioning Monica to a chair.

Monica felt too restless to sit but she thought she'd better do what Todd said. So far he hadn't brandished a weapon, but his very presence felt threatening, and it was possible he had a gun or knife in the pocket of his raincoat.

Todd took a sip of his tea and grimaced. "Hot," he said, blowing on the cup and sending the tea rippling into eddies.

The clock on the wall ticked away the seconds, each ticktock making Monica wonder how much longer it would be before Todd made his move. Because she had no doubt that he was here to silence her. Forever.

"How did you know?" Todd said, looking up at Monica.

"Know what?" Monica played dumb.

"You know perfectly well what I mean. How did you know I killed Betsy? It was written all over your face when we ran into each other earlier today. What tipped you off? I thought I was so careful."

Keep him talking, Monica said to herself. *Play for time and maybe Greg will arrive.* The thought that Todd might try to harm Greg made her gasp.

"You must know," she said, leveling her gaze at Todd. "Wasn't it obvious?"

"You found out that the Pepper Pot is closed on Mondays so my alibi didn't hold water. So what? What else?"

"You kept insisting that you didn't want the anchor position at WZZZ, but that wasn't the truth. Quite the contrary. You all but had the position sewn up when Betsy came along, slept with someone in power and then snatched the job right out from under your nose. That must have stung." Monica thought she might as well twist the knife while she was at it.

Todd's face turned a dusky red color. Monica was surprised steam didn't come pouring out his ears like the steam that had streamed out of the spout on the kettle.

"It wasn't fair. That was supposed to be my job. I'd worked hard for it. And all Betsy had to do was . . . well, you know." He was gripping the handle of the mug so tightly his knuckles had turned white.

"And on top of it," Monica said, taking a certain relish in rubbing it in, "you asked Betsy out, and not only did she turn you down but she made a fool of you in front of the whole station. That must have really rubbed salt in the wound."

Todd gave a half-hearted laugh. "But who is going to believe I would commit murder just because of that? If that's all you have, you're kidding yourself."

"My assistant saw a car pulled off the road a short ways from where Betsy's body was found. He also saw a man walking toward Betsy's parked car. You'd changed your clothes, pulled out your shirt and put on a baseball cap, but you forgot to change your shoes."

Todd looked as if he'd been struck. He suddenly jumped to his feet.

"Betsy didn't deserve that anchor spot. It was supposed to be mine," he shouted, his face turning a purplish red. "And then she was being considered for that job in Washington." By now, Todd was nearly spitting in his fury. "She wouldn't stop rubbing it in. How I was going to be stuck at this backwater television station for the rest of my life while she was going to be on national television." Todd let out a sob. "It wasn't fair." He collapsed into his chair.

Monica looked around the kitchen. Todd was sitting between her and the back door. If she ran it would have to be out the front door or up the stairs, where she could lock herself in her bedroom. The next time Todd sipped his tea, she would make a run for it.

Monica's muscles were tensed for action as she waited for the right moment. She tried to look relaxed, afraid that Todd would sense her tension and guess that she was poised to bolt.

Todd ran his finger around the rim of his mug. *Pick it up!* Monica screamed in her head.

The seconds ticked by, the clock on the wall emphasizing each one.

Finally, Todd wrapped his hand around the mug and began raising it to his mouth.

Monica stood up so fast her chair shot backward, screeching across the wood floor. She was out of the kitchen and crossing the living room before Todd was able to get up and come after her.

Todd must have dropped his mug. Monica heard it bounce off the table and onto the floor.

Hercule obviously sensed something was wrong and sprang to his feet. Monica turned to look long enough to see that his fur had bristled and his teeth were bared. He lunged at Todd and his powerful jaws opened and closed around Todd's pant leg.

Monica turned to run again and heard Todd swear then the sound of fabric ripping. Todd had wrested his leg from Hercule's grip and was coming after her. Hercule was right behind him, his nails scrabbling against the wood floor.

Monica was almost to the front door when she slipped on the throw rug and banged her shin against the coffee table. The sudden sharp pain brought tears to her eyes. She ignored it and kept moving.

She didn't know what she was going to do when she got outside, but if she could reach the processing building, she knew Jeff and his crew would be there. She would have to pray she could outrun Todd.

The door felt as if it was receding with each step Monica took toward it. Finally, she reached it and turned the lock. She grasped the handle but her palm was slippery with sweat and slipped off. She wiped her hand on the leg of her jeans and tried again.

This time she got the door open. Sensing freedom, Hercule shot past her and into the front yard, where he was immediately distracted by a squirrel that had run up a tree to escape him.

Monica was about to slam the front door closed when she realized Todd was right behind her. Instead she began to run. Todd caught up with her and grabbed her arm, causing her to stumble. She landed on her knees and the jolt sent her upper and lower teeth slamming against each other. She barely felt the pain as panic drove her to keep fighting.

As she got to her feet, she felt something warm and wet trickling down her legs. Blood. She'd managed to skin her knees right through her jeans.

She tried as hard as she could to resist but Todd was surprisingly strong and slowly dragged her back toward the cottage, her shoes leaving scuff marks in the dirt. She made herself as limp as possible, knowing that would make her harder to move. She felt a sense of satisfaction when she heard Todd's breath come in ragged gasps.

He shoved her over the threshold and she stumbled into the living room, Todd slamming and locking the door behind him. Monica prayed Hercule wouldn't follow his nose somewhere and be unable to find his way home. He'd already been lost once. He didn't deserve to have it happen a second time.

Finally Todd pulled Monica back into the kitchen and shoved her toward a chair. She fell into the seat with a jolt.

"What are you going to do?" she said, hoping to get Todd talking again. Surely Greg was on his way home by now.

A thought occurred to Monica that sent a chill through her. What if Greg was planning to go back to Book 'Em before he came home? He might not be home for hours yet.

She thought of trying to run again but she was exhausted and knew she had very little hope of making it. Her leg was throbbing from where she'd banged it on the coffee table and her skinned knees burned.

Todd fished around in his pocket and pulled something out. Monica didn't know what was in his hand at first but then she recognized it and a feeling of dread seized her chest, making it difficult to breathe.

"What are you doing?" she said. It came out in a croak.

"Handy little things." Todd brandished the zip tie. "Put your hands together."

Monica remembered what she had seen in the newspaper article and remained passive, holding her hands out, side by side, fists clenched and palms down.

She felt Todd's sour breath on her face as he leaned over her to fasten the tie, and turned her head.

He yanked the zip tie until it had been tightened to his satisfaction.

"I hope that's not too uncomfortable," he said with a leer, "but it won't be for long."

Monica's feeling of dread intensified.

He pulled several more zip ties from his pocket and knelt, tying each of Monica's ankles to the legs of the kitchen chair. He pulled on the tie to test it. She felt panic rise in her throat like bile and had to stifle the urge to cry.

"That should do it," Todd said, standing back to admire his handiwork. "There'll be no getting out of that."

Monica felt her fear slowly turn to anger and she tried to yank her hands and feet from their bonds.

"Don't even bother." Todd laughed. Chills prickled Monica's arms, raising goose bumps.

Todd walked over to the stove. One by one he turned the burners on, then leaned over and blew out the flames. Monica watched in horror as he opened the oven door, blew out the pilot light and turned on the gas.

Finally, he pulled a small squat candle and a pack of matches from his raincoat pocket, put the candle on the counter and lit it.

He smiled with satisfaction. "When the house blows up, it will look like a sad accident. Poor Monica. She must have left the gas on. Tsk, tsk."

Chapter 20

Todd stopped at the door and turned around to look at Monica, an expression of satisfaction on his face. He opened the door and then slammed it shut behind him. Monica was left alone, trapped, in a room quickly filling with gas.

She sat for a moment, not moving. Panic threatened to drown her but she forced herself to breathe slowly—inhale, exhale, inhale, exhale. At first her breath came shuddering out in near gasps, but finally it became steadier and more even.

Her heartbeat gradually slowed as she continued to focus on her breath. When she felt she was about as calm as she was going to get under the circumstances, she began to plan what to do.

First, she needed to free her hands from the zip ties. She tried to remember what she'd seen in the article she'd read. Her hands were tied together side-by-side, her thumbs touching. Slowly she opened her clenched fists. There were half-moon indentations where her nails had dug into her palms.

She flexed her fingers a few times to relax them and then tried to remember the next step. The tie was tight and the plastic cut into her skin, but she managed to turn her hands so that her palms were together as if she was praying. That position decreased the circumference of her wrists and loosened the tie slightly.

The zip tie was still tight and she had to struggle to work one thumb out from under it. She spent several minutes wriggling and tugging her hand, ignoring the bite of the rough plastic into her flesh. She had a moment of triumph when her whole hand finally came free. After that, the tie slipped off her other hand with ease. She dropped it on the floor and kicked it away.

Her ankles were another story. Her only hope was to somehow break the ties. She strained against them frantically but that did little more than force the plastic deeper into her ankles. She'd have to think of something else.

She gazed longingly at the knives in her knife block on the counter. One of those would cut through the ties easily, but there was little hope of reaching one.

She would have to somehow scooch the chair she was tethered to across the floor. She rocked it back and forth and back and forth until it began to move forward with frustrating slowness. It took several minutes to move a couple of inches. She rocked the chair again and held her breath as it tottered and nearly toppled over onto its side.

Inch by inch, Monica crossed the kitchen floor to the counter. The effort was exhausting and the smell of gas was beginning to make her feel woozy. She wanted to close her eyes and rest for a moment but she forced herself to continue.

Finally, she was within reach of the counter. She needed to grab the candle and blow it out. She stretched out her arm as far as she could, but try as she might, it was just beyond her fingertips. She wanted to cry and stamp her feet in frustration.

She'd have to make her way over to the stove.

It was slow and laborious, and by now the lure of closing her eyes for a moment was so strong she could barely fight it. She was tempted to give in—just for a minute—but every second the burners were on meant more noxious gas was pouring into the room. The house was shut up tight—no windows cracked or doors open. One spark and the house would blow up. With her in it.

That was enough to get her moving again and she inched her way across the floor toward the stove, the muscles in her legs screaming from exhaustion. She reached out a hand and stretched out her fingers as far as she could. Her fingertips brushed the knobs but she wasn't close enough to grab them and turn them. A few more inches though and she would be there.

Monica rocked the chair back and forth, moving closer and closer to the stove with each motion. She reached out an arm again but her fingertips only grazed the knobs, which were still tantalizingly out of reach. One more push, one more effort, and she'd be able to turn them off.

But she was so terribly tired. Monica let her head drop onto her chest and her heavy eyelids close. She was on the very edge of unconsciousness when some primitive instinct roused her and she forced herself awake.

She shook her arms out and gave a last great push. This time she was finally in reach of the stove. She closed her hand around one of the knobs and turned it. She did the same with all the other burners and the oven before sagging in the chair in relief. The gas was no longer pumping into the room. But there was still danger. The gas was still trapped inside and she needed to open a window or a door to clear the room.

Once again, her head dropped onto her chest, but after a few minutes rest she began her slow crawl across the kitchen floor, this time headed toward the back door. She was almost there when she heard a noise outside—it sounded like Hercule scratching frantically to be let in. He began to bark furiously. It *was* Hercule. Monica felt a rush of relief and called to him.

"I'm coming, buddy, just hang on a few more minutes."

She had almost reached the door when sleepiness finally overcame her and she could no longer fight it. She slumped in the chair, closed her eyes and drifted into blissful unconsciousness.

• • •

Monica first became aware of the noise—someone shouting, sirens, other voices. Then she felt herself being lifted up and carried in someone's arms as she tried to claw her way back to consciousness. Finally she opened her eyes to find she was outside, surrounded by Greg's and Jeff's anxious faces.

"What's going on? What happened?" she asked. Slowly her memory returned and she gasped. "How did you find me?"

Greg gave her a reassuring smile and reached out to hold her hand.

"Hercule was barking furiously outside the back door. Jeff heard him and knocked on the door. When you didn't answer, he became worried and called me. I came home immediately to find you tied to a kitchen chair, unconscious." Greg shuddered. "For one terrible moment I thought we were too late." His face was pale.

Everything was coming back to Monica now—Todd chasing her, being tied up, gas pouring into the room. She began to shake.

"It's shock," Greg said. "I'll get you a blanket."

"Wait," Monica called after him. "What about Todd? Someone has to stop him."

"The police are here," Jeff said, pointing to a patrol car in the driveway. Monica recognized the car parked behind it as Stevens's. "I called them."

"Is Detective Stevens here? I need to talk to her," Monica said, trying to stand up. The world began to spin and she sat back down again.

"Are you sure you're up to it?" Jeff asked, frowning.

"I'm fine." Monica gave a rueful smile. "As long as I don't try to stand up."

"The dizziness should pass soon," Greg said, returning with a blanket, which he draped around Monica's shoulders.

She pulled it around her, luxuriating in the warmth.

"It sounds like we almost lost you," Stevens said, coming out from behind the patrol car and walking toward Monica. "What happened?"

Monica took a deep breath. It made her cough.

"Are you okay? Do you want some water?" Greg said.

Monica shook her head. "I'm fine."

She began to explain to Stevens how she had deduced that Todd Lipton had been the one to kill Betsy DeJong. As she told the detective about Todd tying her up, lighting a candle and turning on the gas, she began to shake again.

"You'd better rest," Stevens said. "You've had a bad shock." She gave a quick grin. "Although not for the first time."

"But what about Todd? What if he goes after someone else?"

"I do have a bit of experience, you know," Stevens said dryly. "We were already on to him. A patrol car has gone to pick him up and bring him in for questioning."

"You know he faked his alibi," Monica said. "The Pepper Pot is closed on Mondays."

There was a twinkle in Stevens's eyes. She squeezed Monica's shoulder. "Yes, we know. It was to our advantage to let him think he'd fooled us. It looks like we were right behind you."

"What about Dan Polsky?" Monica said, plucking at the blanket wrapped around her. "Have you let him go?"

Stevens nodded. "He's been released. Someone came forward to say that he saw Dan and his daughter, Melinda, sitting on a bench down by the harbor when the murder occurred."

"And Bob Visser?"

Stevens frowned. "He's being investigated for money laundering, and from what I've heard, they have nearly enough evidence to charge him."

"What about his first wife's death?"

Stevens shrugged. "I'm afraid there's really nothing we can do at this late date. There isn't enough evidence for a conviction." She smiled. "But if they do prove money laundering, he's still going to go away for a good long time."

• • •

"You don't have to fuss over me," Monica said, watching Greg stir a pot at the stove. He'd insisted on cooking dinner for her while she put her feet up. "I'm perfectly fine now."

Greg turned around and smiled. "I enjoy coddling you a bit. You deserve it."

Monica felt a rush of emotion that brought tears to her eyes. She brushed them away quickly.

"This stew is going to take awhile," Greg said, putting his spoon down on the counter. "Why don't we go turn on the evening news?"

Greg put his arm around Monica's waist as he led her into the living room.

"You take the chair," he said, pulling up the ottoman for Monica's feet.

Monica felt perfectly fine, albeit a bit shaky after her ordeal, but she decided she would let Greg fuss over her for this one evening.

Greg picked up the remote, pressed the power button and the television came on.

A commercial for the Cranberry Cove Inn was playing, and when it ended the WZZZ newsroom came into view.

Todd Lipton was behind the news desk as usual. Monica was surprised. She had assumed Stevens was going to bring him in for questioning immediately.

Todd looked unbearably smug tonight. He was obviously comfortable with his new job now as an anchorman and his delivery was smooth and professional. Monica wondered when the hammer was going to fall. He wouldn't look quite so self-satisfied then.

Todd was in the middle of a report on a fire in a Dumpster behind the local post office when there appeared to be something going on just offstage. Todd kept taking his eyes off the camera and glancing in that direction.

Monica leaned forward. "I wonder why he keeps looking off to the side like that," she said to Greg.

"Something must be going on."

The smug look on Todd's face had been wiped off and replaced by one of terror. He stood up from the news desk and appeared to be about to run off camera.

Suddenly two policemen burst onto the set, guns drawn and at the ready. Monica gasped.

Todd began backing away from them. He looked around frantically, as if he might find someplace to hide. He was heading toward the opposite side of the set when a third policeman emerged from the shadows.

He was cornered.

Monica thought she would feel a sense of satisfaction knowing that Todd was going to pay for his crimes, but for some reason she didn't. She felt pity instead.

Two of the policemen had grabbed Todd and were escorting him off the stage. There was a moment of silence, the camera trained on the empty news desk, and then the station cut to a commercial for a local car wash.

Monica and Greg looked at each other in astonishment.

"What on earth?" Greg said.

"That was rather fitting, don't you think?" Monica said.

"Yes, definitely." Greg stood up. "Time to see how the stew is coming along."

"I'll set the table," Monica said, following Greg out to the kitchen.

Chapter 21

The Pepper Pot was full the following evening when Greg and Monica arrived, but Welch had saved a special table for them. They followed the hostess through the restaurant to a slightly secluded spot, where their table was screened by a large potted fern. They were about to sit down when they saw Gina standing by the hostess stand waving to them.

She made her way through the tables to where Monica and Greg were sitting. She was wearing black leather pants, a leopard-print top and high-heeled suede booties. Monica had to smile. No one would ever mistake Gina for a native resident of Cranberry Cove.

"I'm here," she said when she reached them, going around the table and giving each of them an air kiss. "Are Jeff and Lauren coming?" she asked as a waiter pulled out her chair.

"Yes," Monica said. "Jeff said they might be a few minutes late and we should go ahead and order drinks."

They decided on wine, and Greg ordered a bottle for the table. The waiter had just opened it and begun to pour when Monica looked up to see Jeff and Lauren walking toward them.

They were holding hands and both were smiling.

Lauren took a seat on one side of Monica and Jeff on the other side.

Jeff was deep in conversation with Gina when Monica leaned closer to Lauren.

"Did you and Jeff have a chance to talk?" she said in a low voice.

Lauren grinned. "We did. I feel so much better."

"So everything is okay between the two of you now?"

Lauren nodded. "Definitely." She leaned closer to Monica. "You were right. We had a good talk and well, it really helped." She glanced at Jeff, a small smile playing around her lips and her eyes sparkling. "Everything is definitely fine."

"I'm so glad." Monica smiled.

"Does everyone know what they want?" Greg asked as the waiter hovered near their table.

The waiter took down their orders, collected the menus and headed toward the kitchen.

"How is Dan doing?" Monica said to Jeff as she reached for the basket of rolls the waiter had left on the table.

"He's still a little shaken by his ordeal," Jeff said, pushing the butter dish toward her. "Being arrested really scared him. I think it will be awhile before he forgets that experience." Jeff drummed his fingers on the table. "There is one good thing that's come out of all of this though."

"Oh?" Monica tore off a piece of her roll and buttered it. "What's that?"

"Dan and his daughter, Melinda, are getting to know each other. They've been spending some time together. It turns out they both like to hike so they've planned a hiking trip for Saturday."

"That is good news," Monica said. The thought of Melinda finally having a relationship with her biological father made her happy.

The waiter arrived, balancing a huge tray on his shoulder. He lowered it to a tray stand and began serving their dinners.

"You really had us scared there for a bit, Sis," Jeff said as he tucked into his steak. "I'm sure glad Hercule raised the alarm in time. The whole house could have gone up."

Greg speared one of his French fries. "You can say that again." He reached out and squeezed Monica's hand.

"I'm just as glad as you are," Monica said. "That was a close call. A little too close for comfort." She picked up her hamburger and bit into it.

They were finishing their entrées when Welch came over to them. He stood in back of Gina, his hands on her shoulders.

"Have you told them our news yet?" he said to her.

Gina smiled coyly. "Not yet, no." She swiveled in her seat and looked at Welch. "Why don't you go ahead."

Welch cleared his throat. He looked slightly nervous.

"Gina and I are getting a place together," he said. "We found a house nearby. It's not big but it should suit us perfectly."

"You can see a little sliver of Lake Michigan from the kitchen window," Gina said proudly.

"Congratulations," everyone at the table chorused.

"I think this calls for some champagne," Welch said, snapping his fingers at a passing waiter. "I'll have them send over a bottle and some glasses. On the house." He grinned.

The waiter reappeared with a chilled bottle of champagne and a champagne bucket filled with ice on a stand. He poured champagne all around and then nestled the bottle in the ice.

Welch pulled out a chair, picked up his glass and held it aloft.

"To all good things," he said and took a sip.

"Hear, hear!" everyone responded.

An hour later, champagne and dessert long finished, they began to get up to leave.

Greg took Monica's arm and they were walking toward the exit when Monica spotted a familiar face. Stevens was sitting at one of the tables talking intently to her companion, who Monica recognized as Dr. Russo, the medical examiner who had been at the scene of Betsy's murder.

Was this a date? she wondered. She did remember noticing that Russo had seemed quite friendly with Stevens — flirtatious even.

"Excuse me," she said as she tapped Greg's arm. "I'll be right back."

Monica walked over to where Stevens and Russo were sitting.

Stevens seemed slightly flustered to see Monica. This was definitely a date then, Monica thought.

"Monica, this is Frank Russo. He's the new medical examiner. I think you met him at your farm when Betsy DeJong was murdered." She turned to Russo. "Frank, this is Monica Albertson."

"I don't want to disturb your meal," Monica said. "I just wanted to say hello."

She said goodbye and joined Greg, who was waiting for her by the door.

Monica found herself dozing on the way home in the car and didn't wake up until they pulled into the driveway of the cottage.

"Tired?" Greg asked, as he held the car door open for her.

"I guess so," Monica said. "I think I dozed off for a bit."

They heard a thud as Greg put the key in the lock and pushed open the back door.

"Sounds like Hercule must have been sleeping on the sofa," Greg said with a grin.

Hercule came flying into the kitchen, skidding to a stop at their feet.

"Come on, buddy, let's have a quick walk," Greg said, fastening Hercule's leash. "We won't be long," he said to Monica as Hercule pulled him out the door.

Monica was almost too tired to go up the stairs to bed. She sat in a chair in the darkened living room and soon her eyes closed and she was asleep. The next thing she knew, Greg was gently shaking her arm to wake her.

"Let's go up to bed," he said, helping her to her feet.

They paused in front of the spare room and Greg put his arm around Monica. "I noticed you didn't have any of the wine or champagne tonight," he said. "Are you feeling okay?"

"I'm fine. I don't know anything for sure yet—I haven't taken a test—but I've been having some symptoms lately," she said. "I wonder . . ."

Greg grinned and gestured at the spare bedroom. "Maybe we'll be putting this room to good use after all."

Recipes

Old Dutch Sand Cookies

3 sticks butter
1½ cups granulated white sugar
3 cups flour
1 teaspoon baking soda
1½ teaspoons vanilla extract

Preheat oven to 350 degrees.

Cream butter and sugar until light and fluffy.

Sift flour and baking soda and add to creamed mixture. Add vanilla and mix well.

Shape dough into rolls, cover with wax paper and refrigerate overnight.

Slice into ¼-inch thick rounds and place on parchment-lined cookie sheet.

Bake approximately 10 minutes. Do not let cookies get too brown.

Recipe provided by Mary VanderVelde

White Chocolate Cranberry Orange Cookies

3 cups all-purpose flour, unsifted
½ teaspoon baking soda
1 teaspoon salt
2 4-ounce white chocolate baking bars
1½ cups dried cranberries
1 cup unsalted butter, softened
1½ cups granulated white sugar
1 cup light brown sugar, firmly packed
2 extra large eggs, at room temperature
1½ teaspoons orange extract
½ teaspoon vanilla extract

Preheat oven to 350 degrees.

Place the flour, baking soda, and salt in a medium bowl. Using a spoon or whisk, blend the dry ingredients together and set aside.

Break or chop the white chocolate baking bars (using a serrated knife) into chunks onto a sheet of parchment paper.

Add the dried cranberries and chopped chocolate to the flour mixture and lightly mix the ingredients until all cranberries and chocolate are coated with flour. Set aside.

Cream butter and sugars in a large bowl until fluffy. Add eggs, orange extract, and vanilla, and beat well.

Add the flour and cranberry/chocolate mixture to the butter, sugar and egg mixture and blend using a wooden spoon or stiff spatula. If dough appears too dry, add 1 tablespoon milk.

Either drop by spoonfuls, or lightly roll the dough into a rounded ball shape and place on an ungreased or parchment-paper-lined cookie sheet.

Bake at 350 degrees for 10–12 minutes. The size of the cookies will determine baking times. Larger cookies may need an additional 2 to 3 minutes.

Recipe provided by Mary Matthews

About the Author

Peg grew up in a New Jersey suburb about twenty-five miles outside of New York City. After college, she moved to the City, where she managed an art gallery owned by the son of the artist Henri Matisse.

After her husband died, Peg remarried and her new husband took a job in Grand Rapids, Michigan, where they now live (on exile from New Jersey, as she likes to joke). Somehow Peg managed to segue from the art world to marketing and is now the manager of marketing communications for a company that provides services to seniors.

She is the author of the Cranberry Cove Mysteries, the Lucille Mysteries, the Farmer's Daughter Mysteries, the Gourmet De-Lite Mysteries, and, writing as Meg London, the Sweet Nothings Vintage Lingerie series.

Peg has two daughters, a stepdaughter and stepson, a beautiful granddaughter, and a Westhighland white terrier named Reggie. You can read more at pegcochran.com and meglondon.com.

Made in the USA
Las Vegas, NV
08 September 2021